Broken Brain Books Presents

SCREAMS FROM THE OCEAN FLOOR

A Horror Anthology

Edited by Heather Ann Larson

Contents

Introduction

Ahoy! Welcome to what we hope will be the first in a series of anthologies from Broken Brain Books. Thank you for joining us on our maiden voyage for this high-seas adventure.

When coming up with the theme for this anthology, I had a lot of different ideas pulling me in all directions. With so many possibilities, there was one that kept circling back around, and it wasn't only because of the Titan submersible disaster dominating the news at the time (although that was admittedly part of it).

There's just something about the ocean. It holds so many amazing wonders, as well as providing a source of food for people and animals all around the planet. The entire world's ecosystem depends on the ocean for survival. But at the same time, it is powerful, unrelenting, unforgiving, and extremely deadly.

Most people don't even consider how massive the ocean is. It makes the majority of our planet completely inhospitable to oxygen-breathing creatures like us. Even with all of today's technology, more than 80% of the ocean has never been mapped. In addition to that, over 90% of marine species have yet to be classified. Due to the near zero visibility and crushing pressure, most of the ocean floor has never been visited. In fact, we have mapped greater amounts of the Moon and Mars than the ocean floor. Modern humans have been on the Earth for hundreds of thousands of years, yet we have literally just scratched the surface of this undiscovered world.

Being underwater is often compared to being in space. They are similar in many ways. A lot of it is due to the lack of oxygen, which is our most vital need for survival, but I think the darkness, solitude, and general fear of the unknown also have something to do with it. The main difference between outer space and the deep sea is that most of us will never visit space. We couldn't even if we wanted to. But the ocean is right here, ready to spit out alien creatures and swallow you whole.

We received over 50 great submissions for this anthology. We wish we could've accepted them all, however we are proud to present these 16 salty tales of terror. Thank you to everyone who submitted a story and to all the readers for giving this book a chance. We hope you enjoy this collection of ocean horror stories curated and edited by Heather Ann Larson. And without further ado, it's time to set sail. I hear there are some rough waters ahead, so hold on to your hats.

Your trusty captain,
LM Kaplin
Just a reminder, this is a one-way trip.
First stop, Davy Jones' Locker.

DARK WATERS

BY WIL FORBIS

*P*OSEIDON BLADE, THE DEEP-SEA *submersible carrying billionaire Richard Vanderplas and crew, is still missing in the depths of the Atlantic.*

Dan Korris snorted a bitter laugh as the chyron slid across the television mounted just above the Tuff Luv Saloon's liquor shelf. The blonde anchorwoman furrowed her brow—almost as if in response to Dan's derision—but the Morrissey song blasting out of the corner jukebox drowned her words out. Not that Dan had any interest in the woman's blathering. He took a sip from his New England IPA and swiveled his stool around to face the small crowd waiting for The Rejectors to finish tuning their guitars and plugging in their amplifiers.

Zane Padilla emerged from the throng of bodies and signaled the bartender for another rum and coke. Dan mused that the leather jacket stretched over his friend's lanky frame had to be stifling in the cavernous environment.

"Yo man, you hear about this?" Zane yelled, nodding at the television. "This super rich dude disappeared, and now, like, everybody's freaking out."

"It's bullshit," Dan shouted back. "Why the hell should we give a crap about some billionaire douchebag wasting sick cash on an underwater carnival ride? Motherfucker could be feeding the poor with that money. Or paying off folk's college debt."

Zane chortled. "I know, right? Like those rich pricks would ever give a fuck about people like us."

"And Vanderpussy is worse than most," Dan said. "His cancer drug company was going broke until he got some cash infusion that allowed him to redesign his labs to mass-produce painkillers. But all those pills did was get people so sick that they..." He choked to a stop, unable to finish.

Zane looked confused, then his jaw dropped. "Oh man, you mean your dad, right?" He paused. "You got a lot of righteous anger, bro. You should express it. Everyone on TV is crying about this sub."

"Sure thing." Dan rolled his eyes. "I'll have my agent book me a spot on CNN right after I finish this beer."

Zane slapped him on the shoulder. "I'm talking about putting it on your socials, dude. You got the journo degree and a way with words. People out there might listen."

"Nobody pays attention to me there. Whenever I put something on social media, I feel like an old man shouting at clouds."

"Can't hurt to try, bro. You might go viral."

Dan shrugged. He pulled out his iPhone,

thumb-tapped the screen for a half minute, and held it up for Zane to see.

> I'll shed no tears for a man whose dirty drugs killed good people. I hope the submersible and everyone in it sinks to the bottom of the ocean.

"Awesome," Zane enthused. "Post it, dude."

Dan's finger was hovering over the submit button when someone new sidled up to the bar. Karla Herrera wore a plastic corset over a black dress, her thick legs snuggly fit into fishnet stockings and army boots. "What are you gents up to?" she asked.

"My dude Daniel is speaking truth to power," Zane said. "He's dropping a post about how it's bullshit we're supposed to care about these rich scumbags drowning in that submersible."

When Karla leaned over and read Dan's screen, her eyes narrowed. "You can't say that. What about the other men on the sub? The crew? They've got to be terrified, wondering if they're ever going to see their families again."

"Fuck 'em," Dan growled. "They should've known better than to work for Vanderplas."

The fire in his gut cooled a bit when he saw the soft gaze Karla cast on him. He knew the look from back when they were a couple and she would curl up next to him and ask why the world was so unkind, why people were so cruel.

She pulled his hand away from the screen. "I know

you loved your dad, Danny. But you're better than this."

"Whatever." He clicked out of the app and took another swig of beer, leaving the post unsent.

A grinding guitar chord blared. "All right!" Zane shouted. "The Rejecters are kicking it off!"

Dan swiveled around to the sea of bodies that now filled the club. People cheered as Lilith Moretti, lead singer and keyboard player of The Rejecters, climbed onto the stage.

"Are you fuckers ready to get aggro?" Lilith yelled into the microphone. She pumped her fist in the air, and the band launched into their latest digital single, "Scavage This!" A wave of guitars, synths, and drums crashed against Dan's chest, pumping adrenaline into his veins. He sucked down the last of his IPA.

When the band moved to their second song, "Blood Fist," a tap came on Dan's shoulder. "Awesome, no?" Zane yelled into his ear.

"I love this one," Dan said. He hopped off his bar stool and cleaved into the crowd, his gaze set on Lilith's angled face and athletic, tattooed arms.

Goddamn, she is hot. My frickin' dream woman right here.

The club got hotter and more humid as the audience packed closer to the stage. For over a dozen songs, Lilith shrieked lyrics about racist cops and broken institutions, her energy never waning.

Finally, as the ending cymbal crash of the last song faded, she leaned into the mic. "You guys ruled tonight. And I got one more thing to say. You've all heard about this billionaire, Richard Vanderplas, and his toadies getting lost in the Atlantic, right? I want y'all to join me in giving those scumbags a proper fuck you." She jabbed her middle fingers in the air.

Dan laughed and mimicked the gesture with the rest of the crowd. "Fuck you!" everyone shouted.

The club emptied, and Dan soon stood with a group of people watching The Rejectors load gear into their beat-up van. He yearned to tell Lilith how much he had loved the show and how her final words had resonated with him.

Get over it, dude. Lilith Moretti's a superstar in this scene. She's not gonna care about some dork who blends into the crowd and never makes a mark.

It struck him how he could change that, how he could take a stand for something he believed in. He grabbed his phone and looked at the unsent post in his social media app.

Had Karla been right? Were his words too callous, too cruel?

Goddammit, don't over-analyze shit. Take some action for once.

He pressed the submit button.

The aqua murk of the ocean floated on the other side of the five-foot-wide porthole built into the *Poseidon Blade*'s bow. Algae, krill, and pieces of plankton flickered and undulated in the glow of the LED lights mounted on each side of the submersible.

The scene inside was not so copasetic. Dan gaped at crewmembers whose faces contorted in fear, their hands clawing at a steering arm rising from a center console. But when their mouths fell open, no cries came forth. In fact, Dan could hear nothing at all; it was as if the surrounding ocean devoured all sound.

A white-haired man with a well-trimmed beard stood near a row of computer screens on one side of the vessel's tubular interior. Ducking his head to avoid hitting the ceiling, Richard Vanderplas glared through the porthole as if he sought to burn the sea with his rage-filled eyes.

Dan followed the billionaire's gaze to an ethereal black mass floating ahead in the distant waters. As he watched, clouds of algae and schools of fish were pulled into the whale-sized blob, as if drawn by invisible tractor beams.

It was then Dan understood why the men so frantically clutched the controls. If the *Poseidon Blade* was absorbed into the caliginous ooze, none on board would ever set foot on the surface world again.

"Ghaaa!" Dan jolted awake, choking on the scream in his throat.

Sunlight sliced through the blinds, warming him on the pullout sofa bed in the middle of his living room. His guts gurgled and churned as if a swarm of eels slithered through his intestines.

Jesus. What a weird fucking dream... Gotta watch those IPAs.

A clock on a night table read 7:18 a.m. He had just

under forty-five minutes to get to work.

When he grabbed his phone off the mattress and swiped to his social media app, his eyes nearly popped out of his head.

Last night's social media post had 122,354 views, 11,230 reposts, and hundreds of comments. His follower count, which had hovered around 670 for months, was at 9,563.

No, wait, now 9,565.

He cackled uproariously. His posts never received more than a smattering of comments and likes from friends and family. But now he was looking at pages of replies from people cheering him on, including a few from famous musicians and actors.

Of course, there were many unfavorable comments—angry missives from right-wing blowhards telling him he was an amoral bastard or godless socialist. But the ratio was incontestably in his favor, and he delighted in knowing he had frayed the nerves of people he detested.

After dressing, Dan microwaved a bowl of oatmeal

and ate, all the while checking the app and watching the numbers rise. He was too lost in his excitement to register the busy streets and heavy traffic as he walked from his apartment building to the Java Bean Café.

Inside the employee room, Dan was pulling on a barista's apron when his shift leader popped through the door. Tyrone Clarke had his long dreadlocks pulled back into a bun.

"Yo, Danny. I was checking the socials, and I saw this post going viral. And all of a sudden I'm saying to myself, 'I know that dude.'"

Dan smiled. "Yeah, I don't know what happened. I posted it last night, and it just exploded."

"You gotta capitalize on that, my friend. My cousin's tweet blew up, and now he's like a major influencer in Kingston."

"Capitalize? Like how?"

"Send off more posts, man," Tyrone enthused. "You got the world's eyes on you now." He ducked out the door.

Dan still had a few minutes until his shift started. He pulled up the app and began to type.

> I bet Vanderplas is sweating bullets now. How long until the walls come crashing in and he gets turned into fish food?

Chuckling to himself, he walked to the front of the café and began taking orders for macchiatos, iced chai lattes, and other caffeinated delights. Throughout the morning rush, however, he snuck peeks at his phone and watched the original post continue to explode as the new one found traction as well.

Maybe Tyrone's onto something. This could be the start of a new career: Dan Korris, activist and influencer.

Eventually, the breakfast crowd faded. Dan found himself leaning against the pastry case and staring at his phone. As he parsed his stats, a husky voice cut into his focus.

"Hey, I know you."

He looked up to see Lilith Moretti smiling at him from across the counter. She occasionally came into the café but never spoke to him.

"Umm, oh, y-yeah," Dan stammered. "Hi."

"Checking your stats?" She grinned. "I saw your post went big time."

His cheeks warmed. "I guess I am. You read it?"

"Sure. It was all over my feed this morning. It was even shared by this *Rolling Stone* journalist who said she wanted to talk with you. I looked at your profile pic and I was like, 'Wait, that's the cute guy from the Java Bean.'"

Face burning, Dan decided to change the subject. "You guys rocked at the Tuff Luv last night."

She nodded. "You know, I like to give back to people who help with the cause. I could put you on the guest list for the next show. Just give me your number." She pushed her phone across the countertop.

Dan held his fingers steady as he typed his name and number into her contacts list.

"Awesome," Lilith said. "I gotta get going. But maybe we can hang out sometime?"

"Totally. You know, you kind of inspired me to make

that post. With what you said at the end of the show."

"Cool." As she walked out of the café, the closed-lip smile on Lilith's face was both beguiling and inscrutable.

Dan chewed a fingernail. What had she meant with her offer to hang out? Like a date or something?

And what about her comment about the *Rolling Stone* journalist? After searching through his DMs, he found a note from a writer named Nadja Haruni who wanted to schedule an interview about his post and the attention it had drawn.

Goddamn! I'm hitting the big time here.

He needed time to get his thoughts in order, so he replied to Ms. Haruni with a proposal for a call tomorrow afternoon. She immediately returned a thumbs-up sign.

For the rest of the day, Dan floated in a haze as his social media stats continued to rise.

The black mass was closer now, drifting a dozen yards ahead of the *Poseidon Blade*'s porthole. The chill it radiated passed through the submersible's hull, burrowing into Dan's flesh and settling in his bones.

Not literally, of course. He now understood he did not exist in a corporal form on the craft; rather, he floated as an invisible specter sent to observe the growing terror of men he had mocked.

The crewmembers lay about the quarters, fatigued after days of stale, sour air. Only Vanderplas stood upright, his lips muttering inaudible curses as he gazed into the abyss.

A violent motion pitched the *Poseidon Blade* to one side, tossing several crewmembers against the starboard wall. After the vessel leveled itself, the men rose and stared through the porthole as if the source of the disturbance would appear in the gloom.

What did they expect to see, Dan wondered. A giant squid out of a 1960s horror movie? The collapsing ruins of an Atlantean city?

Another spasm jolted the craft. Everyone but Vanderplas flopped to the port side, their mouths rounded in mute cries. Then a slow hiss began, the first sound Dan had heard in these visits to the vessel. It came not from the ship but from the stygian depths outside its metal walls. Or perhaps from inside Dan's skull, he couldn't tell. The sibilant moan grew louder, as if mimicking the doomed mariners' screams.

Inside the black mass, a red ball flamed to life, pulsing and throbbing like a beating heart.

The hissing squeal came in waves, each vibration like a pair of steel thumbs pushing at Dan's eardrums.

He jerked awake to his iPhone buzzing beside him on his sofa bed.

Several text messages had just come in. From Lilith.

Dan quickly typed an invitation, followed by his address.

He closed the sofa bed and took the next several minutes to sweep the floors, wipe crumbs off the kitchen counter, and generally tidy the apartment. A punk rock goddess like Lilith Moretti probably didn't require absolute cleanliness, but why look like a slob?

When the entry intercom buzzed, he pressed a button on the wall that unlocked the downstairs entrance. He pulled open the front door and peered into the hallway. Within seconds, Lilith emerged in the stairwell, a bottle of vodka periscoping out of the paper bag in her fist.

"Hey," he said. "So, umm, what's up? Were you—?"

She bounded up to his door, wrapped her arms around him, and mashed her lips against his. A warmth surged in Dan's chest as he stumbled back into his apartment. He guided Lilith to the sofa, where she pushed him onto the cushions.

He looked up at her looming over him. "Wow. That was—"

Lilith raised a finger to her lips. "Don't talk," she whispered. She took a long sip from the vodka bottle, then climbed onto Dan's hips, straddling him and leaning down to kiss him again. He felt like he was back on the dream vessel, floating in an undulating sea, but this time beset not by soul-quaking terror but waves of pleasure. That euphoria continued as he and Lilith wrestled their way out of their clothes and began exploring each other's bodies.

The glow of outside street lamps filtered through the blinds and dripped over Lilith's moaning form as she thrashed on top of him. When they finished, he unfolded the sofa bed and lay beside her, his arms wrapped around hers.

For the rest of the night, Dan was plagued by no further nightmares.

In the morning, he woke to Lilith sitting beside him on the sofa bed in her black bra and panties, a mug of steaming coffee in her hand.

She ran a hand over his scraggly beard. "Morning, sleepyhead."

He rubbed his eyes. "What time is it? I've got a 10:00 a.m. shift."

"You're fine. It's just past eight." She sauntered into the kitchen, poured a cup of coffee, and brought it back to him.

"Mmmm. This is delicious." He gazed at Lilith. "Just like you."

Sticking a finger in her mouth, she imitated gagging. "Barf. You are such a cheeseball." But he could tell she was flattered.

Lilith squinted at the light coming through the blinds, then cocked her head at him. "Hey, did you ever talk to that *Rolling Stone* journalist?"

"I sure did. I'm doing a phone interview with her after my shift today."

"That's awesome. You think you could do me a favor?"

"Depends. Now that I'm a big internet star, I've got a lot of people making requests."

She rolled her eyes. "Maybe you could tell her about The Rejectors? Like, maybe she could get our release in front of some reviewers?"

"Of course. You guys totally deserve to blow up."

"Cool." Lilith took a sip and set her cup on the end table. "We've got some time before you go to work. Any ideas on how to waste it?"

"Hmm, I dunno, nothing comes to mind. Wait! You like Parcheesi? Or how about—"

But she was already gliding a hand down his chest and smothering him with kisses.

At 4:30 p.m., Dan sat on the sofa in his apartment. His iPhone buzzed.

"Dan Korris here."

"Mr. Korris, this is Nadja Haruni," a voice replied. The *Rolling Stone* journalist wasted no time with small talk and began peppering Dan with questions about why he felt his post had struck such a nerve and what it said about modern society. Dan did his best to answer and managed to squeeze two Chomsky quotes into the space of five minutes.

After a brief lull, Nadja said, "This is all great, Dan. I

really appreciate you taking the time."

"No problem." He sensed an opportunity to bring up Lilith and The Rejectors.

"One thing," Nadja said before he could speak. "Do you have any regrets about what you wrote? If the men on the *Poseidon Blade* are rescued, they will certainly see your posts. What would you say to them if that happens?"

A surge of bile burned Dan's throat.

"Dan?"

"I, ummm, I dunno..." he croaked out. "I mean, I guess I hadn't thought about that."

"Well, perhaps it's something to consider. Anyway, thanks again. I'll let you know when the interview's up."

The line went dead.

At 10:30 p.m., the intercom buzzed as Dan paced across the living room floor. Lilith had promised to come by after her band rehearsal for what she called "round two."

Moments later, she strode into the apartment and held up a new bottle of vodka. With an excited expression on her face, she said, "How'd the interview go?"

"Pretty good, I think. She hit me with a weird question at the end and I—"

"Did you tell her about The Rejectors?"

Dan let out a nervous laugh. "I kind of forgot. Like I said, she asked me this weird question and—"

"You fucking forgot? What does that mean? How could you forget?" Lilith's words nipped at his throat.

He swallowed hard. "I dunno. I just got flustered. I'm sorry."

She looked away and took a swig from the bottle.

"Babe, I'm sorry." Dan wrapped a hand around Lilith's waist and pulled her close. He nuzzled her neck and kissed her cheek.

She yawned. "To be honest, dude, I'm kind of tired. Can we just pull the sofa out and hit the sack? Maybe we can pick this up in the morning."

"Umm, sure." Dan unfolded the bed. Lilith lay down and took several sips from the bottle.

"Want to just snuggle and talk?" he asked.

"Not really."

A cannonball swelled in his stomach, squeezing acid up his esophagus.

Dammit, I've fucked it up already. Like with Karla.

With nothing left to do, he brushed his teeth, stripped to his boxers, and lay next to Lilith in the dark. The weight in his chest settled into his guts, and it took him an hour to fall asleep.

The hissing was unbearably loud now, a surgeon's blade slicing through the air. The crewmembers clawed at their ears, fingers slick with blood. They fell about the cabin as the *Poseidon Blade* lurched back and forth. Only Vanderplas was able to hold himself upright and continued staring through the porthole.

The giant red ball floated a dozen feet ahead of the vessel, pulsing with aortic regularity.

A crack appeared in the porthole's glass pane, followed by splintering spider webs. Then the window's bottom half gave way and water sloshed into the cabin. Within seconds, the crewmembers' boots were soaked.

For the first time in his nightmares, Dan heard the mens' screams. Howls of terrors daggered into his ears as the rest of the window broke free and the water climbed to the crewmembers' waists.

All the while, Vanderplas stood in angry silence.

Five gigantic tentacles extended from the red orb and slithered towards the vessel. A thick appendage slipped through the shattered porthole, plucked a man thrashing in the water, and yanked him into the black depths. The fear-drenched cries grew louder.

A different tendril, mottled with suction cups, coiled around another man, squeezing him until his bones cracked and blood spattered from his mouth. Then he, too, was pulled into the dark.

Dan wanted to cover his eyes, to blind himself to the horrible sight. But in this dream state, such a thing was not possible. He watched as more tentacles ensnared the men and pulled them into the ocean. Until only one remained.

Vanderplas's chin bobbed above the water that nearly filled the cabin. He turned and beamed eyes of rage at Dan.

"You!" the giant man bellowed. "I know what you did. *And I'll have my revenge!*"

Dan's heartbeat thrummed in his neck as he awoke in the dark. Cool sweat drenched his forehead.

Goddamn. That one was the worst of all. What's going on in my brain?

The cause of his unease was obvious. Nadja Haruni's last question implying his guilt had found a loose piece of psychic filament and had started to pull.

He sat up and pushed a hand into the shadows next to him. Perhaps Lilith could give him some comfort. Not necessarily sex. Just soothing words.

The other side of the bed was empty, the mattress not even warm.

"Lilith?" he called into the dark.

A new dread, different from the nightmare's terrors, stabbed his chest. He had blown it with her. Because he had failed to promote her band to *Rolling Stone*, Lilith had no more need of him.

So that's it? She was just using me?

The suspicion stung twice. First, because he knew he had been duped. Second, because he knew that if she gave him another chance, he would forgive her betrayal. Anything to stave off the loneliness that filled his days and nights.

But no second chance was coming; she had fled while he slumbered, leaving him only his haunted dreams.

A shudder glazed over him. Maybe a warm bath would help?

He peeled off his underwear and padded naked across the carpet to the bathroom. He flipped on the light and filled the tub with steaming water. When he got in, the liquid enveloped his body, muting both the cold air and the pang of Lilith's rejection.

But the bath's curative properties were short-lived and his turmoil quickly returned. What would happen when he saw Lilith at shows or at work? A vision of her cool, distant gaze emerged in his mind, and he clenched his eyes shut to staunch the tears threatening to roll down his cheeks.

His eyes were still closed when a *squelch* came from the hallway. He looked up at a thin figure moving through the gloom.

His heart lurched in his chest, followed by a swell of relief when he recognized the woman approaching the doorway. Lilith's naked skin was almost luminescent in the light escaping from the bathroom.

"Jesus, babe," Dan said, releasing his held breath in a rushed exhalation. "I'm so glad to see you. I just had one hell of a crazy dream. Been having a lot of them lately."

She said nothing, floating towards the door.

"Wanna join me in the tub?" he asked hopefully.

The pungent smell of rotting seaweed wafted into the air.

Why did Lilith seem... different?

Dan's throat clenched when he realized what had nagged at him since she had appeared. Lilith's legs were not ambulating as she moved forward. Rather, they dangled from her torso as if she was a marionette hanging off a puppeteer's strings.

Thick, gray fingers peered out from the sides of her neck. Someone was holding her aloft from behind.

Lilith's form jerked forward, sailing through the doorway, crashing through the shower curtain, and landing on Dan. Dead eyes stared at him. Blackened veins etched winding paths beneath alabaster skin.

Screaming and thrashing in the bathwater, Dan pressed his hands onto cold flesh and heaved Lilith's corpse onto the tiled floor.

A low chuckling sound came from the hallway. A giant shape stepped out of the shadows.

"No…" Dan choked out. "It… it can't be."

Richard Vanderplas stood in the doorway. Or at least a contorted mutation of the billionaire sea explorer did. A shirt and trousers—wet and torn—clung to his tall form. His puckered, decaying skin held a sickly gray pallor. A bloodless gash ran from his temple down to his stubbled chin.

A tiny eel emerged from the exposed orifice that was Vanderplas's right eye socket. The creature slithered down his cheek, fell to the floor, and disappeared into a corner.

"Good evening, Mr. Korris," Vanderplas rumbled. "I imagine you're surprised to see me. After all, I'm supposed to be… how did you put it? Fish food?"

Dan's jaw froze, his terrified thoughts eating themselves.

The ghoul in the doorway smiled. "Twice during my far-reaching explorations, I've come across a gateway to Hell. The first such discovery was many years ago in the mountains of Tibet, and I took the opportunity to make a deal with the Devil. He granted me vast wealth, and I agreed to provide him with a steady supply of souls. Souls such as you father, for instance."

"My… father?"

"But there was one caveat to my Devil's bargain. I was told never to return to Hell, and that if I did, the Devil would take ownership of my soul. I dutifully honored that request until a few days ago, when the *Poseidon Blade* stumbled across another portal in the depths of the Atlantic." Vanderplas sighed. "But you knew that already, didn't you? You've been watching us in your dreams."

The bathwater suddenly cooled. Dan's quivering knees slapped against the sides of the tub. "Then why aren't you there?" he screamed. "What are you doing in my bathroom?"

Vanderplas laughed. "The Devil is not so cruel that he does not offer an occasional favor. He knew I raged at your words, so he granted me one last visit to the surface world. To take my revenge."

A suffocating, squeezing muscle spasm gripped Dan's chest. "No... no..."

"But *au contraire, mon frère*. I say yes... yes." Vanderplas kneeled and pressed his cold palms on Dan's shoulders. Dan clawed at the giant hands pushing him under the surface. The stinging bathwater forced his eyelids shut. Salty liquid and briny particles filled his throat.

His lungs, losing oxygen, cried out in agony. How bad would it be? Drowning? Dying?

Then he realized Vanderplas's paws no longer held him down. He blinked his eyes open.

Empty chairs and a console of dials and a bent steering arm came into view just past a plankton haze. Dead computer monitors hung off rounded walls. The porthole, edged with shards of glass, looked like an open shark's mouth framing the red orb pulsing in the distance.

A thick, gray tentacle darted in through the porthole.

The appendage probed the chamber, gliding over the interior until it found Dan. Smooth, gray muscle coiled around his torso and quivering suction cups affixed to his skin. Then the tentacle was pulling him through the water, out the porthole, into the frigid darkness.

Straight into the beating red heart of Hell.

And Then They Eat Your Eyes

by Leigh Kenny

T HE BOAT SWAYED AND bobbed upon the dark ocean as Max came to with a groan. Shadows stretched and coalesced in the cramped cabin. He lifted his head from the cushioned bunk space and winced as a headache announced itself with the force of a jackhammer. He knew drinking on a boat was never going to end well, had told Brett as much, but his friend was never one to miss an alcohol-soaked opportunity.

"Brett," he croaked, glancing with squinted eyes through the grimy window.

Max paused, listening to the sounds from beyond the small, dark space he currently occupied. He could hear the thumps and creaks of the small cabin cruiser as it moved upon the water. Beyond that he could hear nothing but the gentle slap of the ocean against the sides and the occasional screeching of the gulls that had circled overhead all day.

It was eerily quiet.

No tinny music from Brett's battered old radio. No Brett singing along enthusiastically but dreadfully off key.

Dragging himself outside, Max could see he was alone on the boat. He lifted the bench lid and saw the rods and tackle boxes still tucked neatly away where they had left them after a drunken attempt at fishing. The large cooler full of beer and snacks was still parked by the bench. Even Brett's stupid cowboy hat still rested where he had last seen it.

But no Brett.

Fighting back an increasing feeling of panic, Max grasped an upright rail and leaned out as far as he dared, scanning the water. Nothing but gentle waves and sprays of foam. The last of the day's light was bleeding into the water in a spectacular display of fiery reds and opulent golds, the sun slowly sinking beyond the horizon. It was a breathtaking sight, and Max wished he could appreciate it in all its splendor. But the nagging unease that tugged at him like a dead weight wouldn't allow it.

"Brett!" he called again, loudly enough to aggravate the dull, throbbing pain in his head. Reaching into the cooler, Max dug past wrapped sandwiches, chips, and beer bottles, searching for some water. His fingers touched plastic through the melting ice, and he felt his parched throat click in anticipation as he drew the bottle out. He held it up and groaned. Less than half of the small plastic bottle remained.

He took a sip, his throat constricting as the icy liquid traveled down, instantly relieving the scratchy dryness. Max hugged the bottle between his knees and dug around the cooler some more. He found another plastic bottle, this one only a quarter full. *Plenty of beer though*, he thought, silently cursing his friend before being overcome with worry.

Max stood, shielding his eyes from the dying glare of the melting sun, and turned slowly, scanning the area around him for any sign of his friend. His concern wasn't just for Brett, but for himself. He had no idea where they were and no idea how to turn the boat on, much less navigate it back to shore.

Whenever he visited Brett in Florida, Max felt like their adventures got a little more out of hand each time.

They had met in college, and upon first laying eyes on his roommate, Max thought there was zero chance of them getting along. Brett was loud and obnoxious. Max was more of an introvert. But spending so much time in close quarters had drawn the two together, and a shared love of video games and all things horror had bonded them.

After college, Max had moved to Dallas for work, and Brett had moved to Florida. Brett had grown up in a small farming community and had always said that the minute he was done with college, he was heading for sunny shores. He dreamed of living out his days working on fishing boats or in a small beach shack selling shiny crap to gullible tourists. College for Brett had just been an escape route from his dreary life and the expectation from his parents that he would continue to run the family business, a small hardware store that also sold livestock feed. Brett always said the most exciting things that happened in his hometown usually involved tractors or cows. Sometimes both.

And so, he had escaped to Florida right out of college, just like he said he would. Max almost envied him. Max had gone through the hard grind of college with aspirations of becoming a writer, just to end up in a multi-story office block in downtown Dallas. He flew out to Brett every year for a week of drunken debauchery. Every year when he arrived home, Max promised himself he would finally start chasing his dreams, just like Brett had.

He would fire up his laptop enthusiastically, only to find himself staring at a blank page an hour later, the tiny cursor blinking at him accusingly. Max would take that laptop out every evening after work for a few weeks before finally admitting defeat once more. Until the next time he visited Brett.

"Do something you love, and you'll never work a day in your life!" Brett had always told him.

Max had met a pretty waitress in one of the bars he frequented, and they had fallen in love and got married. He and Michelle were living the American dream: a big house in the suburbs and two beautiful kids, one boy and one girl. Hell, they even had the family dog and the picket fence. Max loved his wife and kids. He was happy with his life most of time, except for those few weeks after visiting his friend. His bubble never quite burst, but it sure did deflate some.

And now he was stuck on a small boat somewhere in the Atlantic Ocean. He had no idea where his friend was and no idea where he was.

Max could feel the beginning of an anxiety attack. It

was a creeping tightness across his chest and lungs, the icy prickle at the base of his skull, the tingling sensation in his fingers and toes.

"Calm down," he muttered to himself.

Max sat heavily on the bottom of the boat, one hand to his chest. He forced himself to take some deep breaths, dragging the salty sea air in through his nose until his lungs burned, then pushing it back out through his mouth.

Eventually, his focused breathing, along with the gentle motion of the boat, reduced his heart rate to a slow, steady beat once more. Releasing one final, deep breath, he stood and tried to take stock of his situation.

He headed for the helm of the boat, and one look at the multitude of dials and gadgets told Max there was no way he'd be driving the boat out of there. He was pretty sure Brett had started the thing with a key in the first place, and there was no sign of one in front of him. Brett must have pocketed the keys for whatever reason, and now he was nowhere to be found.

With a heavy sigh, Max searched around the boat, taking stock of what he had at his disposal. There was very little water but plenty of beer. He wasn't stupid though. He knew drinking alcohol would only serve to dehydrate him further.

There were a couple of sandwiches, a large bag of nacho-flavored chips, and a lone stick of beef jerky in the cooler. The fishing rods were there, but that was a non-starter. Outdoor pursuits had never been his strong suit.

Rooting around in the benches, he found a couple of lifejackets. It stopped him in his tracks because Brett had told him before they set off there was a lifejacket each for them. They had worn them as they traveled out to sea but had removed them once the boat was stationary. The fact that both of the orange vests were still in the bench meant wherever Brett was, he was without a life jacket. He had most likely fallen overboard, and Max, in his drunken state, asleep in the tiny bunk section below deck, hadn't even awoke to the sound of splashing.

Had Brett shouted for his help?

Wouldn't he have heard *something?*

Probably not, he conceded. The amount of alcohol he had drank combined with the heat of the sun had left him in a bad way. The cooling darkness of the bunk area along with the gentle motion of the boat on the water had lulled him to sleep quickly, and not even a siren's call would have roused him.

The thought of sirens left a lump in Max's throat as he thought of the wild tales Brett had told him as they raced further away from dry land.

Brett had worked on a lot of fishing boats during his years in the South, and all the men he worked with had tales of sirens, mermaids, and other fantastical sea creatures. Max had brayed with laughter as Brett's second-hand stories had become increasingly more ridiculous. His friend had reveled in the tales of strange, feminine water creatures that lured men with their beautiful songs and strangely alluring bodies. They would draw up alongside unsuspecting boats, especially smaller ones, where they would entrance the men aboard with their melody. The men would unwittingly move closer, closer, ever closer to the edge of the boat, and once they were within reach, the sirens would snatch them into the water.

"...And then they eat your eyes," Brett had said solemnly.

A beat of silence, and then they had both howled with laughter.

That had been about halfway through a cheap bottle of tequila, right about the time they had given up on fishing.

Running his hands through hair stiff with sea salt, Max hissed out a frustrated breath.

He had no idea what to do. Pulling open the small door to the cabin, he hunted through the few small storage spaces. What he found was mostly junk, but he did find a small first aid kit and a hard case he was pretty sure housed a flare gun.

Opening the first aid kit, he fingered through its meager contents; a few waterproof plasters, a half empty sleeve of Tylenol, a roll of Tums, and a raggedy bandage with a few rusted pins still stuck in it.

"Jesus Christ, Brett," he whispered, reminded of his friend's irresponsible attitude to life, and not for the first time.

He stuffed the contents back in the kit and tossed it into the storage bench. Placing the gun case carefully on the cushioned bench, he stepped back outside, his mind reeling with the suddenness of the situation he found himself in.

An idea struck, and Max cursed himself for not thinking of it sooner. He raced back to the helm, hunting around the various controls and knobs until he found what looked like the closest thing to a radio. Praying it was already tuned to the proper frequency, Max hit the switch. Relief washed over him as the radio crackled to life.

"Hello? Is anybody out there?" he called desperately. "Mayday! Mayday!"

He was sure that was what they said in the movies. Who cared about radio etiquette, anyway; it only mattered that he got in contact with someone who could help him.

The radio hissed, but no voices came through. Max rolled the dial, hoping for a miracle.

"Can anybody hear me? Hello? HELLO??!!"

As he stared anxiously at the fizzing radio, his mind recalled something Brett had said earlier as he had cut the boat's engine.

"This is it now," he had said, "The Bermuda Triangle. If anything goes wrong out here, we're on our own, buddy!"

He had waggled his eyebrows at Max, a wicked grin on his face.

"Ah shit, Brett," he had replied, "Why couldn't we just stay around the bay?? Why does everything have to be done to such extremes with you?"

Brett had laughed.

"Chill, bro! Everything is under control. I come here fishing all the time; it's where the best fish are. I'm telling you man, if you want to actually catch something worth taking home, the Triangle is the place to do it!"

"You literally just said that if anything goes wrong, we're on our own," Max had replied pointedly.

"I'm just messing with you, bro! The radio doesn't work great this far out, not on this shit heap anyway. Its cool though. I'm an expert in these things. Few hours fishing, few beers, and we'll be back in time to hit Santiago's up before the good tables are gone. No harm, no foul, and plenty of fun to keep your motor running long after you go back to Dallas."

Brett had delivered the last line with a wink.

Max tried the radio a few more times until, eventually, even the hissing static disappeared and the radio was silent.

"FUCK!!!" he yelled. He got no response because there was nothing out here but him and blackness.

He gazed out into the abyss, searching frantically for something, anything. The lights from a nearby fishing vessel or, better yet, the coastguard. But he was greeted with nothing but a stygian darkness.

With a sigh, Max rested his elbows on the cold metal rail and dropped his chin, peering out at the undulating waves.

As his eyes adjusted to the dark, he became aware of a glow within the water.

It seemed to lay just below the surface, a short distance from the boat but stretching far beyond it. *Bioluminescence*, he thought. He'd heard of it, seen plenty of pictures on the internet, but had never seen it in person.

Up close, it was really quite beautiful.

He hadn't known it was a thing in Florida and was surprised Brett had never mentioned it. It made for a jaw-dropping spectacle. The ethereal glow soothed his frazzled mind, and the gentle motion of the boat upon the waves was calming. If he didn't think about Brett's whereabouts, or the situation he was in, it was almost peaceful.

BANG!

Max was jolted from his seat, realizing he had somehow fallen asleep as he had watched the water sparkle and glow. He scanned the horizon, but the glow had disappeared. All he could see was darkness again, the separation between sky and sea barely discernible.

A loud splash broke the silence, and another heavy thud rocked the small cruiser.

Hands shaking, Max grasped the rail and peered over the side.

A shape rose before his eyes in the water, cutting through the water like the blade of a knife.

A shark!

Max dropped to the bottom of the boat as the creature collided heavily with the side of the cruiser. A loud crack sounded, and the vessel shuddered slightly.

Holy shit, though Max, *I'm in the middle of the fucking Bermuda Triangle on a shitty boat that's not working, and a fucking shark is trying to eat me!*

This trip was going down as the worst experience of his life so far. Max realized with horror that whatever fate Brett had met in the water, it was probably at the jaws of something similar to the monster now stalking him.

With a whimper, he crawled across the boat to the storage bench and wrenched out one of the life jackets. He pulled it on and stood just as the boat was rammed again. He tumbled to the hard floor. The lights on board disappeared, plunging Max into absolute darkness.

Stumbling blindly across the boat and through the cabin door, Max could feel his clothes sticking to his skin.

The cruiser was taking on water. His clothes were half

drenched from stumbling and slipping around on deck. Panic coursed through him as he fanned out his hands, feeling around blindly for the hard case that contained the flare gun.

It was his last hope if he had any chance of being rescued.

The cabin door crashed open behind him, and as Max turned to close it, he noticed the stern of the small boat was shattered. Through the gaping hole, the ocean greedily lapped at the deck. Terrified, Max could see the boat was slowly sinking. The backwards tilt had caused the cabin door to fly open.

Bracing himself against the small cabin wall, Max could hear nothing beyond the roar of his own heartbeat in his ears. His blood ran like fire and ice through his veins, drowning out everything around him. Panting, he tried to pry open the case, his fingers slipping along the smooth plastic.

He had never used a flare gun, and he hoped it was easy to operate.

His life most definitely depended on it!

Another deafening crash knocked Max from his feet, and with a pained cry, he watched as the gun case slid along the wet deck and disappeared into the water.

"Shit!" he yelled, hauling himself up from the sodden floor.

He reached for the rail like it was a lifeline. As his fingers grasped the cold, wet metal bar, the boat suddenly tipped furiously in that direction. Max sailed through the air, his grip useless, and landed in the sea with a loud splash. The life jacket pulled him straight back to the surface, and as his head emerged from the briny water, he spluttered and coughed.

Terrified, Max turned his head, hoping to catch sight of the shark. He let the life jacket do its job of keeping him afloat, afraid to flail his limbs but inwardly desperate to do so. Adrenaline screamed through his body as he fought the panic rising in him like a volcano on the edge of eruption. Max was no outdoorsman, but he knew enough to understand controlling the urge to panic could be the difference between life and death in this situation. The boat was only a short distance away, but the ocean had begun to claim it as its own. Max's heart sank. What little chance he had of survival before the boat began to sink was evaporating before his eyes.

Something brushed heavily against his legs as they gently tread water, and Max yelped, his movements becoming erratic as the panic overcame him.

"Help!!" he screamed out into the dark, his voice drowned out by the roar of the ocean.

The moon peeked out from beyond the clouds, illuminating his horror. Ahead of him, that familiar, dark shape rose in the water, the silver light glinting off its crescent fin. It began to cut a path directly towards him, disappearing below the waves once more as it swam closer. Max sobbed, closing his eyes and bracing for the pain he expected to feel at any moment.

But nothing happened.

Daring to open his eyes, Max could see nothing in the water around him except the glow of the bioluminescent organisms that had come alive once more. The shark was nowhere to be seen.

Maybe he's circling me, Max thought to himself. *Any minute now, he's gonna grab my leg and drag me under.*

Michelle will never know what happened. What will she tell the kids?

The frigid cold made his teeth chatter, and he continued to bob along, his mind a tumultuous jumble of panicked thoughts. Max had no idea how much time had passed, but miraculously it seemed as though the shark had given up.

The sea glowed around him, like an underwater Aurora display. It was spectacular to behold and soothing to his fractured mind. Thoughts of Brett, of Michelle and the kids, slowly melted away as the cold pierced his skin, seeping right into his weary bones.

Something bumped against his arm, and Max yelped again, sure he was about to meet his end. A hard plastic case floated alongside him.

Max laughed with relief as he reached for the case. A noise in the distance pulled his attention in the opposite direction, but he held fast to the precious flare gun case.

Lights!

They were a great distance away, but he could see lights. It looked like a large ship, and it was lit up like a Christmas tree. *A cruise ship*!

Max hollered and yelled, waving his free arm over his head. He quickly realized the distance was too great for them to have any chance of spotting him. He was just a dark speck in an even darker ocean.

Chewing on the already broken skin of his lips, he made the decision to fire the gun. If they were close enough for him to see their lights, they were close enough to see the flare. His hands were heavy and trembling with the cold, but Max knew his life depended on how the next few minutes went. The bioluminescent water around him offered no advantage to his vision. Just as he was growing desperate, the clouds sailed past the moon again. Celestial light fell across him, allowing him to finally see where the catches were on the case. Max offered up a silent prayer of thanks to anyone who cared to listen. Things had taken a turn for the worse, but he finally felt like the universe was smiling down on him, offering him a lifeline out of this terrible situation.

He noticed the glowing water growing closer from the corner of his eye as he concentrated on the weapon. Was the luminous matter moving towards him, or was it him that was on the move? He hoped the current was taking him closer to the ship, but the case was open now so it didn't much matter.

Lifting his arm straight up in the air, his muscles shaking, Max closed his eyes and pulled the trigger.

The flare shot straight up before trailing off in an arc. The sudden explosion was blindingly wonderful, and Max cheered at the sight.

Then froze.

The flare illuminated the ocean around him, and Max could finally see the source of the ethereal glow he had so admired.

Hundreds of eyes watched him from just below the surface of the water.

Maybe thousands.

Whatever they were, they surrounded him completely and stretched as far as the flare's light reached and beyond.

With barely a sound, one of the creatures emerged from the water a few feet from Max, its huge, gleaming eyes studying him.

It looked almost human but too grotesque to ever be confused with a real person. It had those massive eyes and a mouth but no ears or nose. It appeared to have hair, but at a second glance the strands that fell from its head were thick and slimy, more akin to seaweed or some other organic matter. Its skin was tinged a bluish-grey, almost translucent. As it reached out an arm towards him, Max could see the webbing between its digits, something wet and slimy dripping from them.

Before the creature could touch him, Max pushed himself backwards through the water. His movement stopped as he met with an obstacle. With a whimper, he felt something pin his arms by his side. It held itself close to him, and his nostrils filled with the scent of the sea and rotting flesh. It made a sound in his ear, almost like a whisper but unintelligible. Max's eyes darted around in panic as he watched the first creature glide silently through the sea towards him. The creature reached out with both hands this time, cradling his face almost tenderly as it joined the one that held him in place with whispers.

Max's shoulders shook as silent tears streamed down his terrified face. He lifted his eyes towards the creature once more, noticing the cruise ship was no longer as distant. It loomed larger than it previously had and was clearly heading in his direction.

They were coming to save me, Max thought, his heart aching at how quickly his hope had withered and died right there in the Atlantic Ocean.

He screamed as the creature probed its webbed fingers around his left eye, a sharp pain flooding his senses. The scream died on his lips as he watched the monstrous thing pull its hand back, his eyeball caught between its fingers. A thin, gray, tongue-like appendage slithered from the creature's mouth between rows of needle-sharp teeth. The tongue rolled over the eyeball, and the creature made a satisfied groaning sound deep in its throat. Then it tossed the eye into its open mouth and bit down with a sickening crunch.

Bile rose in Max's throat as fluid gushed from his separated eyeball and ran from the creature's mouth. It chewed for a moment before swallowing, then wiped its hand along its glistening chin and licked the goo clean. It threw its head back, its throat ululating in some bastardization of celebration or song.

Before Max could react, the creature behind him deftly lifted one arm and plucked his remaining eye from its socket. There was no hesitation with this creature; he heard the nauseating crack as it bit down instantly and chewed noisily on his eyeball. Max shrieked as pain flamed from his empty sockets. The creature behind him released him suddenly, and Max floated freely on the surface of the ocean, crying out from the blinding pain. He could feel cold hands, colder still than the water that wanted to claim him, tugging and scratching at his skin. Sudden sharp pains stabbed at him, hot as fire, and with dawning horror Max understood that more of the creatures were consuming him in tiny nibbles and scratched off pieces of flesh.

With a sudden jolt, his body began to submerge, and Max pulled a final breath of the salty night air deep into his burning lungs. As his head dipped below the surface, the open wounds where his eyes had been only moments ago burned as though someone had filled the cavernous sockets with fire ants. His mouth gaped in a silent scream, bubbles of air filling the space around him. His throat filled with the salty ocean water, and Max didn't fight it.

Drowning would be peaceful compared to dying at the hands of these abominations!

But he wasn't the first human the creatures had hunted. They had taken another just like him only hours earlier in this very spot. They circled Max's dying body, teeth and talons in a frenzy as they stripped the warm flesh from his bones before he could steal the delicious warmth from them. By the time Max's heart finally stopped beating, he had experienced a thousand lifetimes worth of suffering at the hands of the sirens.

As light flooded the water's surface just meters above their heads, the creatures descended into the darker depths of their home, dragging what was left of their prize with them to the bottom of the ocean.

SAND

BY DEREK HEATH

D IM SPANGLES OF PHOSPHORESCENCE preceded the creatures as they moved sluggishly across the seabed. There were two of them: two bulbous figures with flesh that was halfway rubber and halfway coppery foil, enormous, reflective orbs for heads.

Long, black cables connected them to a spherical submersible, a dull and scratched machine lying tilted in the sand, anchored by protruding metal arms. The vessel was large and lay like a dark moon, round windows about its circumference letting out faint clouds of light. As the glass-headed creatures moved farther from the silent steel bulb of their submersible, the cables snapped and coiled like snakes. The light that bloomed from banks of dazzling blue LEDs on their suits was soft and warm and allowed them to see a few feet into the dark. Dark clouds of silt exploded around heavy lead boots with every step.

"I still don't see anything," Orla called, following the second suited figure into the black. The eerie silence of the trench was interrupted by knots of static that burst through the radio in the young woman's helmet.

The blue light of her helmet illuminated a school of tiny, iridescent fish as they skittered around her head, and for a moment she was distracted, her whole body lilting back in the pressurised pseudo-gravity as she gazed up into a mass of flitting, transparent bodies.

It was a moment before she realized she had heard no reply. Sighing, she looked forward and watched as the second figure plodded awkwardly onward. The cable snaking from his back drew billowing clouds of sand up from the seabed. Before he could disappear completely into the pitch, Orla pressed forward. "And let me guess," she sighed quietly, "your radio's down again. Either you're not hearing me, or I'm not hearing you."

The bloated suit ahead of her continued forward, offering her no hand gestures, not even a turn of the head, and she surmised it was the former.

"Well," she said, lifting each leg like it weighed a ton, planting it in the sand and letting the silt bloom around her. "I guess since you can't hear me, I may as well tell you something." Oxygen pumped gently into the bulky glass ball of her helmet, and Orla breathed as she had learned, regulating the movements of her chest without thinking about it.

Her radio squawked suddenly, and David's voice filled her helmet; it wasn't the comfort it should have been down here in the pressurised dark. "Just a little farther," he said flatly. "There's a small mound of rock coming up on your left. I remember that. It can only be another twenty feet."

It was an odd sensation, listening to the disembodied words of the man she had spent the last eighteen months working with while clots of dark, silky nothing swirled in the void around them; it was like the ocean itself was talking to her. "Well, at least I can hear *you*," she said quietly.

She slogged after him, wading through the ice-cold depths in pursuit of a silhouette. Twenty feet might not have been very far on land, but down here it was a mile. She was excited to see what David had seen, but she would have liked to be back on the submersible and moving freely. It would be easier to talk to him too.

"Listen, I may as well get it out. Something about saying it out loud, you know? Even if I'll have to repeat it for you sometime. Gives me a practice run, I guess."

She breathed deeply, inevitably, recovering from the exertion of using her vocal cords. Everything down here was heavy, an effort. Another cluster of tiny, translucent fish fluttered past her head, their eyes tiny points of light, their tails bolts of electricity.

"I don't know how you feel, David, but the last year and a half has been the best time of my life. I know it's been a lot of hard work, and a lot of waiting, and watching, and wondering, but... I've loved every minute of my time with you. I think—"

"Here. Look."

David had stopped. He turned his head, the shining orb of his helmet whirling around painfully slowly, his arm coming up through the water like an iron rod through tar. His fingers beckoned, curling inward inside the thick rubber clumps of a fat, black glove.

"Come on, you'll miss it."

She moved as quickly as she could, kicking up a storm of sand that floated around her, a dense, wheeling cancer of grainy black blossoming at her back. On her left, she noted a smooth, pointed plate of granite half-buried in a ridge of sand that seemed to writhe and shift around it. On a low dune beyond the boulder, David stood staring into the black, his bulky arms hanging by his sides. The ocean wept in a bleak kaleidoscope of silt and saline around his thick figure.

Orla kept her eyes on the back of his helmet as she moved. "I just think you're great," she said. "That's all there is to it, really. And you know how difficult it'd be for me to say that if I thought you could actually hear me.

"But I do, David. I think you're really... beautiful. And kind. And I wonder if it's possible to spend eighteen months in a deep-sea research laboratory with one other person and *not* fall in love with them, but..."

She smiled weakly in the cloying ball of her helmet.

"Yeah. That's it. I'm in love with you. I love you, David. I think we should try it out, see if it works."

She reached his side, trudging slowly up the slope of sand upon which he stood. Together, they stared out into a faintly blue-lit clearing of sorts, a smooth bank of sand at the very bottom of the ocean illuminated with patches of gloom.

"Maybe when we get back to the sub, I'll tell you all that for real."

"Do you see it?" crackled the voice in her ear. Her eyes darted sidelong; his helmet was a smooth haze of tinted black and she couldn't see his face, but she could hear the smile in his voice.

Orla turned her attention back to the flat pane of sand before them and peered into the grim near-distance. There was nothing. Occasionally a tiny geyser of dust plumed up from the seabed and dissipated, but otherwise nothing at all. Even the tiny, iridescent fish had disappeared.

"You big dumb pillock," Orla said, "there's nothing here. I love you, David—more than you could know—but for Christ's sake—"

"Wait," David said quietly, oblivious to every word. "Wait... wait... *there*."

Orla saw it. Her eyes widened as she watched. Beside her, David slowly raised a chunky finger, the glacial movement of his arm a delayed signal that was entirely useless to her.

Now that she had seen it, she couldn't take her eyes off the thing in the sand.

It rose slowly from beneath the seabed, a tiny triangle of pale grey becoming a speckled, serrated dorsal fin about the size of a teacup. As it rose, it bent and swayed in a wide circle, its movements widening with each rotation so that it knifed a slow, hypnotic spiral through the sand.

"It's beautiful," Orla said. The fin's posterior was completely smooth, its anterior chipped and ragged like a broken fingernail, and it was exactly the color of the sand—or the grey-bluish color that the sand appeared in the weak light their suits were transmitting—and as it carved its path through the seabed, it seemed to move *with* it, rather than through it, the only sign that it had passed through at all a slight shifting of the grains around it. A flattened, fleshy point of flecked and gritty colourlessness, she might have missed it altogether if not directed toward it.

"This is the best bit," David whispered right in her ear. "Look..."

As the circular movements of the fin grew wider, something else appeared behind it. Another fin. At first a tiny point rising from the silt, then a blade of sandy grey the same size as the first. For a moment, Orla thought there was another creature moving beneath the sand behind the first, but she realized the speed at which both fins were circling was exact, was identical—that this second fin belonged to the same beast as the first—and as she drew in an awed hitch of oxygen, a third began to lift from the sand, and then a fourth—

"Wow," she breathed.

After a moment, there were twelve of them, varying in size, large to small from the lead of the file to the small, sharp point bringing up the rear, a snaking spiral of sandy shapes that swam slowly underneath the seabed and that moved like magic, like nothing she had ever imagined.

"I can't believe it," she said. "This is... huge. This is something new, David. You've found something nobody's ever seen before."

But something stirred uncomfortably in her stomach, a tingle of fear she knew was rational, was sensible, and she wished he could hear her.

The creature was narrow and snake-like, that much was obvious without being able to see its body—and it was large, at least four or five meters long, a little more if she assumed the fins of its tail were still somewhere beneath the sand—and there was something else, something incomprehensible, something wrong. Something she couldn't put her finger on.

"We should go back," she said, instinctively raising her hand to grip his. Their gloved digits bumped together awkwardly, and she turned her head, nodding in his direction and hoping he would get the message. "Come back out here prepared. All right?"

David shook his head; he couldn't hear her. But he didn't seem to care, anyway, and she watched with a growing sense of unease as his helmet twisted back in the direction of the creature, unfazed. Hypnotised. In awe of it.

She couldn't help but look too. The creature had ceased its spiraling, and it snaked away from them, the serrated fins along its back cutting easily through the sandy floor as they bowed left and right. Just before it left the field of light their suits created, it darted to the left, and after swimming that way for a moment, it turned back on itself, temporarily creating a slender *U*-shape and hooking back to the right.

"David," she whispered.

It wasn't moving through the sand. It wasn't *beneath* the sand.

She put her finger on it, and it felt like death. She prodded him hard with her hand and clutched his arm as best she could, tugging backward. "David, we need to go back."

"What's wrong?" he said breathlessly, his eyes on the creature. "Orla, just another minute..."

"It's in the sand," she said. "It *is* the sand, it's... David, please—"

The thing looped back on itself again, and Orla's breath hitched in her throat as it arced toward them, moving fast, slicing forward, a row of knife blades cutting a silent path through the silt.

"David!" she yelled, grabbing him with both hands and stepping back, the weight of her body and suit propelling them down the dune. They tumbled back into the black, and the sand clouded around them, plumes of light tipping upward. For a second that dragged for miles, they fell. She landed in the sand, somehow tangled in the black cable fused to her back and lying on her front, her unwieldy hands pressed into the seabed. She looked up.

The creature shot toward them like a bullet train, a dozen fins tilting back as it screamed forward.

"No!"

Then it exploded.

She blinked, her brain unable to process what had happened, but somehow she understood. All at once, as though a button had been pressed, the fins sunk back into the sand—except they didn't fall back into it, like the spines of a creature moving beneath the surface—they burst into grains and filtered downward, floating back into the seabed from which they had risen.

Dissolving.

"It's the sand," she yelled, pushing her body upward until she was standing on bowed, unsteady legs, thrusting the cables away from her. She bent to grab David, helping him to struggle onto his feet, and his voice crackled through her radio:

"—going on—*fzzzt*—back to the—*szzzk*—now!"

A shrill electronic whine pierced her skull, and she yelled, turning her body through the thick, cold tar of the ocean to launch herself back toward the submersible. She felt David moving beside her but could not see him; the LEDs of her suit were blinking, flickering dangerously so that the sea around her flashed in various shades of pitch and blue. Oxygen rushed into her helmet, compensating for her frantic breaths, and she wondered briefly how much was left—enough to make it back, surely—but what if it wasn't?

"—hand—*szkkkzt*—come on!"

She looked in his direction and saw he was reaching for her. Without thinking, she grabbed his hand and felt the pressurised vortex of the depths bend and mould around them as they lurched forward, two cumbersome shapes in the void ploughing through dreadful blooms of space.

His light was flickering too.

Orla frantically scanned the seabed for movement and saw shapes racing through the sand alongside them, a scattering of fins—no longer arranged single file but in a herd, at least half a dozen of them moving independently of each other—and before she could stop herself, she looked in the other direction, past David, and saw another half-dozen were beating through the sand on their right too. Racing them toward the submersible.

"What the fuck is it?" she yelled, more to herself than anything. She drew in a deep breath, and her heart skipped a beat as she heard something rattle in the pipes that filtered oxygen through her suit. Felt it, more than heard it: something grainy slipping through the system.

Sand in her suit.

"David, it's everywhere—"

"I know!" he yelled in her ear, his voice fused with

static. Gripping her suit by the wrist, he lunged forward, each of them pulling the other a step at a time through the mire. "Come on!"

Her skull bounced against the glass of her helmet and she cried out. The sand beneath their boots rippled suddenly, and she nearly tumbled forward again, but he steadied her, slowly twisting his body until he was almost beneath her and throwing her back up onto her feet. They were weightless and a million times too heavy all at once, and as they crashed forward, the seabed trembled and bowing underneath them, flexing like the back of some enormous creature, powerful and soft at the same time.

"You can hear me," she realized. "You bastard, how long have you been able to hear me?!"

"I didn't know what to say!" he yelled, the radio squawking with him. "I was going to talk to you about everything when we got back!"

"How much did you hear, you pillock?!"

Suddenly, David's body was wrenched backward as a great blanket of sand exploded upward and enveloped his suit, coils of dusty black curling around his waist and legs and ripping him out of her reach.

"David!" she screamed, turning her head as fast as she could, peering terrified through a thick sludge of nothing. "*David!*"

A thick pillar of sand sucked itself into the seabed, and a cloud of black erupted from the whirling hole it made. Then the hole filled in and he was gone. Slamming her face into the glass of her helmet, Orla looked frantically left and right scanning the seabed for movement, but there was nothing. The sand ruffled and shifted, but the fins were gone.

Nothing at all.

She slowly backed away, stumbling toward the sub with her eyes on the ocean. It suddenly felt very large and very empty, and she realized the lights coming from her suit had almost died; they weren't flickering but had dimmed to an utterly insignificant cyan, basically useless.

"David," she said softly. She was sobbing, she realized, tears running down her face into her mouth. "Please... David, please..."

A gloved hand crashed up from the sand, rounded fingers clawing at nothing. She lunged forward, crashing to her knees and scrambling for him. His forearm thrust through the seabed and swiped madly at the ocean. She grabbed, pulled as hard as she could.

"*DAVID!*"

She saw an elbow, inches of suit spearing out of the sand—folds of coppery material laid through with silver piping, then a shoulder, then the first glimpse of a glass helmet—and then the sand around them roared.

Clouds of silt burst into the water and became snapping, darting shapes, fins beating at the ocean as they ploughed forward and smacked their bodies into his suit, where they erupted and dissolved around him. Thick knots of sand clotted together and grabbed at his body like hands, thick fingers wrenching him back, a dozen arms pushing him down. "No!" Orla screamed as the sand sucked him in, a black hole of particles tightening around his neck, dragging at his arm. She felt her grip loosening and realized the sand was bulging between her fingers, forcing her away as it drew him down, down,

down—

"—love—*fzzzzzzzzzzkkk*—too—"

And then he was gone, and she reeled back from the seething whirlpool of sand, scrambling back toward the sub. Turning over, she gazed up at the great metal ball and calculated the distance; she could make it, she just had to get up, get on her feet, get *away*...

"David..." she whispered, crawling through the sand. It writhed madly about her, grainy fists smashing at her legs, thick tangles of it sifting through the filtration systems of her suit and sliding inside, ruining her oxygen, suffocating her. "No... please..."

Six feet ahead of her, a figure rose from the sand. It was bulbous and unwieldy, its head a perfect sphere, each of its hands a useless mass of clunky digits. It was made entirely of sand, and it moved like a school of independent creatures, a hive of bees coming together into one unearthly silhouette, a silhouette that the seabed had borrowed, had copied, had *taken from her*.

She forced herself to her feet and screamed, rage billowing through her entire body, her teeth smacking the glass as she propelled herself forward. She burst through the sandy figure and it dissolved around her, individual grains dispersing, the shadowy, half-formed shape breaking into atoms. Then she was running, moving at half a mile an hour through the deep but every bit as hard as she could, and for a moment she knew she would make it to the sub, make it home.

The seabed shifted beneath the submersible, and she bellowed in protest, tumbling onto her hands and knees, helpless to watch as every fiber of hope in her body ripped itself apart.

A great black pit opened around the sub, and walls of sand shot upward, rupturing, becoming teeth. The seabed rippled as it yawed open, a wide maw of jagged points crashing into the submersible and bursting, drawing back again and gnawing inward, each murmuration—each powerful, deadly bite—slamming the vessel deeper into the sand until it was buried. For a second, Orla saw the true face of the beast, a gargantuan mouth that shifted and twisted and snapped; it was blind, eyeless, but it was all the same creature, the same enormous beast, a beast that was all around her, was everywhere, every*thing*.

Orla slammed her great glass head into the sand and screamed, praying to God that she could smash it hard enough that the glass would break; praying that she would drown and die a slow, suffocating, and ice-cold death before she was sucked into the seabed.

OCEANLUST

BY RJ ROLES

Captain Higgins stood at the stern of the schooner staring out at the calm, flat ocean. The wind had died a week prior, and he and his crew were drifting aimlessly, not knowing which direction they were currently heading since starless skies blanketed the night's sky.

They were due to make port in three days, but Higgins knew any committed date of delivery was a lost cause now. Nevermind that he and his skeleton crew—along with the contents of the cargo hold—were strictly off the books with the delivery on this run.

"Cap'n. He's up there again." Petey Sullivan—the ship's first mate—stood a few feet behind the captain.

Higgins turned, bypassing Sullivan, looking directly toward the bow. Three days after they had lost the wind, Bosun's Mate Jack Billings took to sitting on the ship's bowsprit, staring into the water while muttering to himself about the lights calling to him from the depths.

Higgins had heard such tales before. About men losing their minds when hopeless dread had set in. Stir crazy, some called it. Others called it oceanlust—a sickness of the mind that few recovered from once befallen. Either way, Higgins recognized the signs early and tasked his first mate with the job of keeping an eye on the potentially troublesome crewmate.

Higgins grumbled before leaving the rear of the ship, making his way to the bow. The few crew members currently topside scattered before him, clearing a path.

"What are ye doin' up there, Billings?" Higgins asked, raising his hand to shield his eyes from the blinding sun.

The bosun's mate either ignored the question or simply didn't hear the captain over his own utterings. Billings continued to stare into the depths, lost to all around him.

Higgins checked his anger despite wanting to yell at the man. "Billings!"

Jack slowly came out of his daze, turning to look at Higgins with empty eyes. "Yes, Cap'n?" he asked absentmindedly.

"What're doin' up there, sailor?" Higgins asked again.

Billings looked back into the water for a moment before turning back, confusion washing over his face. "The lights... They speak to me. They know things no one else should know—could know. The deepest of secrets I've not told a soul. You should have a look. See for yourself, Cap'n."

Higgins hesitated for a moment but stepped to the railing, slightly leaning over and looking at the water. The midday sun illuminated the placid ocean deep into the murky fathoms below, but he didn't see anything he hadn't seen a thousand times before.

Reeling back, he addressed the bosun's mate. "Billings, I need you to go with Sullivan. There's a special detail that requires your immediate attention."

The captain saw the man's hands claw at the wood he was sitting on, his nails digging into it nearly to the point of ripping from his fingers, then finally relaxing.

"Yes, Cap'n," Billings replied solemnly.

Higgins backed away as the man climbed onto the deck. Billings's eyes met with his before the man hung his head and followed the first mate below. He turned and stared out over the glassy sheet of water, sunlight sparkling in a serene glitter of aquamarine diamonds. He said a silent prayer for the wind to come. For salvation to find them in the form of a gust or gale. He would even settle for a slight breeze if it was enough to fill the sail and set them on their course again.

The looking glass sea turned Higgins's thought to Lenore. She had stolen his heart—if only for a moment—enough so for him to question his commitment he had made to the ocean long before their chance meeting. She was the reason he had taken on this voyage. With its bounty, he would have sufficient wealth to feel confident enough to ask for her hand in marriage.

Slipping the thoughts of Lenore to the back of his mind, Captain Higgins looked up from his position on the bow, loathly eyeing the limp sails with contempt.

Another prayer unanswered. Another day stranded. One more closer to death, he thought.

Pacing the length of the ship, he climbed below deck and entered his private quarters. Map charts and manifests littered his desk, but the folded note sitting on top of everything was what weighed heavily on his mind.

Settling into his chair, Higgins stroked at the long scruff of beard on his face—normally shaven down to his cheek, had they made it to port when expected.

Hand moving away from his face, it hovered over the note—hoping the words had changed since he had last read them. Picking it up, Higgins slowly unfolded the scrap of parchment, his heart sinking deeper into despair.

Seven - three

Five - four

Three - five

The note chilled him as he reread it—more so now than when it arrived to him earlier that morning. Cryptic enough to anyone that may've happened upon it, Higgins knew it was an ominous warning from the ship's quartermaster—Harold Raife.

A hollow knock came at the door, causing the captain to startle. "Enter," he said as he folded the note and stowed it in his shirt.

"Did as ya said, Cap'n. Billings is scouring the ship for rats, will give 'em to Raife when he's done."

Higgins nodded. "Thank you, Petey."

His first mate lingered in the doorway, no doubt with something else to say.

"Something else on your mind?"

Taking a quick look behind him, Petey said, "Mind if I have a minute of your time?"

Wetting his lips, Higgins inclined his head and raised a hand to the seat on the opposite side of his desk.

Closing the door behind him, first mate Sullivan quickly occupied the chair. "Raife says the stores'll run dry soon. Water first. Food can be half-rationed, putting them down to a quarter of normal size." He kept his voice low as he expressed his concerns to Higgins.

The captain grumbled to himself before replying. "Raife would do well to leash his tongue when it comes to conversing with others." Higgins's words held more venom than he intended, but discipline amongst the crew had become too lax since the ship had halted its progress.

Sullivan averted his eyes, looking at everything in the small quarters except his captain. "I just meant... What are we to do once the stores run dry? Even if the wind does come—"

"When," Higgins interjected.

"Course, Cap'n. *When* it returns, we still won't have enough to see us through the rest of the voyage."

Higgins sat straighter in his chair, his right hand briefly touching the fabric of his shirt where the note remained hidden, and interlocked his hands on the desk between the two of them.

"I'm well aware of the direness of our situation, Sullivan. When I fully realize the best course of action, you'll be the first to know. In the interim, toss the crew's effects for anything felched from the galley."

"Aye," the first mate replied and stood. "And... knowing it's not a topic for discussion, but you don't suppose somethin' in the hold'd be of aid to us?"

The look Captain Higgins gave the man was enough to know he had been dismissed without the words needing to be said. Hanging his head, Sullivan left to complete his task.

Higgins took a deep breath and let it out slowly. Since

they had set sail, speculation was abound of what it was they were transporting. Higgins himself was the only crew member on board the vessel that had been present when the cargo was stowed away in the hold below. It had been done in the cover of night, a stipulation put in place by the financier of the trip.

He and Lenore had just finished their evening meal the night before his departure when he told her he had to return to the shipyard until they cast off to oversee and ensure all agreements were upheld.

"I do not understand. Would it not be more apt to wait until at least daybreak, when the sun's light would make it far easier to load the ship?" she asked, each syllable of her serenading voice a constant reminder of why he had fallen in love with her in the first place.

Higgins offered a soft smile. "I am simply a servant to those who pull the strings."

Lenore had become despondent when he had first told her of the sudden trip to America which fell into his lap. Slowly, Higgins had been able to melt her icy exterior, ensuring her it was the best thing for their future if he was to follow through and make the delivery as instructed. Though she was slow to come around, Higgins believed she and he were seeing the same possibilities upon his return.

After one final farewell, an embrace shared between them that Higgins could've stayed in until his heart ceased its beating, he made his way to the shipyard and oversaw the precious cargo board his ship.

It wasn't the queerness of the all the secrecy which gave him the most apprehension but seeing what he and his crew would be transporting, or more precisely, the lack thereof.

A single crate—double nailed and the rough hewn wood burnt black—was loaded by two men dressed head to toe in the purest black robes he had ever seen. No one spoke as they maneuvered the crate to the hold—as per instructions—and they left as soon as they saw the captain put a lock on the hold's door and pocket the only known key.

Higgins spent the rest of the night on watch, making sure no one disturbed the cargo, until they left port later that morning.

Since then, as far as he knew, the crate remained unmolested, safe behind the locked door. An uneasiness crept into his mind, and Higgins decided to check for himself and cast away all doubt.

Pulling out the note and placing it in one of the drawers of his desk, he left his quarters and climbed down to the hold, unseen by the rest of the crew. As he approached the door, his heart clenched in his chest when he saw the fresh claw marks in the wood next to the plate that fastened the lock to the door.

Without thinking, he reached up, matching his hand perfectly to the gouge marks where his fingernails would be. Pulling open his shirt, Higgins retrieved the key that was still safely fastened around his neck and breathed easier.

Someone had obviously attempted to gain access, but without the key, the craftsman who installed the formidable door assured him no one would be able to break in, short of firing cannon point blank at the lock itself.

After climbing topside, Captain Higgins took to standing at the stern again, staring out over the water where, in his mind, Lenore sat waiting for his return. The dead-calm made for long days, and as the sun hung low over the horizon, he decided to retire for the night, hoping that tomorrow would see them on their way.

Higgins had foregone his rations, and as he lay in bed, his stomach rumbling in protest of his decision, he slowly drifted off to sleep.

"CAP'N!" a voice cried, intermixed with pounding at the door, pulling Higgins from a restless slumber.

Squinting around the room in the dim candlelight, he asked, "What is it? Who's there?"

"It's Sullivan, Cap'n. You are needed at the helm." Higgins could detect the sense of urgency in his first mate's voice and rolled out of his rack.

Still trying to gain his bearings, the captain walked over to the door and opened it.

"What's going on?"

Sullivan swallowed hard. "It's Billings, sir. He's back on the bowsprit. And he's not alone."

Higgins nodded for the first mate to lead the way as he grabbed a lantern hanging by the door, following in Sullivan's wake. The night was as close to pitch as he had ever seen when he walked onto deck.

The swaying light from the lantern did little to stave off the encroaching darkness, leaving little room for error as the captain and his first mate navigated their way to the bow.

Higgins held the light higher to see who was present and thought Billings had certainly done his due diligence in capturing rats on board his ship.

"What's the meaning of this?" he asked, he and Sullivan standing shoulder to shoulder.

Neither Evans, nor Fairchild, nor Handscomb, nor even Billings—who was sitting high on the bowsprit uttering something that was more akin to animal noise rather than humanistic vocabulary—paid any attention to the captain's inquiry.

Pulling Sullivan in close, he said, "Get Raife," in the man's ear.

The first mate left without hesitation, leaving Higgins to contend with the other four. Billings's voice grew louder, and the other three men seemed to respond by swaying from side to side to the almost melodic sounds.

"I command you all to cease this insufferable chicanery immediately and return to your racks for the remainder of the night." Higgins's words held a sternness he seldom needed to use with his normally cooperative crew.

With the lantern still held high, the captain walked closer to the men, stopping when Handscomb rose to his feet and turned to face him. Higgins shivered when he saw the man's eyes had lost all color and were staring at him through a milky white film. Handscomb's mouth began to open and close like a fish struggling to breathe when pulled from the water.

He watched in horror as his crewmember scratched at his own throat, raking his nails against his flesh until streaks of dark blood began to coat his fingers. Handscomb backed to the railing on the port side and gasped one final breath before throwing himself backwards into the water.

"No!" Higgins yelled and rushed to look over.

The lantern he held did little to illuminate the ocean below, but it didn't matter. Strange lights shining from the depths lit the plunging man, forming a watery halo of full-spectrum colors around him. Higgins didn't know if his eyes were playing tricks on him, but he swore he could see the man smiling.

Feeling something bump into his back, he turned to see the same milky eyes looking at him from Evans's face.

"Pull yourself together, sailor!" Higgins snapped.

His words fell on deaf ears as Evans mounted the railing, throwing one leg over the side until Higgins grabbed him by the shirt, pulling him back onto the deck. The man landed with a loud thud, his head bouncing off the wooden planks. Billings's voice rose even more shrilly, and Evans began to stand, his face as blank as the sky above.

Captain Higgins stepped between the rising man and the railing, prepared to stop him at all costs.

"I order you to stand down, sailor!"

Standing eye level with Evans, Higgins braced himself for conflict. Evans's head tilted forward, just enough for a face to be seen clearly in the lantern's light. The opaque sheen eyes boring into him flashed suddenly to slits with mossy green pupils.

If it hadn't been for the warmth spreading over the front of his pants, Higgins would have been unaware he had pissed himself. Evans's eyes flashed again to dull white as he headed for the rail. The captain remained planted to the spot, unable to move as his mind worked to comprehend what it was he saw—trying to decipher the overwhelming sense of dread that filled every fiber of his being.

He heard the splash behind him and turned slowly,

his hands shaking. Higgins stepped to the railing and leaned over, looking as Evans willingly sank into the lights, which were now glowing brighter than they had with Handscomb.

Hearing shuffling on the deck, Higgins turned to see Fairchild on his feet, looking at him with the same dead eyes, the same emotionless expression. Backing away a few paces, the captain knew it was futile to try and intercept him.

Fairchild walked forward without a sound and disappeared over the railing, a splash the only indicator he had gone overboard. Higgins looked on as another one of his crew was rendered into the service of the great deep, the lights below even brighter than before.

Strange as it all was, an odd sense of relief washed over him as he remembered the note residing in his pocket.

Five. There are Five of us left now. Left to linger on in this godforsaken doldrum, he thought.

Realizing the sounds from Billings had stopped, Higgins turned and was startled to find the man standing next to him. Billings's arms shot up and grabbed him by the shoulders in an iron-clad grip, his fingers digging into the fleshy parts.

The bosun mate's eyes had a strange look to them, almost reptilian, like the alligators the captain had seen on one of his previous crossings to America. Billings opened his mouth, and Higgins could see that same array of lights in the back of the man's throat. Slithering tentacles began unfurling from the gaping maw, undulating and reaching toward the captain.

Higgins lost himself as he stared into the lights, his mind blank and all sense of knowing gone as the feeling of euphoric bliss emanated from the pit of his stomach and spread through the rest of his body. He wanted nothing more than to journey into the brilliance of their pulsating rhythm.

Leaning forward to better feel the warmth of the lights, one of the tentacles latched onto the captain's face and started to pull him closer. Before he knew what was happening, the butt end of a rifle collided with the side of Billings's head, and Higgins fell to the deck, unconscious.

Heading pounding, Captain Higgins's eyes fluttered open, the dim interior of his quarters greeting him. He turned his head and saw Sullivan asleep at the chair behind his desk. Groaning as he rose to a seated position, Sullivan woke and kicked his heels off the desk, rising to his feet and rushing to the captain's rack.

"Easy, Cap'n. You've had an ordeal. All's well. Well, as well as well could be 'siderin' the loss o' men."

Higgins looked at his first mate with questions on his mind. "So it wasn't a bad spell, then? Handscomb, Evans, Fairchild?"

Sullivan looked away before answering. "All belongin' to the deep now, Cap'n."

Rubbing his hands over his face, Higgins looked up. "And Billings? What of that... abomination?"

"In the brig, sir. Been there for a day now. Waitin' to see what you'd want done with him."

Higgins's brow furrowed into a knot. "Bri... We don't

have a brig on this ship."

Sullivan reached into his pocket and retrieved a familiar looking key that made Higgins reach for his neck. "That hold? You put him in the hold with our cargo?"

Before the first mate could answer, the captain grabbed the key and rose to his feet but swayed as if the ship had a heavy list. Sullivan reached out to steady him, but Higgins brushed him aside, making his way out of the quarters and to the ladder that would take him below.

Nearly falling all the way down, Higgins managed to keep his footing, though unsteady, before planting himself on the keel. He moved to the locked door and inserted the key, hearing a loud click as it popped open.

Entering the hold, the remnants of the crate lay scattered everywhere—and no Billings.

"Dear God in heaven," Sullivan said from behind. "Where's he gone to? Raife, search the ship, we've a mad man on the loose."

The quartermaster left without hesitation, leaving the captain and his first mate to search among the rubble for any clues. Higgins felt the strength leave his legs and dropped to the hold floor.

"It's all for naught..." he said.

"Wassit, Cap'n?" Sullivan turned and asked.

"It's all for naught," he repeated. "Every last god damned minute of this insufferable crossing has been cursed from day one."

Sullivan shuffled his feet a few times before approaching the captain. "Let's get you back to your cabin, sir. If Billings is still on the ship, Raife is sure to find him."

Higgins didn't protest. He allowed himself to be corralled back to his quarters, lying back down in his rack.

"I'll report back soon as I have somethin'," Sullivan said as he was leaving.

"Yes. Thank you," Higgins replied.

With the cargo compromised and missing, everything he had been working for was now a fool's errand. Moreso, the fact that mother nature was conspiring against him left his mind plagued with shadows of deepening despair.

At some point in his worrying, Higgins drifted off, and his thoughts lingered on his beloved Lenore, whose voice was calling to him.

"Yes? I'm here," he said, causing himself to wake.

The candles on his desk were burning low when he looked around the cabin.

"Lenore, is that you?"

"Come to me, darling..." her voice said from somewhere distant.

Rising, Higgins strode to the desk, pulling out a fresh candle from the bottom drawn and using one of the dying ones to light it. Holding a cupped hand around it, he searched for a lantern but was unable to find one.

"Sullivan? Raife?" he called out into the lower deck of the ship after opening the door.

When no one replied, he stepped out and went to the first mate's room.

Empty.

Next, he walked to the quartermaster's quarters and searched for Raife, calling out for anyone that could hear him. There were no signs that the man had been there recently—even his personal effects that normally littered the shelves were nowhere to be seen.

Walking back to his quarters, Higgins entered and

saw a strange book sitting on his desk that he didn't recognize. Its binding looked to be that of black leather, and metal clasps kept the book firmly shut when he tried to open it.

Bending low, holding the candle close, Higgins could just make out the strangest markings he had ever seen. A circle with many overlapping stars that didn't quite line up perfectly were engraved into the cover.

Just as he was about to pull a knife from his desk and try to pry it open, Lenore's voice called to him.

"Are you coming, darling?"

Higgins stood up straight and looked through the open doorway. Her voice had been clearer this time, and she sounded closer.

"Lenore?" he said weakly.

Stepping out from behind the desk, he moved over the wooden flooring, feeling as if he was gliding. Holding the candle high, Higgins looked down the corridor and then up the stairs that would take him topside.

"Lenore?" he called, louder this time.

"I am waiting..."

Her voice came from the direction of the staircase, and he moved as fast as he could until he found himself standing on deck. Higgins stood next to the rudder wheel and looked around, still not seeing his beloved. Grabbing the wheel, he felt it move freely, giving no resistance as it should have.

When he bent to inspect the linkage, Lenore's voice entered his ears.

"It is time, my love. We will be together forever."

Jumping up, Higgins squinted as he looked around the deck, seeing the faintest wisp of movement toward the bow. Sprinting forward, the candle nearly went out and he had to slow and protect the withering flame. At a steady, brisk pace, the captain continued on until he was at the front railing.

"Where are you? I can not see you."

A splash sounded. He leaned over and looked and finally saw her looking up at him from the water. The lights Billings had been obsessed with twinkled from the depths, casting an eerie aura around Lenore as her white gown spread out around her in the water in rippling waves.

"How did you get in the water? Are you hurt?" he called to her.

Lenore cooed softly and spread her arms out, leaning back to float on the ocean's surface.

"Join me. We have been waiting for you for so long. I have missed you, my love."

Her voice was honey in his ears, and he felt a warmth spread throughout his body he hadn't felt since that last night they had spent together.

"Come out of there. It can not be safe." Higgins cast his gaze to the starless sky, lamenting the lack of light.

Bending over the railing, he brought the candle down as low as he could reach, shining its flickering light on her. Her skin held a pale green hue that caused him to recoil slightly.

"Are you well?" Higgins asked.

"I need you," she replied flatly.

As he straightened, the pattern in the lights beneath her altered and caught his eye, tugging at his chest. Higgins stared—unblinking—at them, his mind void of all thought. Dropping the candle to the deck, he kept his eyes locked on the lights as he shucked his overcoat off.

"I am coming, my love," he said before mounting the railing and diving off into the water.

Lenore vanished from the surface when he came up.

"Lenore? LENORE?! Where are you?"

Plunging his head in the water, he looked about and saw her sinking into the lights, her arm outstretched, reaching for him.

Rising up to take a deep breath, Higgins dove down, swimming with all his might to get to her. The deeper he swam, the farther she seemed to get from him. His lungs started to burn as he kicked and cut through the water with his arms, building on the pressure from the water that seemed to be squeezing him.

Lost in motion, Higgins looked to where he thought the surface of the water should be and found nothing to differentiate it from the rest of the ocean. Looking back down, he saw Lenore's mouth move, inaudible from the distance between them.

Searing pain spreading through his chest, he dove on, determined to reach her before she was lost to the deep. His kicks became weaker and weaker, and his vision started to blacken around the edges. The lights in the depths grew brighter, but Lenore never seemed to grow closer.

Visions of faces clouded his mind, the faces of his crew. Billings was first, a look of shock as Higgins plunged a knife into his chest. Handscomb, Evans, and Fairchild were next, all similar to Billings's face, all murdered in the same fashion. Raife's now cycled in, the look of anger and fear on the man's face as Higgins's hands wrapped around his throat, choking the life out of him.

Last came Sullivan's. His first mate's face wore the unwavering look of betrayal as his captain carved out his internal organs and chewed on them for the man to see.

Realization washed over Higgins as it all became clear what he had done. Something in the back of his mind came to the forefront, visions of him sitting at his desk, pouring over the strange book during the night he was supposed to be watching over the ship before setting sail.

The language depicted on the pages made no sense to him, but it didn't matter by then, their untold knowledge had already imprinted on his soul.

Floating listless in the deep ocean, Lenore disappeared from his waning vision, and the lights beyond blinked once, then twice.

As Higgins felt his heart beat slow and then finally cease, he heard Lenore's voice in his mind.

Finally.

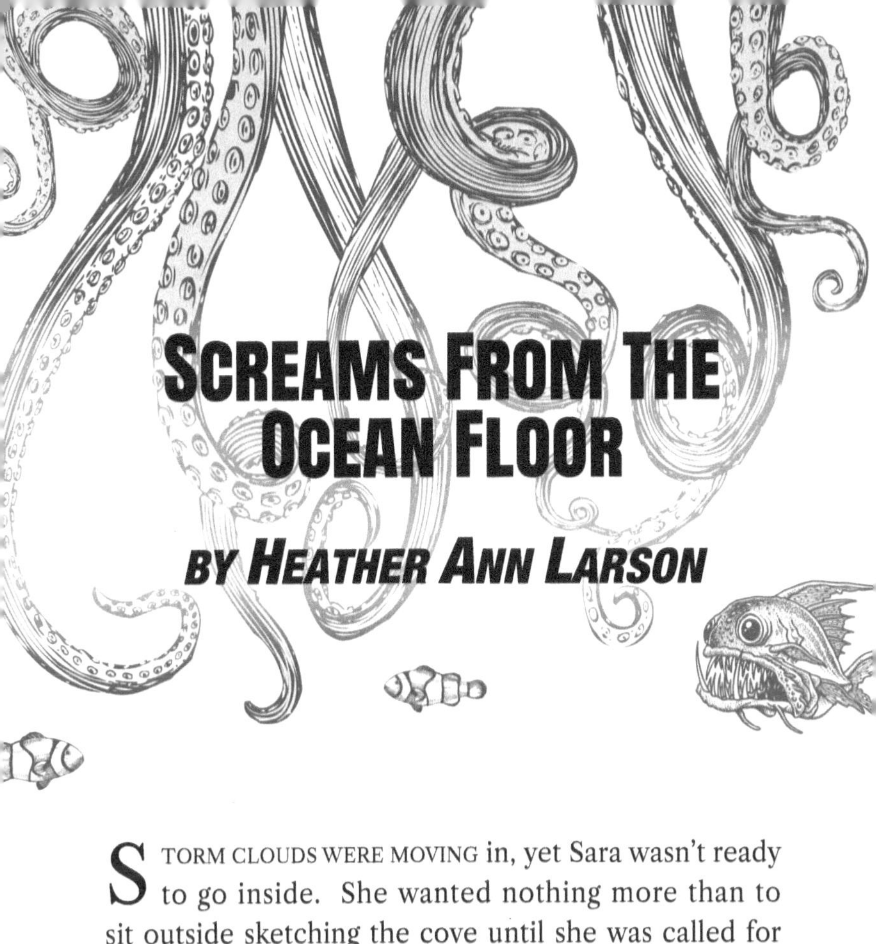

Screams From The Ocean Floor

by Heather Ann Larson

S TORM CLOUDS WERE MOVING in, yet Sara wasn't ready to go inside. She wanted nothing more than to sit outside sketching the cove until she was called for dinner. The ominous-looking clouds overhead told her she would be doing no such thing.

She had been summering at this cottage in the cove every one of her thirteen summers; she had actually been coming here since before she was born, according to her parents. She looked forward to it every summer, until Grandpa was gone, vanished without a trace. After that it wasn't the same.

The wind was picking up, but until it started to rain, Sara was keeping herself planted where she was. She wanted to stay lost in her memories, mesmerized by the giant crests of water slamming into the rocks. Sara had inherited Grandpa's love of this stormy weather, a gene passed down to her from her favorite grandparent. She would sit out here with him in the wind and rain, the sky lulling them with its crescendo into a full-blown storm.

Mom interrupted her plans. "Sara, get in here before you catch cold!"

She sighed her biggest sigh, mostly so Mom could see her dislike, and turned to do as requested. But as she turned, something in the water caught her attention. She saw a silver-streaked fin slapping down into the water as a large, turbulent wave slammed into the shore.

She blinked several times, unsure if her eyes were playing tricks on her. There wasn't anything there now, but she was certain of what she saw.

As she mounted the porch steps, she swore she heard a haunting melody hummed on the gales.

As she slept that night, the haunting ocean melody danced through her dreams. She dreamed of a silver tail gliding effortlessly through the crashing waves. She dreamed of a creature come to shore, sitting on the large ocean rocks, waiting for the next giant wave to roll through. The creature continued to ride the giant swells, resting on the rocks in between.

Her grandfather appeared in her dream too. He sat on the shore, watching the being play in the ocean. He didn't appear frightened. He had a smile on his face, and his posture was relaxed. He was familiar with this entity.

Suddenly the thing was right in Sara's face, unleashing a harsh, quiet scream.

Sara bolted upright, breathing heavily. It took her a very long time to fall back to sleep.

Sara found herself at her same perch on the shore day after day. She wanted desperately to see that silver fin again, to know she wasn't imagining things. She also continued to dream of her grandfather and the creature. The dreams were different every time, but every one indicated her grandfather and this thing were friendly.

Ten days had gone by with no sightings. Sara gave up and refocused on her drawings. She sat as she did that first day, awaiting yet another storm coming in and awaiting the call from her mother to come inside. She was concentrating on a particularly detailed sketch when she heard the humming again.

She slowly looked up from her sketch. In the crashing waves, she saw the creature from her dreams. It was splashing through the roiling water, surfacing between the enormous swells. Sara gasped, and through the wind and the crashing water, it seemed the being had heard her.

The creature made its way closer to the shore, watching Sara as it would a predator, eyeing her warily. As it got closer, the haunting melody gained volume. The creature stopped when it reached a depth it was no longer fully submerged in while laying flat. It maintained its gaze on Sara, cocking its head as if curious and interested.

Sara stood, unsure she was really seeing what she was looking at. Her sketchbook forgotten, the pages fluttering in the wind, Sara took step after cautious step closer to the thing. When she was five yards from shore, she stopped.

The entity continued to look at her. The haunting melody was so loud it hurt her ears. She knew now the melody was coming from the creature – she was so close she could see the vibrations on the thing's throat. Just as she was going to speak to the being, the sky opened and her mother was hollering at her from the porch. Sara looked to her mother, then back at the ocean.

The creature was gone.

Sara did what research she could in the local library when she went into town with her mom. She researched as much local legend and lore as she could get her hands on. She concluded it was some type of mermaid. She was surprised. The only mermaid she had ever known was the red-haired one from the movies. This was definitely not like that.

This mermaid did not have a half-human, half-fish appearance. It was grey-green, a sickly pallor, really, with sagging skin. Its tail was a darker shade of that same grey-green, and it certainly didn't sparkle (or it didn't appear it would if the creature would ever come out when the sun made its rare appearance). The sparse hair it had was lanky and stringy, not lustrous and full. The only beautiful thing about the creature was its stunning silver fin. It otherwise looked absolutely disgusting and terrifying. But Sara wasn't scared of it.

She also read it was believed mermaids lived in colonies. She had only seen the one; where were the others if they lived in such large groups? Was this one an outcast? Were the other members of its colony gone?

Sara found herself obsessing over the creature. She would sit near the water for hours every day, waiting for the creature to make its appearance. She played this charade with the being for several weeks. The thing would only come out during storms, would get close enough to the shore to have a stare down, then retreat back to the sea after ten minutes or so. It seemed curious, never coming any closer than it had that first day, and seemed to be nonaggressive. It never made quick movements, it had a neutral look on its face, and it appeared relaxed as it sang that haunting melody.

Her heart leaped when she saw it surface, and she felt joy when she watched it play about in the waves. Watching as it dove through the swells gave her a feeling of calm. As it came near and sang its hymn, she found herself hypnotized. It entranced her so much she would forget everything around her. She longed to see this creature more and more every day. And every day it didn't come, she found herself deeply saddened, like she was missing her best friend in the whole world.

She decided the next time it came, she was going to meet it.

"Sara, I found this for you when I was going through Grandpa's dresser. It's addressed to you; it looks like a journal of some sort," Sara's mom said when Sara came in for dinner that evening.

Sara placed it on her bed and went back to have dinner with her mother. When dinner was finished, they decided to watch a movie together. It was "Shark Week," Sara's favorite, and *Jaws* was playing on tv. She forgot about the journal.

It was late when she finally got to bed, and she was exhausted. She set back the covers, climbed in, and fell right to sleep. The journal lay forgotten on top of the spread.

Morning came with a violent crash of waves against the rocks. *A storm! I bet it comes today!* Sara thought. She threw the covers back and heard something hit the floor. She reached down and picked up the journal. She decided to take it with her and read by the shore until the rain came. She would keep a ziplock in her pocket to keep the book dry.

She opened the journal as soon as she was seated on her perch. A letter nearly blew away in the wind, but she caught it before it took flight. It was addressed to her, just as her mother had said.

Dearest Sara,

If you are reading this, then I have moved on from this existence. Know that wherever lies beyond, I am thinking of you. I imagine you miss me, too.

I have been keeping this journal for many years, and I feel you are the only one who will accept and attempt to understand what is written within the pages. Do I have your curiosity piqued yet? Knowing you, you're having a hard time not skipping ahead!

But enough jesting. The contents of this book are of a creature I have befriended in the sea. Its name is Kai, and it is a mercreature. It came to me one day during the beginning of a storm. Since that day, I have mercilessly researched this creature. The findings are slim, and what I have found and experienced are within these pages.

I have known about it these many years and have had no one to share this exciting discovery with. I pass this knowledge to you in the hopes you and Kai find each other. Do not be afraid; Kai has been nothing but inquisitive and docile during our times together. Revel in the discovery of something unknown to nearly every person in this world.

I love you, child, with all my being. I wish you the very best in your life.

Love,

Grandpa

Sara sat and stared at that letter for a long time. Her grandfather knew about this creature, and he even gave her its name. *Kai.* She repeated the name a few times and liked how it sounded. *Kai.* Her being had a name. She decided to read through the journal in search of how to communicate with it.

As she waited for the storm, she read. She learned how her grandfather had met the creature – Kai, she kept telling herself, its name was Kai – and it was very similar to her own discovery of Kai. He had been collecting shells along the beach, instead of drawing as she had been, when a storm rolled in. He heard a splash too big to be one of the local marine life. He stood and watched for a long time, eventually glimpsing that beautiful, silver fin among the crashing waves. That was all he saw that first day.

He did the same thing Sara had done and gone into the local town to research. And he found the same lack of information Sara had. Grandpa took it one step further and went to the large city nearby. There he found a bit more on sea folklore and also contacted a university professor known for her study of folklore. The professor sent him as much information as she could find on the sea creatures of tales. He was able to deduce from all the research the creature was some type of merfolk. She had determined this much on her own, but he included copies of all his research in the journal, highlighting the high points.

As she sat there reading, she didn't notice the clouds becoming darker or the waves crashing more violently. The storm was upon her before she knew it. The sky let loose, hard sheets of rain pounding down on her. It was raining so hard she couldn't see the cottage from where she sat. After jamming the journal into the ziplock and putting it in her pocket, she stood up to run to the house. She found herself flat on her face, having slipped on the rock when she stood. She lay there for a moment, stunned, when she felt a tug on her ankle.

She turned and was face-to-face with Kai. She didn't know what to do. She didn't want to move in fear of scaring it away, but the rain was getting harder and colder. She made to stand when Kai pointed to a little shelter not thirty yards away. Sara had never noticed it before; it was on the back side of the rock she always sat on. Had she not fallen, and had Kai not pointed it out, she never would have known it was there.

She made her way there and sat inside in relief. She was soaked to the bone and freezing, but the small shelter was enough to keep her out of the rain. She looked around; someone had been here before. There was a small pile of burned wood and a larger pile of unburned wood. There was even a small box of matches. Surprised the matches were dry, she was able to use a few blank pages from the back of the book to coax a small fire to life.

Grandpa was here, she thought. It was close enough to the water to see Kai but out of the weather to stay dry. It had to be him. She could sense her grandfather's presence, although she couldn't say exactly how.

Kai stayed nearby, almost like it was standing guard. It stayed that way until the rain had let up to a point Sara could run inside. As soon as she took off, Kai was gone. She glanced over her shoulder midway to the cottage to see Kai's tail disappearing in a swell fifty yards out. Sara sprinted the rest of the way to the house.

The weather stayed stormy for the next five days. Sara saw Kai every one of those days, waiting for her off the shoreline. She snuck down to her rock perch as often as she could, but her mom made her stay in for the most part, spouting about the cold, wet weather and illness.

The times she could get away, she and Kai sat with each other. Sara told Kai about her grandfather's journal, unsure if Kai understood or not. Kai simply sat, seemingly content to be near Sara; it seemed to express its only emotion when Sara spoke of her grandfather. It almost seemed to purr at those times. Kai expressed no other emotions nor needs and did not try to communicate in any type of language.

Sara spent that time sketching Kai, feeling Kai's surprisingly smooth grey-green skin, it's bumpy, scaled tail, and its beautiful silver fin, which felt like fine strands of silken hair.

On the fourth day, Sara caught sight of more shiny tails. She couldn't believe it - Kai wasn't the only one. It did have a colony. She hoped she would get to meet them.

On the fifth day, Sara asked Kai if she knew where her grandfather was. His disappearance had been sketchy at best – he had come to vacation at the cottage, and no one had heard from him again. It was believed he had gotten caught in a tide from the ocean, the weather had snuck up on him and caught him off guard. Sara hadn't believed that. Her grandfather had been on or near the ocean his entire life. There was no possibility he was taken unaware by it.

Kai perked up at this, indicating to Sara it had been understanding her all along. It pointed at the ocean, a smile upon its face. Had her grandfather been taken in the ocean then? Was the story true? Kai grabbed at Sara, tried to pull her along, to pull her into the water. Sara panicked. She couldn't understand what Kai wanted from her, why it was pulling her into the water. She couldn't breathe down there, and Sara assumed Kai lived quite deep under the surface.

Sara tried to tell Kai she couldn't go with, that she didn't have the ability to live under the water. But Kai pulled harder and harder. Sara was terrified of drowning in the depths of the ocean; there was no way she was going in that water any further, regardless of an implied meeting with her grandfather. Sara yanked back as hard as she could, falling into the water and releasing her arm from Kai's grip. She scrambled backward as fast as she possibly could, like a crab scuttling from a rambunctious child, getting onto the beach where she couldn't be reached.

Kai stared at her, its normally relaxed gaze hard, cold like the water. Sara had angered it; it had been determined for Sara to come with it. Sara again tried to tell Kai she couldn't go, she couldn't breathe under water. She fled that icy stare.

Sara avoided her rock perch after that, instead choosing to draw on the small, grassy hill to the back of their cottage. They only had a week left before returning to the city, and Sara decided she would not try to find Kai before leaving. She was afraid of what Kai would try if it got ahold of her again.

Even in her attempt to forget the mermaid, Sara found herself humming its tune. She would find herself in a trance, the tune sending her ito a daze, and when she snapped out of it, she found she had sketched images of Kai in her drawing book.

The night before their departure, Sara dreamed that

same dream with the same haunting melody. As the song crescendoed with the crashing waves, she could see Kai's tail glinting through the grey haze. When Kai surfaced, Sara's grandfather was there, too, holding Kai's hand. There was a second mermaid to his other side. He let go of the second mermaid's hand and beckoned Sara to come to him. He opened his arms to her, a small wave of one hand letting her know it was okay to join him. Sara took two tentative steps forward, a smile forming on her face at seeing her grandfather for the first time in so very long.

As she took a third step, Kai's face changed from neutral to eager, like it wanted her to come to her grandfather. It was an eagerness that was untoward, not the eagerness of meeting a long lost friend but that of need, of anticipation of something it wanted badly.

Sara stopped in her tracks, but she had gone farther than she thought. She found herself calf deep in the water, just within reach of Kai and her grandfather. She tried to step backward, but it was too late. Kai was lightening quick, and Sara found Kai's hand wrapped around her ankle. Her head slammed into the water and sand as Kai dragged her into the deep. Her grandfather floated in the water, watching, his face frozen in a silent scream.

Sara's body slammed up in bed, her body drawing in huge breaths. Once she calmed, she noticed her feet and the bottom of her sheets were wet.

"Are you sure you have all your things packed?" Mom asked for the 708th time. Sara rolled her eyes and nodded yes in response.

Sara looked one more time at the ocean, a longing in her soul pulling her toward it.

"Mom, I'll be right back. I just want to make sure I didn't leave any of my drawing stuff down by the little cave I found," Sara told her mom. "It'll only take a moment."

Although she had stayed away, she had felt a strong pull toward the water over the last seven days. She needed to see Kai again, needed to say goodbye. But she was also terrified.

She had only ever met with Kai during a storm, so she felt it unlikely Kai would present itself on this rare day of sunshine. She found herself looking cautiously around anyway, looking for any signs Kai was present. The water was calm and as clear as it ever got; she would see Kai if it came. She got within two yards of the shoreline before she turned around to leave.

It came from nowhere. Sara found herself face-planted in the sand before she had even taken a step away from the water's edge. Blood rushed into her mouth, and she could feel space where a tooth had come out. A sharp pain spiked through her head, and she realized she had come down upon a small rock.

Before she could holler out to her mother, she was under the water. It was everything she could do not to take a breath, not to fill her lungs with that frigid, salty water.

Kai swam faster than anything Sara had ever seen. Before she knew it, they were deep at the bottom. She saw a carcass of what could only be a mermaid lying on the bottom. She also saw the second mermaid from her dream, along with several others.

And there were chains floating in the water, held down by heavy, iron balls, floating upward and taut in a way Sara couldn't comprehend nor attempt to explain. There were people attached to the chains, floating in the water with silent screams on their faces. One of them was her grandfather, exactly as she had seen him in her dream. His mouth was a wide-open cavern, fear etched on his face for eternity.

Sara felt the chain clamp around her ankle. She didn't want to see any more. She opened her lungs, welcoming the glacial chill that filled her body.

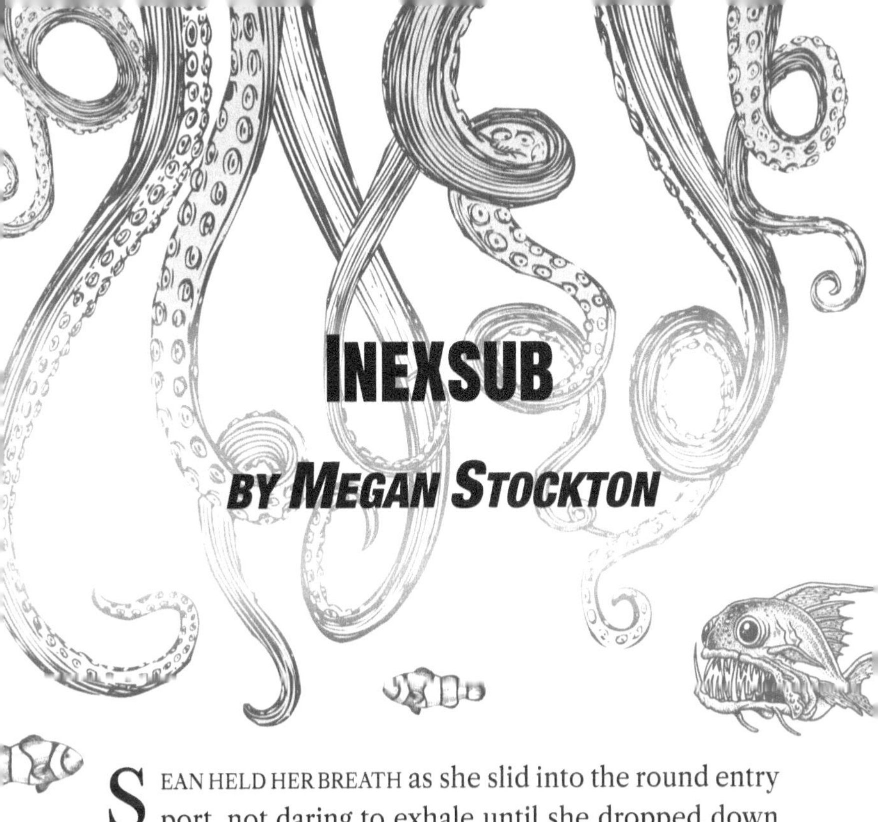

INEXSUB

BY MEGAN STOCKTON

S EAN HELD HER BREATH as she slid into the round entry port, not daring to exhale until she dropped down inside and her feet hit the floor. When a space was this small, it really didn't matter if you had claustrophobia or not. You were suddenly aware of how much space you occupied, of the miniscule distance between you and everything that contained you. Sean wasn't a big person; standing barely five-two and lacking any real width or girth on any part of her body, she was half the size of most of the ship's crew.

She took a deep breath and looked up at the face smiling down at her from outside.

"You good?" Charlie's blonde hair fell downwards past his face as he peered down at her.

"I'm good," Sean confirmed with a thumbs up.

"Great. Get settled in. I'll go touch base with you from the command station before you are set off. They're going to close the hatch now."

There was a finality to the way Charlie said that. Sean knew she shouldn't be apprehensive. Was it apprehension? Or was it fear? Sean's eyes scanned over the knobs and levers and buttons, and for a brief and panic-inducing moment, she forgot what everything did. She was suddenly a child inside one of the most state-of-the-art vessels in the oceans today.

The Independent Exploratory Submersible, Inexsub for short, was Sean's second home these days. She had been on trial runs inside this little spherical vessel at least a hundred times over the last eighteen months. She was the only person who knew how to fully operate it. Although its design seemed overwhelming, it was very intuitive and user-friendly.

She laid her palms across the control panel, trying to ignore the sound of the maintenance workers fastening the bolts that would protect her from the pressure of the ocean. They were already over forty thousand feet down, and there was always the risk that the Inexsub would immediately implode. She took some comfort in knowing that if that *did* happen, she would die instantly, before she ever realized anything was wrong. That was the worst case scenario, right? Not too shabby for the worst possible outcome in a scenario.

The Inexsub had been tested time and time again, but never at these depths. They were in unknown and unexplored territory here. They had reached a depth that was officially deeper than the lowest known point of the Mariana Trench.

But they wanted to go even lower.

She took several deep breaths, clicking a few buttons

on the control pad as she waited for a series of eight green lights to appear across the dash. One by one they illuminated. One, two, three, four, five, six...

"Can you hear me, Sean?"

Sean blinked, shaking herself out of her worried day-dreaming, and put her headset on. She adjusted the microphone then flipped the switch to aux in.

"Yes, I can hear you."

Charlie's voice was calming on the other end. "Per-fect. We are testing all of your system functions now, and everything looks good. Any concerns on your end? Have you performed a systems check?"

"All clear," she said, tapping the radar control as it continued to blink orange. Everything else was greenlit and ready to go. She chewed the inside of her cheek as she stared at the blinking orange bulb. The radar was very simple and had never failed before. If she told Charlie it hadn't booted up successfully yet, they would delay and she would have to start the nerve-wracking loading process all over again while they troubleshoot-ed. Or worse, they would cancel or postpone this explo-ration.

"Alright. This is the moment. Do you want me to do a countdown?"

"No," Sean responded too quickly. Her heart lurched into her throat and she put her hand over her chest. She was glad they couldn't see her inside the little inox and titanium sphere, the way the color had surely drained from her face at the mere question.

"No. If something is going to go wrong, I don't want to be waiting for it. Just d—"

The Inexsub suddenly lurched forward, a rapid popping noise echoing in the chamber around her, and she gripped the joystick in front of her like she could outmaneuver the inevitable... and then the submersible rocked backwards and dropped away.

She let out a long exhale, grinning broadly.

"You son of a bitch, Charlie!"

"Sorry if I scared you, just doing what you asked," he chided, friendly humor thick in his voice. His laughter came across her headset.

She allowed the vessel to descend on its own for several more yards, watching as the light of the ship above became smaller and smaller, until it disappeared.

"Leave the light on for me?"

"Always. Going silent. Talk to you in an hour. Good luck, Sean."

Sean closed her eyes as she allowed the sub to continue the natural descent, flinching as she heard the gangway compress, collapse, and then fall away from the ship. That disposable gangway allowed Sean to enter the Inexsub and enabled both the submersible and the main ship to be sealed off safely without water or pressure exposure from opening the hatches.

She heard the contained propeller kick on, and she opened her eyes, enveloped in darkness that was disorienting but also somehow... comforting. This wasn't the career field for someone with anxiety. Everytime a hatch was opened, every time the ship descended, every time even the smallest thing went wrong, there was a risk of instant death... or becoming unrecoverable, which could have been an even worse scenario. Dying slowly with no escape somewhere miles beneath the surface. Sean found the solitude in the Inexsub not only comforting, she was also exhilarated by the prospect of being in control of where she went and how she explored.

She flipped the lights on outside the sub, leaving the interior dark aside from the green and orange glow of the control panels around her. Two beams illuminated the path in front of her, and she pressed the joystick forward, allowing the Inexsub to pass through a cloud of debris that was dark and inky. She wondered if she had passed through a layer of some microspecies, but soon she was on the other side and the water was crystal clear.

She felt like she was floating through the air, suspended in darkness that had so little life. Normally the water was alive with small creatures, some the size of a pinhead. These depths did not often lend to large species. Large predators would mean there had to be large prey, and it just wasn't feasible. But this wasteland she was passing through now was highly unusual.

"Checking in," Sean heard Charlie's voice over the speaker. "Everything alright?"

Sean smirked, putting the Inexsub on autopilot with a crawling pace as she leaned back in her seat. "I thought you were going silent for an hour. Was that too hard for you?"

"Do you have anything on your radar?"

She realized there was something in Charlie's voice that wasn't right. There was no good-hearted humor, no friendliness. He almost sounded scared. Sean suddenly sat bolt upright, flipping the radar on.

"Sean?" Charlie croaked through static, pitch increasing.

"I'm looking, I'm looking..." she insisted. "I didn't have

it turned on."

She heard Charlie say something, garbled and crisp with static. She couldn't understand him, and she frantically tapped at the radar, watching as it slowly loaded. A light green ripple pulsed across the screen, mapping the area around her with sonar. It was mostly empty, and then...

"What the fuck is that?" Sean whispered to herself, voice catching as she noticed the massive object between her and the main sub. She couldn't see the other ship on the limited radar, but she could tell that whatever the blob was, it was moving quickly. The radar barely had time to appropriately map it before it was blinking closer and closer to her.

She froze, hair standing on end, muscles burning like they had been pumped full of acid. She was unable to move until she heard Charlie scream her name once, crystal clear, over the radio before he disappeared into a wave of static again. She was spurred into motion by his panic, reaching down with both hands to grasp the joysticks on either side, moving them expertly to spin the ship around and dive down.

The Inexsub began beeping at her, flashing tiny red lights as a warning as she both descended too quickly and was being approached by an unavoidable impact. She thought she could feel the ripple of water around the submersible before she was hit by the creature, the slightest wobble of the controls in her hand as she prepared for the hit.

She gritted her teeth, screaming as she felt the ship spin out of control. She gripped the arms of her chair, head pinned back against the headrest with the force of the spiral. Something obscured her viewing window in the turmoil, and she thought she could make out the form of something black clicking against the glass. The ship gave her another alert, this one even more alarming: pressure warning. She was being crushed. Something more than the pressure of the ocean's depths was bearing down on the Inexsub.

Suddenly, the creature pulled away from her, and the ship's rapid pirouette became even more out-of-control and erratic. Her eyes watered as she tried to look down at the radar. It was coming back for her, whatever it was. Outside the window, she could see the wild sweep of her lights and the way they briefly illuminated the pink, scarred skin of a massive squid.

It was *gigantic.*

She knew colossal squids could get forty or fifty feet, but that was more tentacle than anything. The mantle on this specimen could've been one hundred feet on its own.

The sight of its pale flesh and dilated, searching eye made her realize everything down here was probably photosensitive. She quickly reached over to shut off the headlights. She flipped off the exhaust fans and the engine; she was suddenly enveloped in silence. It wasn't comforting anymore, it wasn't empowering... It was suffocating.

She steadied her breathing, hands clenching the controls with white-knuckled nervousness. She took several small, slow breaths between her lips before she reached over, tapping the radio paging system. When no one responded, she spoke.

"Hello? Charlie? Anybody? Can you guys hear me?"

She tapped the pager again, but there was nothing. Even the static she had heard earlier was gone. She felt the sickening sensation of the Inexsub rolling backwards, turning her upside down. The ballast tanks must have been damaged by the squid. She clenched her eyes shut, stifling the warm and acidic sick that threatened to rise in her throat. She could right the ship with the engine if she turned it back on, but she might draw the squid back to her. Did she have a choice though?

Sean kept her eyes closed, stomach spiraling in tune with the slow rotation of the ship. She felt her hair fall upwards, and her body slid against the shoulder strap of the seatbelt as she briefly dangled. She dug her toes in under the dash, hooking them so she didn't fall upwards quite so far. She counted with slow and deliberate dedication as she waited for the Inexusb to come back to a correct configuration. As it began its downward turn, she opened her eyes briefly, catching sight of a light in the darkness. It was a pinprick of light, like someone had torn a hole in the fabric of the deep sea.

"Charlie," she breathed. "I could fucking kiss that ugly face."

He had left the lights on so she could find her way back to the main ship. Could they get her loaded back onto the main ship? She would normally have to be hauled to the surface on the Inexsub, but she didn't know if she could handle it. She was on the verge of another panic attack, and the small interior suddenly felt even smaller. Regardless, the first step would be to get to the main ship.

She looked at the radar again, breathing a sigh of relief when she didn't see anything else on the radar...

right now, anyway. It was fuzzy, and every pulse sent a scrambled pattern across the screen. She was lucky the squid hadn't damaged the hull or ruptured the window. She could've been dead, a mist of human flesh from the implosion.

She clicked on the engines first, letting them whir to life as she kept a close eye on the damaged radar. No sign still. The ship wobbled until it had corrected its malposition. Her mouth was dry, and every swallow reminded her of how nauseous she still was. When the radar remained empty, she reached for the headlights and hesitated, hand hovering in the air. Her fingertips quivered and she retracted them to her chest. She lucked up on the engine not attracting the attention of the squid, but did she really want to risk the lights?

She fixed her eyes on that tiny globe of white up above and gently pressed the Inexsub towards it, crawling through the dense black of the ocean. She hunched over, drawing into herself as she wrapped her free arm around her rumbling gut.

"Charlie?" she asked again, tapping the radio's pager. She was met with only silence. It didn't seem right, and she was filled with a sense of both inexplicable dread and worry. If the communications system was down, she should have had an error code of some sort. Maybe they had a problem on their end. Had they been attacked too? Why wasn't the squid going after their light? It could have had something to do with the depth. Maybe the squid wasn't comfortable at higher elevations...

"Jesus Christ, you are losing it," Sean muttered to herself, cutting off the frantic and running thoughts. She increased the speed of the Inexsub now, trying to convince herself she was braver and more confident. The faster she got up there, the safer she would be.

The radar picked up the ship above, warping the shape into something more irregular, but it was there and undeniable. Any moment now she would see its metal hull. The circle of light was already becoming larger and larger.

Then she realized that something wasn't right. She slowed the submersible down as the light loomed so close it blinded her. It was bobbing. Was the main sub also damaged and unable to maintain its position? How would she be able to help the crew from the Inexsub?

She repeated Charlie's name again to the familiar silence. Then she saw what looked like jagged, yellow spikes appear from the darkness behind the light. They parted, a mini abyss appearing that was more than twice the width and depth of the Inexsub's circumference. She noticed there were hundreds of tendrils that emerged with their own, milder bioluminescence. They were attached to the light, body, and face of the creature. She saw its eyes then, on either side of its narrow head: glassy and flat, shimmering coins the size of manhole covers. But it was the teeth that had Sean's blood running cold. They were uneven, jutting, like a child had glued them in.

She flinched at the sound of static over the radio speakers, and she thought *maybe* she heard someone say her name. Her eyes flicked to the radar then back up to the monstrous creature that stared with lidless eyes, mouth opening and closing slowly. The anglerfish jiggled its lure at her again, and Sean jerked the joystick to the side to try and divert her path.

In the depths of the ocean, no one could hear your screams or the sound of the Inexsub imploding from the puncture of fangs through its hull. No one could admire the vapor of vermillion that diluted to cerise in the clear, dark depths: a mist of human flesh, then a particle among millions.

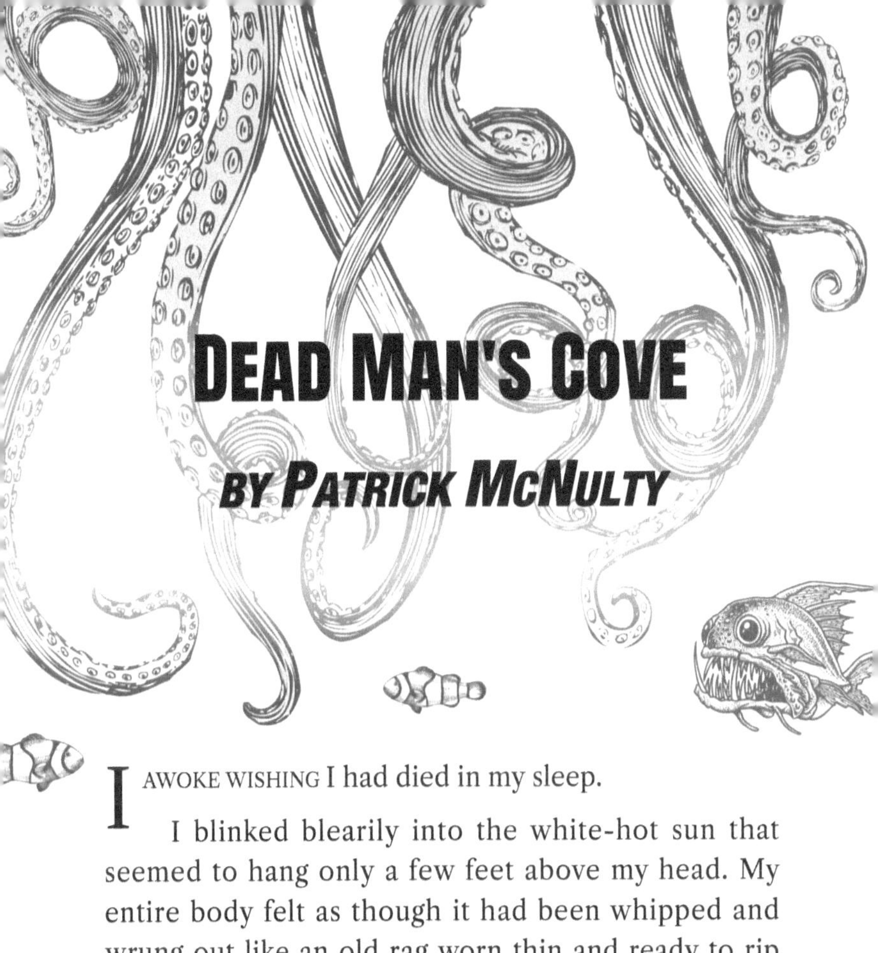

Dead Man's Cove

by Patrick McNulty

I AWOKE WISHING I had died in my sleep.

I blinked blearily into the white-hot sun that seemed to hang only a few feet above my head. My entire body felt as though it had been whipped and wrung out like an old rag worn thin and ready to rip apart.

My joints were filled with shards of glass, as was my head. My exposed skin was burned to a high red sheen that dried and stretched until my flesh lamy so tightly across my bones it felt that even the smallest, most subtle movement would force a tear and allow my insides to spill into the sea.

The sea.

I felt the ocean move beneath me, lifting and lowering my aching body. I lifted my head, and starbursts of pain exploded behind my eyes. But I powered through and found I had been saved from the depths by a few loose ropes and a section of deck boards still lashed together from what remained of the *Marie Clare*.

The rest of the ship and the crew I had sailed with for forty-seven days and nights were gone and swallowed by the sea.

Against my body's wishes, I sat up straighter on my makeshift raft and saw the ragged black peaks of Dead Man's Cove due north, and a new sensation ran through me with a ripple of electricity: fear.

We had been at sea just over forty days when Captain Hale announced he had purposely driven us off of our intended course to Spain and, instead, decided to chase the ghost of Dead Man's Cove.

A magical place, he had told us. A place that held the key to everlasting life. The very fountain of youth. Where the riches were so great that gold and jewels became inconsequential.

As you can imagine, the crew, who believed they were heading to Spain and some well-deserved rest and re-laxation, did not take the news very well. There was talk of a mutiny and even more serious discussion about murdering the one-eyed captain and tossing his ginger ass overboard. But what Captain Hale lacked as a captain he made up for as a salesman, and slowly, over the next few days, he turned the tide of the crew as it were.

Soon, the hushed conversations about this lush and plentiful faraway land that promised to cure all ails, a place that held the secrets of the known universe, became more than a myth. It became a destination. It became the miracle cure desperately needed by Lyle, the ship's cook, who was stricken with gangrene. And to Jim, the nearly blind deckhand whose vision was weakening by the day. It became a paradise that was just a day's sail away.

Still, as the journey to this uncharted utopia dragged on, the rations did not comply. The rum was the first to go, then the last of the fresh vegetables. The livestock was next, until each man's portion could barely satisfy a child, let alone a full-grown man exhausted from a day climbing in the rigging.

And when the rations were gone, tensions returned until the very air on the deck of the ship felt thick with latent electricity. The charged air that hovered close to the earth moments before a thunderstorm.

Tales of miraculous cures and large-breasted women greeting us on the golden shores of this fairy port soured on the tongues of everyone save for the captain, who assured us all we were moments away from spotting those tell-tale black peaks.

Whispered discussions of mutiny and murder resumed.

And then the captain's young son, Will, who could climb to the crow's nest atop the main mast faster than most crows, saw the peaks in the distance. He called it out from his perch, and we all looked. We all knew, right away, that this was a mistake.

The craggy black cliffs and jagged rocks of the cursed place jutted angrily out of the sea like the bent and broken teeth of a monstrous shark.

I think even the captain felt it as he stood on the bridge and gazed out into the growing gloom of an incoming storm. There was no joy in his face. A look of achievement, yes. A satisfied look. But no joy.

Be careful what you wish for, I remember thinking.

You just might get it.

As thunder rolled overhead and lightning clawed at a sky the color of bruises, the captain and his first mate quietly discussed how to proceed. I couldn't hear a lot of what they were saying, but in the end, the first mate did a lot of finger-pointing. A lot of swearing. Then the captain himself took hold of the wheel and steered the ship toward the distant cove, calling orders to the rest of us to raise the sails even in an oncoming storm. He wanted to race the weather to the safety of the cove.

And we almost made it.

The storm that looked harmless at first glance dropped on top of us with the very vengeance of God himself. The *Marie Clare* was built to fight, and she fought fiercely, but no ship could withstand towering waves as high as mountains and troughs as deep as the very sea bottom itself.

When the first mast snapped, it took out three of the crew not six feet away from where I stood. Once the sails were twisted and wrapped around the remaining masts, the sea tossed the crippled ship about the sea like an angry toddler.

There was nowhere to hide. Nowhere to run.

I heard the captain call out to his boy, over and over, until the poor man's voice grew ragged and hoarse. Then the ship rose with a curling wave, turning as it was lifted into the air.

I remember wrapping my arms into a section of rigging. I gripped the remaining mast and prayed to any god that would listen to spare me that night.

As if in spite of my prayers, the sea lifted what remained of our ship on a towering wave until the air thinned and I could feel the first drops of rain as they left the clouds, inches above my face.

The *Marie Clare* dropped just as sharply and rolled over in the curl of the wave. The sudden force and the icy cold water snapped my head back against the deck floor, and with the sound of two billiard balls cracking together, the world went black.

Now, as the sun is setting, the tide rolled me back toward the black peaks of Dead Man's Cove. I started to see bits of the *Marie Clare* and wonder, perhaps for the first time, why a fabled place of everlasting life was given such an infamous name.

That was until I saw the bodies begin to surface.

More and more rose up from the depths as the sun sank behind the peaks. Bloated and bleached white from the seawater, ancient mariners along with a few crew members I still recognized opened their glazed eyes and swiveled their sights toward me.

There was a slight wind at my back, but the raft would not outpace the growing horde of dead sailors that silently surrounded my position.

I screamed out at Collins, a man I had shared dinner with nearly every night aboard the ship—a family man like me, with a wife and a small son at home.

I screamed at the thing who used to be my friend to leave me alone and please go away. Collins opened his mouth to speak, but no words issued forth—only an oily, black filth and what remained of the man's tongue.

The place, this cove, the captain didn't deliver us to paradise. He brought us to Hell.

The horde drifted closer, and I saw that although they were drawing near, they weren't actively swimming. They were simply bobbing in the water, angling themselves toward me like mindless buoys with hands hooked into claws and teeth snapping for a meal.

The sun was nearly down, but I could see a small spit of beach. I prayed these demonic creatures were confined to the sea. Then I prayed I could swim that far without passing out or, worse, being dragged down into the depths. I prayed more in that two-minute gap than I ever had.

Without another word and a final last prayer, I dove into the icy sea and swam. I was never a very strong swimmer, but when pressed and with the wind at my back and the tide in my favor, I swam fairly well. My aching arms and legs were quickly numbed by the frigid temperatures. The current pushed me forward toward the moonlit stretch of beach.

I stole a glance over my shoulder; it was a mistake.

The sea was filled with hundreds of dead sailors all clawing at the water as they awkwardly swam after me. Body after body popped to the surface all around me. At one point, I felt skeletal fingers slip around my ankle. I kicked furiously and was able to shake the dead man's grip as a final wave pushed me into the shallows. My hands clawed through the sand and bits of broken shells as I scrambled onto the beach.

Soaked to the bone, the wind carved through my clothes that stuck to my emaciated frame and knifed away any heat left around my heart.

The rolling tide pushed more and more limp bodies into the shallows and onto the beach. As I found my footing, I watched in horror as dead sailors shakily climbed to their feet and fixed me with their white, moonlit stare as their broken mouths stretched into greasy, hungry grins.

For a moment, I was frozen in place, staring at the horde emerging from the ocean. It was only when I heard footsteps behind me on the beach that I turned and saw a one-eyed man with a ginger beard standing next to a small boy of eleven.

Captain Hale fixed his opaque, pale eyes on me and smiled. "So nice to see you, Mr. Henry. Isn't it nice to see Mr. Henry, Will?"

The thing that stood next to Captain Hale was not the Will I knew. The Will I knew loved sailing and the sea. He could name over a hundred different fish and would spend the day happily jabbering on about everything and nothing.

The feral creature that had taken his place didn't speak, but only issued a low growl from deep within its narrow chest.

"No one believed me," Captain Hale said. "No one. But I found it. Dead Man's Cove."

More dead sailors pushed through the forest behind Hale. Men, children, and even some women. Skin loose and hanging in rags from the yellowed skeletons of the older dead. Some with barely a blemish on their mottled skin.

"Paradise," Hale continued. "Where every need is met. Every need, except one."

Shuffling footsteps grew into a thunderous march as the dead horde from the ocean gathered behind me.

"We're so very hungry," Hale finished. "So hungry. And the dead don't eat their own, do they Will?"

The feral boy's lips curled into a sneer as he bared

his tiny teeth. I stood locked in place as he approached along with the others, powerless to fight as they closed ranks. Hands reaching, grabbing, hooked into claws, teeth snapping at my flesh.

Before the first finger touched me, I prayed again.

I prayed aloud, I screamed at the top of my voice to improve my chances of being heard by some merciful deity hopefully lurking nearby.

And as the horde closed in, I screamed as the greedy fingers dug into my flesh, ripped my mouth apart, and tore my tongue from my body.

And as they tore the sheets of muscle from my chest and broke the bones of my legs to suck out the marrow, I realized that the only magic found here in this cursed place was that death would not take me, for even the reaper avoids Dead Man's Cove.

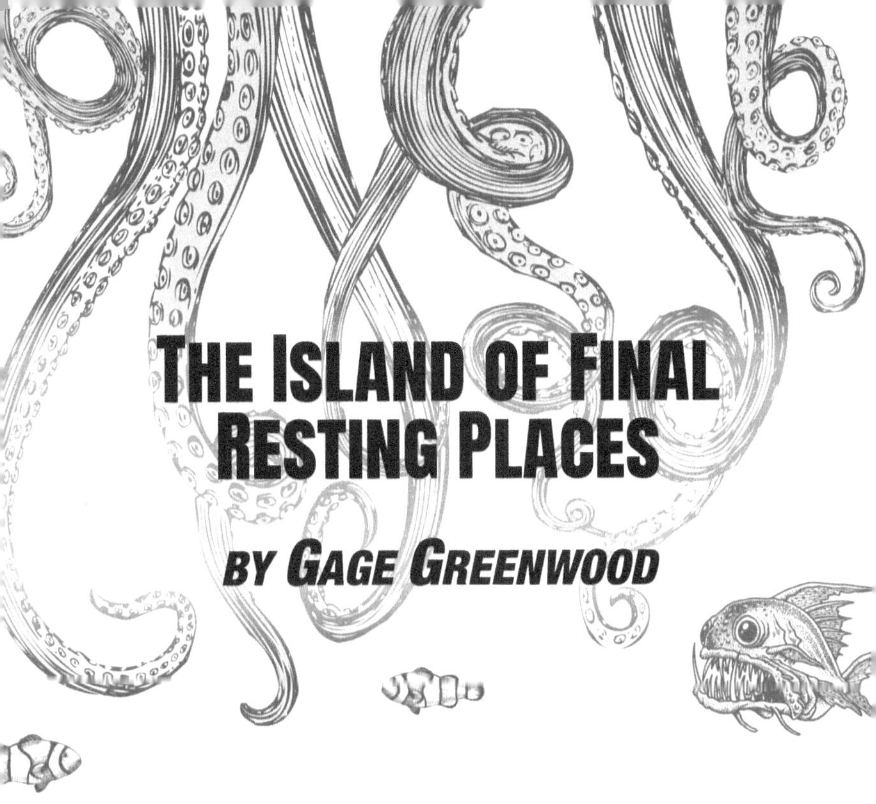

THE ISLAND OF FINAL RESTING PLACES

BY GAGE GREENWOOD

YEAR 20 DIARIES:

COURTNEY: I WADED. OR I waited. Both, I suppose. I'm not sure exactly what I waited for. Anything really. A rupture underneath me so massive it caused a displacement in the ocean, a tsunami, something to wash this all away. To wash me clean off the map of human history.

YEAR 1 DIARIES:

DAY 1
COURTNEY: Okay, I'm not the 'Dear Diary' type, but I thought under the circumstances, I'd start this little written journey solely about our trips to the island. You

all have access to it, and I'll leave it around for all of you to read when you're here. Chester said he hopes we make this a tradition. Every year in August, we all meet up at his ridiculous mansion for two weeks. Seriously, Chester, how did none of us know you were this rich???

Anyway, we're all going away to college. Our lives will change, and inevitably, we'll all move in different directions. I don't know if we'll fulfill Chester's dream of an annual meet up, but I like the idea of it, and I want to document our fun. And I want to showcase what I love about each of you. So I'm keeping this damned diary and you can all laugh at me, but I want one of you to grow old and find this dusty journal in my garage as they wheel my carcass out of my house. I want you to smile at all of the memories, to think of me like this, as I was before I became the most powerful and ruthless woman in the world, which we all know is inevitable.

You all can write in it too. Although I know you won't.

CHESTER: Just to prove you wrong, I'm writing in this. Honestly, I love the idea. And I truly do hope this becomes our tradition. Starting here, the summer after our graduation, and spanning throughout our lives. We can leave the world behind and reconnect.

Some will get married, have children; some won't. We'll shift apart eventually. That's what happens in life. But we MUST make Casa La Douchebag a high priority. Force your spouse to make it a fucking vow at your wedding. "And I promise to allow you two weeks out of the year to become the same type of person you complain about the other fifty weeks: a dooooouchebag."

Now, I think we all know none of us are going to keep

up with this diary, but for the sake of making Courtney happy, I'm going to pester all of you to at least sign it or say something today. I'm sharing a fucking mansion with you. It's the least you could do.

Oh, by the way, Courtney, how did you not know I was rich?

PARKER: Sounds good. Thanks for having me. But I'm with Courtney on this one. We all knew you were a rich prick, but none of us knew you were THIS rich!

JAMES: Seriously, I knew you came from money, but not THIS kind of money. Better idea for your plan: instead of us meeting two weeks a year, why not have us all just move in here permanently and forever? I want this to be my life. Your fucking kitchen is bigger than our high school was.

JULIANA: Oh. My. God. I'm never leaving. If you had told me you literally owned a mansion on your own private island, I would have taken you to prom. I would have married you. At the very least, I would have sucked your dick. I still will if you let me live here forever.

DAY 2

CHESTER: Guys. You all knew my parents were rich. I talked about it. How many times have I whined to y'all about my family? Now, if you'll all excuse me, I have to go meet up with Juliana for a few minutes. Wink.

COURTNEY: Chester, there's a difference between

wealthy and owning an island. Let's not be ridiculous. Also, Juliana once blew a dude in MY BED.... WHILE I WAS TRYING TO SLEEP.... IN THAT SAME BED. So, I have first-hand knowledge that she sucks at sucking. Ew. I'm reading all of this again and realizing we actually are a bunch of douchebags. Sigh. You were right.

But, I have a serious question, and for the sake of this stupid diary, I insist you write the answer here. If your family had this kind of money, why, why, WHYYYYYYY did you live in, and go to school in, Tanner's Switch?

CHESTER: We also have houses in New York City, LA, Miami, Lexington, Ohio, and like five other places. My parents chose Tanner's Switch BECAUSE it's such a small town and because the schools are good. I mean, just look at the caliber of friends I made. Some of them give BJs for living arrangements.

Honestly though, you're all the best people I know, and I feel so fortunate to call you friends.

DAY 8

COURTNEY: Ugh. I made this big stink about this diary, and I totally keep forgetting to write in it myself. Here's some updates. We had a bonfire, where James and Parker cried while we listened to "Nebraska" by Springsteen. They won't admit it, but it happened. Chester makes fancy dinners every night, and my goodness, I had no idea he could cook so well. Ummmmm.... What else happened? James got stoned and slept on the staircase leading to the second floor. Juliana confessed to owning every season of *Saved By the Bell* on DVD, and Jessica told us she's going to open her own restaurant in Tanner's Switch. I'm writing that last one for accountability. Because if we come back here in ten years and that hasn't come to fruition, I will be PISSED.

DAY 10

JESSICA: Okay, I refused to write in here, but Courtney has become obsessed with this stupid thing and insisted I write down what happened to me last night, even though I've already told you all about it. After we drank and smoked the night away, you asswipes passed out, but I decided to sit on the balcony because I'm just a poor Tanner's Switch girl, and we don't got no fancy balconies in our bedrooms. Especially not ones that overlook crystal clear beaches.

Anyway, I heard a weird noise. It was like this cross between a whimper and an owl hoot. I assumed it was just some sort of bird that I'd never heard of because, again, Tanner's Switch isn't paradise, so I don't really know tropical bird calls. But then I saw something moving on the shore. It was like a dog, but its knees bent the opposite way, and they were WAY longer than a dog's legs. It was probably eight feet tall.

It paced the shore for a little bit. And then it disappeared into the water. It didn't really swim away. It kind of just went under.

But again, we drank and smoked a lot. I probably saw James walking to the ocean for a late-night piss.

DAY 14

JULIANA: It's our last day here, and it was the best two weeks of my life. Chester, you're awesome. Thanks for not making me blow you for reals. But honestly, I love you all so much and I hope Chester's vision comes true. I want to see you all next year.

JESSICA: Byyyeeeeee.

JAMES: I didn't piss in the ocean. See you all next year.

PARKER: Sorry I didn't write in here much. I was busy having the best time of my life. See you all next year.

COURTNEY: I love you all. I'm stealing this diary so I can think about each of you throughout the year until we meet up again next summer.

YEAR 20 DIARIES

COURTNEY: I stayed in the water well past sundown. I heard you all laughing inside the house. James sang Backstreet Boys songs while Chester cooked some weird, fancy fish dinner. Juliana danced on the counter while telling us all about her childrens' phobias. Jessica drank wine and made you all promise you'd stop by her restaurant when you were in town next. Parker, of course, just stared out the window at me in the water. He had those glowing blue eyes that begged me to come closer.

YEAR 2 DIARIES

DAY 1

PARKER: Okay, Courtney is obsessed with these diaries, as you all know, so she forced me to wait until we arrived to tell you all the big news. I had to write it in here first. We are dating. We've been dating for five months, and she wouldn't let me tell you.

JESSICA: OH MY GOD!!!! That's awesome.

JAMES: Congrats!

CHESTER: That makes me so happy on a level I can't even describe. I've missed you all so much. Thank you for coming back.

JULIANA: I knew! You can't keep secrets from me. Pretty obvious when you both drool over each other's selfies. And like five out of every seven posts you made were about you two doing something together.

COURTNEY: Friends hang out with each other, you know? We could have just been friends.

JULIANA: Friends hang out with each other, but they don't go to operas together. Only two people pretending to like the opera to impress each other go to the opera together.

DAY 2

CHESTER: I'm making a piccata dish tonight. Trout

with a delicious lemon sauce. You'll love it.

JESSICA: One day, I'm going to open a restaurant, and I insist you work for me, rich boy.

JAMES: Courtney is forcing me to write this in the damned diary. Last night I heard a weird banging on the walls, which I presumed was her and Parker showing off their newfound love for each other in the bedroom, but when I looked outside, I saw a weird figure running from the house into the woods. It reemerged a few minutes later and dove into the ocean.

COURTNEY: Can you all stop saying I forced you to write in the journal. Just write in it and I won't have to force you. Last year we didn't talk about half the stuff we did. No one will even know we had a group cry over a bonfire to Bruce Springsteen's "Nebraska."

CHESTER: I think you and I are the only ones who respect the diary, Courtney. But if you remember, you DID write about the "Nebraska" thing last year.

JESSICA: I don't want anyone to know I cried to Springsteen. THAT'S THE PROBLEM!

JULIANA: I heard the banging too.

DAY 5

COURTNEY: Okay, so Parker and I saw the thing too. Holy shit. My heart is pounding. We woke up a few hours ago and heard something scraping against the outside wall. When Parker opened the shade, it was like right there. It took off down the path to the beach. We didn't see it go back in the water, but that's where it was headed.

I can't tell you how scary it was. Did you see the way it moved? Its legs are so odd. How can it walk like that, let alone run?

JESSICA: The backwards knees!

James: Yup. Same thing I saw.

DAY 7

CHESTER: Everyone is starting to freak out about the creature they all claimed to see. I have stayed on this island so many times in my life, and I have never seen a thing. I think this is a case of group hysteria.

JAMES: STFU. I know what I saw.

PARKER: Same. Definitely saw a creature. Which, hey, we're on a weird island. There's probably land and sea animals I don't know, but it keeps coming to the house and acting weird. That's what's making me freaked out.

DAY 8

CHESTER: You say "keeps" coming to the house, but it hasn't come back since you've seen it.

PARKER: That we know of.

CHESTER: Well, next year I will bring my father's rifle.

DAY 10

JULIANA: I have no idea why I'm writing this in here, but I just feel the need to get it off my chest. My life sucks. I'm not going back to college in fall. Instead, I'll be working at my mom's salon. Not her choice. Mine. But I regret it already. I don't have friends in Tanner's Switch anymore, and I feel alone all the time. We only have four days left, and each second that passes makes me feel more and more desperate to cling to this place. You guys are the best part of my life, and I miss you all.

COURTNEY: We miss you too! Parker and I are only in Connecticut. It's like a forty minute drive. Come visit us whenever you want! You can stay at our apartment. Whatever you need. We'd love to have you around more.

PARKER: Seconded. Seriously. We have plenty of space. Come by whenever.

DAY 14

JAMES: Last day again. Love you all.

CHESTER: Before Courtney steals this diary again, I just want to say thank you all for coming once again. I'll miss you all. I know we'll keep in touch on Facebook, but it's not the same. Can't wait for next summer already.

JESSICA: BYYYYEEEEEE AGAIN!

JULIANA: Bye everyone. Thanks for giving me some fun before I head back to stupidity.

PARKER: Until next year. Love you all. Especially you, Courtney.

COURTNEY: Awwwwww. Love you all.

YEAR 20 DIARIES

COURTNEY: There's an echo in the upstairs hallway. I noticed it the first time I walked toward my bedroom our first year here. It's thin and fragile, but it's there if you listen closely. Sometimes I'll just stand there in that empty space like a dart stuck to a corkboard and I'll listen. I can hear the gentle lapping of the ocean. I can hear my thoughts from years ago still bouncing off the walls. I can hear so much. I just can't hear what I need to hear. You.

YEAR 3 DIARIES

COURTNEY: Parker, I gift this diary to you for two weeks. Take it with you to the island and tell me EVERY-THING I miss. I hate that I can't go. My stomach turns thinking about all I'll miss. Tell everyone I love them. I hope you all have the time of your lives.

DAY 1

PARKER: Well, friends, as you all know, Courtney couldn't make it this year thanks to her new job. So, while we normally looked at this diary as a pain in the ass, this year I insist we all treat it as an obligation so we can fill her in on all the fun she'll miss.

JESSICA: Hi Courtney! Sorry you couldn't make it. Thanks for stopping by the Switch and Grille, which I am totally mentioning so it's documented in our diary that I OWN MY OWN RESTAURANT! But seriously, miss you.

CHESTER: While I have no doubt this will be a fun week, it won't be the same without you, Courtney. Tonight I'm making pan-seared salmon with a lemon garlic butter sauce. Jessica is begging me to make a seafood menu for her restaurant. I probably will.

JAMES: Miss you, Courtney. Glad to see you managed to stay with Parker for the full year. He's been here ten minutes, and I'm already sick of him. You're a real trooper.

JULIANA: Hey, homie. Sorry I never took you up on your offer to come stay with you and Parker. I miss you dearly. I'm hanging out. We should catch up soon.

PARKER: So, it's now three fifty in the morning, and we are all awake because Jessica heard a noise. We all investigated but couldn't find anything. James swears he saw the creature thing dipping into the water. I'm going to try to go back to sleep, but I have a feeling it's going to be a long night.

DAY 2

PARKER: I did get some sleep, but the rest of the house didn't. They were too wired after the startle last night. Instead, they stayed up drinking all night and playing cards, which leaves me alone this lovely morning while they're all passed out on the couch. I kind of like having the place to myself, but I'm also trying to be quiet so I don't wake the dead.

JAMES: It's like five o'clock in the evening and I just woke up. I have a feeling this is my new schedule for the next twelve days. Fuuuuuccckkkk. Anyway, I'm just writing to tell you that I DID see the creature dipping into the water. No doubt about it. I saw it clear as day. Still never got a good look at its face, though. Too hard not to notice those backwards legs. Oh, while I have your attention, I took six thousand dollars from Chester last night in poker. I just made more on this vacation than I would have in the two weeks of work I missed.

PARKER: It's two in the morning now, and we haven't slept yet. I think I'm rotating to their messed-up schedule now. We were all drinking and smoking in the living room when we heard the noise. It was like a scratching on the outside walls. Jessica freaked out. She was like, "That's it! That's the noise."

Because we were all together, we felt a little tougher

than we probably are and we charged outside. The fucking creature was there. He was running away from the house toward the beach, but we all saw him this time. Jesus, he's huge, and we never got that kind of close up before. His skin is all waxy, or I dunno.... Oily? It was fucking weird.

But here's the thing. We thought the scratching was the creature trying to paw his way in, like a cat at the door asking for a treat. Or maybe it was taunting us. Something like that. But James put a light on it. It was writing on the walls. Courtney, I shit you not. The scratch marks look like it was spelling a word.

I don't know if we're going to keep staying here. This is fucked. I need to call you in the A.M. to hear your voice. I might be coming home early, so tell the sailors to get out of the house before I come home and surprise the orgy.

Sorry, I have to joke. You know how I handle tension.

JAMES: I don't mean to be a dick, but if we are using this to document our story, we should write the truth. Courtney, the thing wrote letters on the wall. It looked like it was in the middle of spelling something when we interrupted it. C-O-U-R-T-N. It was spelling your name.

PARKER: We all went upstairs to listen to music in the DJ room, hoping it would quell our nerves. The second we got up here, we heard it again. Louder. Jessica pointed out she thought it came from inside the house. Chester and James just went to investigate. I'm writing this with shaking hands, Courtney. I'm honestly terrified. Jessica's teeth are literally chattering.

I want to call you, but I know you leave the phone on and I don't want to wake you up when you have to work in the morning.

James just screamed.

We ran into my bedroom. Jessica and Juliana barricaded the door with the dresser. I don't know why I'm still writing. I think it's calming me down. Jessica is having a panic attack and Juliana keeps yelling at us.

I don't know what to do, so I'm just writing. I keep telling myself you'll read this when I get home and we'll laugh about it.

Courtney. Something is happening. Before this ends, I just ne

YEAR 20 DIARIES

COURTNEY: I'm calling for the devil from the balcony. He wrote my name, right? So why doesn't he ever come? Why does he never show up when I call him?

YEAR 7 DIARIES

COURTNEY: It feels weird stepping back on the island without all of you. The police gave me this diary years ago, and outside of reading your last entries, I've never been able to open it again. Until now. When I found out Chester gave me this place in his will, I thought I'd never come back here. Not just for my safety, but because I didn't think I could handle being without you here.

The hole grief left inside me hasn't faded. In fact, it's growing. It's devouring me. I'm making this visit to do a little coin toss. Life is unbearable without you. So, I came here, and I'm staying for two weeks in hopes the thing that killed you comes back for me. I want to die where you died. I want to reunite with you all.

And if I somehow survive these two weeks, I'll go back to my life and do everything in my power to move on.

I doubt I'll do much writing in here, though. I probably won't do much of anything.

DAY 14

I stayed up all night most nights, begging the creature to come for me. It never listened. Maybe you all did something to prevent it from coming. Is this your way of telling me to live my life? I don't want to. But I'll try.

YEAR 14 DIARIES

COURTNEY: You fucking assholes can't keep making me do this. Please. I tried. Okay? For a long time, I tried. Seven years! I gave it seven years. WHERE ARE YOU? Come on. You wrote MY name! You called for me. And here I am, calling you back. WHERE ARE YOU???? KILL ME! Please.

YEAR 15 DIARIES

COURTNEY: I went to the water. I sat at the shore and I yelled at the top of my lungs for you to come get me. Why aren't you coming? You can't do this to me. It's torture. It's unfair.

YEAR 17 DIARIES

COURTNEY: Why do I even bother at this point? I'm alone. I'm as empty as this house.

YEAR 19 DIARIES

COURTNEY: I can't do this anymore.

YEAR 20 DIARIES

DAY 14

COURTNEY: I know you're not coming. You never will. So, I'll force you. I made a noose and tied it to the upstairs railing. If you won't bring me to them, I'll find my own way. After I tie this around my neck, I'll wait for you again, but not for long. If you come, I will write down everything. Every detail before you devour me. If you don't come, I'll just step off the railing.

I hear you. You came. Oh my god, I hear you scratching on the outside walls. If I could explain the excitement flowing through me! You're here. But where are you? Why aren't you coming in? Fine, I'll come to you.

This will be my last entry in the diary, and I'm writing to you specifically, Parker. I went outside and saw the markings you mentioned. The ones James insisted were my name. I've passed by them dozens of times now, and I always examine them, trying to convince myself they said something other than C-O-U-R-T-N. The lettering is so weird and frantic, it could have said a million things. But we all know the truth. Of course the thing was spelling my name.

As I sat there on the second floor, planning to jump off the railing, I heard the monster scratching again. I thought it was announcing its entrance, but it left as quickly as it came. Instead, it was finishing its diary.

C-O-U-R-T-N-E-Y I-S W-A-T-E-R D-A-R-K A-N-D D-E-E-P

Do you remember that, Parker? When you said those very words to me? When I came to you and cried for no reason, and ranted about my chest caving in, and how I sometimes couldn't get through a day without collapsing into myself, folding at the seams. Do you remember when I told you about the medicine and how the only time I ever felt okay was when I was with you?

And to make me laugh, you whispered in my ear, "Courtney is water, dark and deep."

I'm going home.

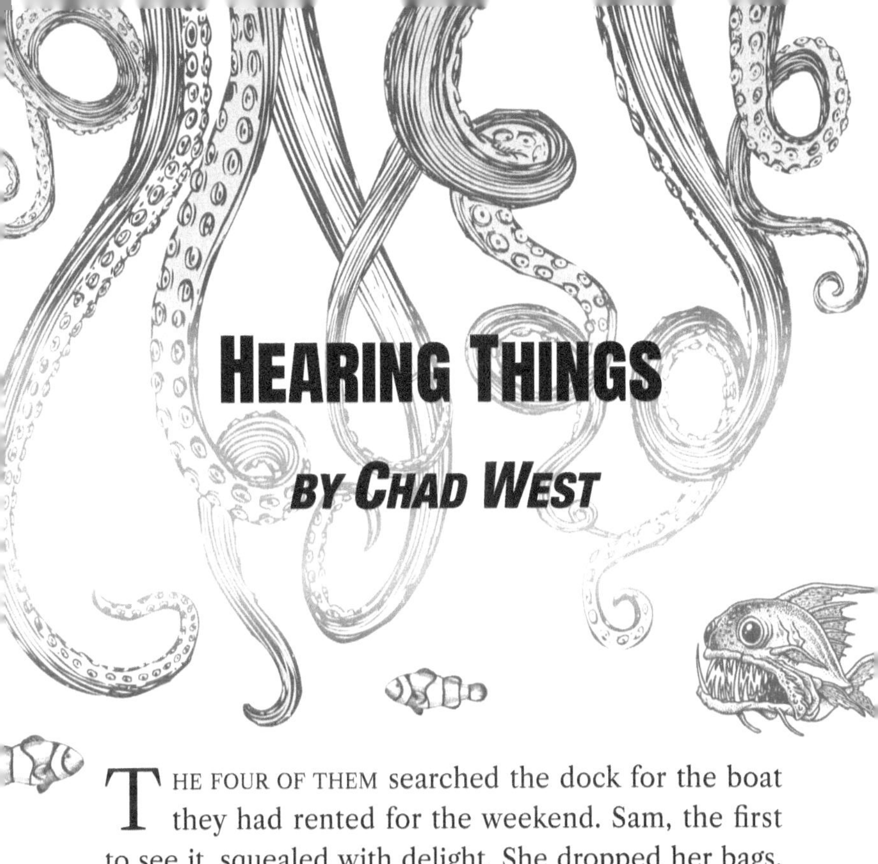

HEARING THINGS

BY CHAD WEST

THE FOUR OF THEM searched the dock for the boat they had rented for the weekend. Sam, the first to see it, squealed with delight. She dropped her bags, grabbed Teresa's hand, and dragged her up the dock and onto the catamaran, where she did a little dance while Teresa laughed, blushing as the others watched. Still on the dock, Megan rolled her eyes but smirked, squeezing her boyfriend, Ron's, arm.

"You big old weirdo," Teresa said, then kissed Sam.

"Somebody grab my bags," Sam said, elongating the last word playfully as she hugged Teresa, swaying with her back and forth.

A few moments later, Megan chucked Sam's bags onto the boat and sighed. "Next time I'm going to give them to the fucking sharks."

Sam reached out and took her arm, helping her aboard. "You would *never*," she said. But Teresa thought she might. Besides Ron, they had all been friends since middle school. But Megan and Sam had spent about a quarter of that time an inch away from becoming enemies.

"Try me, bitch," Megan said, smirking.

"This thing is awesome," Ron said, giving Teresa a high-five. "Excellent job." Ron had given some advice on what to look for, but she had pulled the trigger.

Teresa did an awkward curtsy and gave the boat a once-over. She walked past the cockpit, with its wheel and various buttons and knobs which were mysteries to her. Then she bent to look in the cabin window, seeing a kitchen and large table. A long deck stretched out in front, pontoons poking out from both sides. A tall main sail rose from one end of the roof. She took a deep breath of the sea air and smiled. "Yeah, I think this will do."

Megan sighed. "As long as you guys try to keep your sex volume to a two." She slapped Teresa in the stomach with the back of her hand, raising her eyebrows a couple of times as she walked past.

Teresa felt her face warm and forced out a laugh.

"Just think of it like a dinner bell," Sam said, leaning forward, squeezing her breasts together with her shoulders. "You hear the moans and you come running, you sexy hunk of woman." She then looked at Ron, frowning playfully. "I suppose he could... *watch* or whatever."

"Gross," Megan said, staring out across the bay. "You're the only person who's ever made becoming a sexless monk sound awesome to me."

"Sam," Teresa said, smacking her shoulder, "stop it."

"Oh, I'm joking. I mean, yes, I'd climb her like a redwood if she wanted, but she has the unfortunate status of being straight."

Teresa turned to stand directly in front of her, pointing a single finger at her own chest. "Um, *girlfriend*."

"I said join *us*, babe. Meg is no one-woman conquest."

Megan looked back over her shoulder. "Once again, gross."

"Okay, okay," Sam said. "I'll stop."

Teresa reached out and took Sam's hand, pulling her into a hug and kissing the shorter girl on the top of the head. She always played along but wasn't the biggest fan of the interminable fake flirting Sam did. But they had just gotten there, and she didn't want to start the trip by being *that* girl. So, she reminded herself it was a meaningless game and kept smiling.

"How about," Ron said, "we pick our rooms and put our shit up before we get this party started?"

Teresa watched Ron walk into the cabin and down the stairs to the left hull, where two of the bedrooms were, Megan trailing behind him. If she was putting her frustrations away, she might as well deal with how she felt about him, which was a little miffed he had invaded their girl's trip. But she told herself again that Megan was right. Yes, they were all friends first, but Sam was Teresa's girlfriend now. That meant she would be a third wheel no matter how you looked at it. Besides, Ron was a good guy. Also, he was the only one with any experience with catamarans. So no, it wasn't ideal, and Sam agreed, but they would be landlocked without him. Teresa took in a long breath through her nose and slowly let it out through her mouth. Then she turned her eyes to Sam, who was gathering her bags. Sam sang loudly to herself, shaking her *very* yummy ass in a bikini that would most definitely be the reason for some loud noises later. Teresa smiled, telling herself this was going to be a great vacation.

By nightfall, they were several miles out. The plan was to drop anchor, get some sleep, and set out in the morning for a small, nameless island Ron had found. It would be their own private island to play on for a day or two. Then they would head back to the mainland for even more alcohol-flavored fun.

Teresa washed the last pan from dinner and went down the stairs into a narrow hall. She glanced to her left, glad to see the door to Megan and Ron's room closed, then turned right, seeing Sam in bed, grinning at her.

Teresa shut the door behind her. She could tell Sam was naked, even with the sheets pulled up to her shoulders. Teresa smiled, untying the bikini she wore as she crawled onto the bed, her blonde curls falling around her face. They made love, which was as loud as Megan feared. Then naked, slightly embarrassed by the noise but immensely satisfied, Teresa fell asleep next to Sam.

Dreams were something Teresa hardly ever remembered. So, it was strange to wake with what felt like a full movie still clear in her head. She had been floating in a waveless ocean, staring at the sky. Long, warm fingers slid up her leg. She shivered but didn't startle. She only smiled, closing her eyes, relishing the touch. Then other hands joined. They gripped her thighs, her ankles, another glided onto her stomach, her left wrist, and a final one wrapped around her right bicep. They tightened. A slight gasp escaped her lips. Then she felt herself being pulled under. Once again, she didn't struggle.

She took one last breath and opened her eyes, watching the light shrink above her, the dark of the sea enveloping her. More of them came. Whoever *they* were. One by one, they wrapped themselves around her, but her eyes remained on the shrinking light above, knowing it might be the last time she saw it.

Finally, a pair of lips pressed onto hers. It was too dark now to make out the face, but she hungrily kissed them back. Something not-a-tongue entered her mouth. Several things, in fact. Long, thin filaments slid over her tongue, down her throat, stinging her. She had stiffened, her eyes widened. Teresa tried to scream. Then she was sitting up in bed, damp with sweat, her bangs sticking to her forehead. She looked over to see Sam, a naked pretzel next to her, lightly snoring.

Ron had already made a pile of pancakes by the time Sam and Teresa came up from their room that next morning. Megan was sitting at the table, her hair in a bun, arms crossed, wearing black sunglasses. Ron told them Megan had been up half the night with a headache, and he stroked her hair. Since they weren't sleeping anyway, he decided to get a start on breakfast. While Teresa felt for Megan, pancakes sounded amazing. But even syrup couldn't make up for their dry, mealy texture. She thanked Ron, anyway, commenting on how good they were.

Sam cut her eyes at Teresa, putting her fork down. "What was it you did again, Ron?"

Ron looked at Sam, confused. "Um, coding. Apps and stuff."

"Ah," Sam said, "just making sure it wasn't *professional chef.* Because my girlfriend's too nice to tell you these pancakes suck a limp dick."

Ron blanched. "Oh. Okay. I guess there's other stuff if you want it. Damn."

Teresa gave Sam a hard look. "Stop," she mouthed.

Megan sighed, looking up. "Please don't be a bitch, Sam." She lifted her glasses, rubbing her eyes with the palms of her hands. "I am not feeling your shit today."

Sam held her hands up. "Sorry, sorry. My bad."

"Well, my night wasn't as bad as yours," Teresa started, "but I was up for a while, too, after a weird nightmare."

Megan's head lifted. "Yeah? What was it? What'd you dream?"

"I just remember it being bad." Teresa knew and wasn't quite sure why she hadn't just told them. Except there was something about it that felt personal. Aside from fear, she had woke also feeling something like desire. A pull. That familiar warm tingling in her stomach. She was certain that was thanks to the admirable fucking Sam had given her before they had drifted off, but there it was.

"Oh." Megan turned her fork in her hand, staring at it. "I just... I don't know. Had, like, a ringing in my head. Turned into a headache. And, yeah, when I dozed off,

I'd dream weird shit too."

Teresa nodded. "I've never slept on a boat before. Maybe that's it."

"Maybe," Megan said, moving a bit of pancake around with her fork. She stared at her plate for a moment longer then pushed away from the table. "I'm gonna... I guess I should try and get a nap in, guys. Sorry for being a bummer."

"No way, babe," Ron said. "Get some sleep. I'm just going to be doing my captain duties. I'll wake you when we get to the island."

Megan squeezed his shoulder as she walked toward the stairs. Teresa watched, noticing her jerk to a stop at the last step. She turned, looking lost, confused. Teresa opened her mouth to ask if she was okay, but Megan turned back, disappearing down the hall.

The sun was setting by the time Megan got out of bed. Teresa looked up from the book she was reading in her own bed and smiled as Megan headed toward the stairs. She was about to tell her there had been zero wind and they had had a little engine trouble earlier and hadn't made it to the island as expected, but Megan seemed to look through her, her brow furrowed, as she started up the stairs.

A few seconds later, Teresa sat up at Megan's scream. She scrambled off the bed and ran up the stairs. Ron stood by the sink on the other side of the cabin, his head in his hands. A steak sizzled on the stove across from him. Sam stood in the doorway, her hair blowing in the sea breeze.

Teresa asked, "What happened?"

Sam turned to her, pale, opening her mouth to answer. Another scream from Megan caused them both to turn to the deck, where she was bent over punching the surface of the deck. Teresa looked at both Ron and Sam, wondering why they weren't out there trying to calm her, then rushed past them. She met Megan's eyes, who was pacing now. "Hey, sweetie. What's going on?" Megan didn't stop.

Teresa frowned, confused. "Hey," she said, touching Megan's shoulder. Megan stopped. For a moment, she didn't respond, wouldn't meet Teresa's eyes. Then she brought her head up. Her pupils were dilated, cheeks red as rage. She shook. Her head began to swing back and forth. "What if it's better *there*?" A large tear leapt from her eyelashes onto her cheek.

"What's going on, honey?"

"No. *No*, listen to me."

"What do you mean? What's going on?" She noticed an odd smirk trying to break through the anger. She wondered, for a moment, if this might be a game and glanced up at Sam and Ron. Neither looked the least bit in on it.

Megan's eyes flitted behind Teresa at the ocean, her mouth tightening, then back to Teresa. "I know exactly how it will feel. I know it's—" Her eyes screwed shut and she winced. "And I can't *be* on this fucking boat with liars. I'd rather..." She let out a huff and looked like she might scream again, then it was like something in her broke. Her face went slack. Then the corners of her mouth slowly turned up. A slight puff of a laugh escaped her lips. "You've heard it, too, haven't you?" Her breathing was slower now. "I bet we get to sing too. Once we're there."

Teresa took Megan's hands, clasping them against her chest. "Listen. You're going through something right now. I'm not sure what, but I'm afraid you're not yourself. Will you come back inside with me? Maybe we can lie down together. Rest a little? Would that be okay?"

Megan almost looked sorry for her. Then she stood. Teresa thought she might follow her back to the cabin, but she turned, walking toward the side rail. Teresa jerked her head back over her shoulder looking for help, but Ron and Sam still stood in the cabin looking like scolded children.

She moved to Megan's side. "Hey, can we please go inside?"

Megan ignored her. "I don't even think I'll remember this," she said, then looked at Teresa. "I've been so scared I was losing it. But now I'm just at peace. It's all I want."

"What is?"

Megan scoffed. "To jump for them, silly." She closed her eyes at that, taking a deep breath. "I'm not even angry anymore." She looked back at Sam and Ron, then smiled.

A few things happened next. Something moved in the gathering dark, breaching the water's surface. Large, round eyes gleamed in the scant light. The noise it made felt like an ice pick sliding into the front of Teresa's head, causing her to gasp, stumble. By the time she righted herself, Megan was standing on the other side of the rail.

Megan said something, and Teresa lunged for her but missed as Megan slipped into the water. It took a while for it to register in the pursuant chaos. But as Teresa stared into the ocean, wailing, she realized Megan had said that she would see her soon.

Ron dove into the water several times to search for her. But she was gone. Now he sat on the deck catching his breath, staring at nothing. The realization that the search was done was setting in.

Teresa's skin still tingled from the adrenaline, but she was coming back to herself. The panic attack ending. Sam, she realized, was sitting next to her, holding her. She lifted heavy eyes to her face and asked in a shaky voice what had happened.

Ron's head came up, but Sam gave him a look that turned his head back to the deck. "Ron and I were in the kitchen. He was searing one of the steaks, and I was—" She frowned at the memory, her voice becoming thicker. "Megan came upstairs and just stood there. We both looked at her and she just, like, screamed. Then ran out here."

"We need to call this in," Teresa said.

Ron was shaking his head. "We both tried. We're not getting any signal for some reason." He stopped, his lower lip starting to jump. "She's gone, isn't she?" His body tensed; his breath picked up. "Fuck. No, no, no." His wide eyes went to Sam, pleading.

"Stop," Sam said, sitting up straight. "This isn't our

fault. Something else happened. You heard her. Something was wrong with her."

Teresa shook her head wildly. "Why would you even think this was your fault? We can't do that to ourselves." Her words felt like syrup in her mouth.

"Just get the motor going," Sam said, her voice flat now. "We have to get back."

Ron looked frightened by the suggestion. "We can't leave her. She's here. We can't just leave her."

Sam stood, walking over to him. She took his face in her hands and pointed it at hers. Teresa could hear tears and anger in her voice. "She's gone, Ron. I'm sorry, but us going home is what happens next. Maybe if we fucking hurry, they can at least recover her body. Understand?"

As Ron got up, Teresa remembered the thing in the water. The sound. She opened her mouth to ask if they had heard it too but thought better of it. It had seemed so real and important when it was happening, but now she thought it might not have happened at all. At least not in the way she remembered. It didn't make sense. So much was going on. Maybe Ron or Sam bumped the horn. Or a stupid bird was flying over. Something. *Anything.* Even normal noises sounded so much different, more intense—frightening even—when you were stressed. That, she decided, was probably it.

Ron looked like he was sleepwalking to the cockpit. He stood there a moment in front of the steering wheel, staring. Then he sniffed, wiped his left cheek, and turned the key. His shoulders dropped when it did nothing.

Without looking back, he mumbled, "It did something like this earlier. I know what to do."

Sam asked, "What if it won't start? There's no radio."

"It's fine," Ron said, sounding perturbed now. "It's a freaking sailboat. And there's more wind now."

"Oh." Sam scooted next to Teresa, resting her head on her shoulder. "I don't like this. I know that's stupid to say. But I don't understand, and I'm scared and sad and angry. And I hate everything." She paused, and Teresa put an arm around her. "I just want to go home. To our bed."

"Everything's okay," Teresa said. "We'll be there soon. Just... try not to think about it."

Sam brought her head up, looking at Teresa. "What do you mean? How do you *not* think about it? Our friend is dead."

Teresa winced, looking away. "No." She felt her hands ball into fists. "Megan said—" She stopped, collecting herself, turning to face Sam. "The last thing she said was that she'd see us soon."

"What? Baby, you're in shock. Megan went under and didn't come back up. That was, like, an hour ago. Nobody comes back from that." Sam put a hand over her mouth, trying to stop the flood of emotion. "I don't need this," she said after a moment, her words thick with tears. "I can't deal with you being Miss Silver-Lining right now. Our friend *died*. Over a stupid misunderstanding. I need to be able to talk about that."

"Wait. *What* misunderstanding?"

Sam's cheeks reddened. She stood. "I don't know! Whatever was going through her head when she woke up. Whatever weird mental break she had. That's all I meant to say. Damn."

Ron returned from the back of the boat. "It's not working. Last time the cable had just slipped off the battery post. Now it's—" His eyes went to the side of the boat. His eyebrows drew together, and he began chewing his lower lip.

"What?" Sam asked.

"Sorry. I... can't stop seeing her... *jumping*."

"Just try to think about getting us home," Teresa said. "Let's get the sail up again and get back to shore."

A loud splash on the port side caused them to turn. There seemed to be nothing there. For a moment, Teresa imagined Megan popping out of the water, laughing at how good she had gotten them. Her eyes searched the darkening waters for a few seconds too long, then she looked back at Ron. "What do we need to do first?"

Ron was readying the sail. Sam and Teresa were huddled silently together. Then all three of them were turning toward the sound again. First to one side, then the other. Sam whined, pulling Teresa closer as the squealing wails grew louder.

"That's the same sound as before, isn't it?" Teresa asked, her body tingling.

Sam tucked her head under Teresa's, onto her chest. "When?"

The sound intensified. Teresa put her hands over her ears. "It was so loud. Right before Megan..."

Sam stiffened. "I *do* remember that. Holy shit. It's so much louder now." She covered her ears too.

The water churned. Teresa narrowed her eyes, just able to make out the dark shapes diving in and out of the water.

Sam yelled, "Just raise the damn sail. Let's get the hell out of here, please."

Ron shook his head and pulled at a rope, attaching it to the top corner of the sail. The shrieks grew even louder, not so much in her ears but in Teresa's head. The splashing was closer, becoming almost as loud as the shrieks. She dropped her head again, could hear the winch cranking, could see the tears falling from Sam's eyes onto the deck. But it would be over soon. Ron would raise the sail and they would be away from this place.

The boat heaved suddenly, and Sam fell backward, pulling Teresa over with her. Ron yelped. Teresa sat up in time to see the horizontal pole coming off the mast swing forward, slamming into his stomach. Her eyes widened as he was pushed off the side of the boat. The wailing grew, and the sea boiled as the things around them seemed to move all at once to where he had landed. She crawled forward, Sam balling up behind her.

Once at the railing, she saw Ron dazed but treading water. The ocean around him swarmed with movement, but nothing seemed to be touching him. She looked around, unhooking a life preserver from the side of the cockpit and tossing it to him. He began swimming toward a ladder at the front of the boat. The things in the water seemed to make a path as he moved but were always close, always screaming. She watched, trying to make them out, walking toward the ladder to help Ron back aboard. She jerked, turning at Sam's hands on her arms.

"He's going to be okay," Teresa said, her hands over her ears again.

Sam smiled. "I hear it now." She cocked her head. "It's pretty once you hear it."

Teresa dropped her hands, grabbing Sam by the wrists. "No. We're going to get out of here. It isn't beautiful, it's horrible."

Sam put a hand on Teresa's cheek. "I do love you. In my way." Her eyes went to the water. "But I think I'll be better out there. Whole." Her smile widened. "I don't think I've ever felt whole." She looked back at Teresa, both hands on her face now, her forehead lowering to rest on hers. She whispered, "Tell Ron we shouldn't have. And... it was never you. You were always enough. I just thought I needed the whole world to prove I was loveable."

Teresa raised her head. "Please stop. I don't know what you're saying. You're acting like Megan. Please, just stay with me."

Sam nodded. "I am. We all are. I think that's what they want." Her eyes widened as if she was having a revelation. "I bet I fall in love with you again, even if I don't know you down there." She smiled more broadly than Teresa had ever seen.

"Help," Ron moaned from the front of the boat. "I think my ribs are broken. I can't climb, and these things are everywhere."

Teresa looked at him then back to Sam. "Please come with me. Please help me save Ron." She swallowed hard. "*Before.* Before you go. Okay?"

Sam's head bounced back and forth as she considered this. "I wish I could. I probably owe you that. But it won't matter soon."

Teresa growled, turning, pulling Sam along behind her. Sam tried to pull away, giggling. Ron held onto the ladder, wincing, watching the slick dark skin of the creatures breach the water around him worriedly. When Teresa reached out to Ron, Sam tried to pull away again, her bare feet slipping on the deck. She landed on her backside, almost pulling Teresa down with her. But Teresa held on. She continued to yank her forward, her eyes on Ron. He was staring back at her, even raising a hand for her to take, until something seemed to get his attention and he looked that way, his mouth falling open.

"Oh," he said. The pain in his face dissolved to peace. He let go of the ladder, falling backward into the water. The agitation in the water closed in on him. Teresa bent forward, calling out his name, but stopped at the sight of dark, slick tentacles sliding up over his floating form. She gasped, falling back, tripping over Sam, who let out a gust of air and a yelp when she landed on top of her. When Teresa turned back to where he had been, Ron was gone.

The shrieks seemed to grow louder.

Teresa screamed in frustration, flipping herself over and straddling Sam. Her head throbbed. She pushed Sam's wrists onto the deck."Ohh, I do wish I had time for this, baby," Sam laughed.

"Stop! He's gone. Ron's gone. Megan's gone. We've got

to get the sail up and go. Get out of here. Everything can still be okay if you just stop doing this."

"Being me? Because this is me. I'm not crazy. Neither was Megan. I'm doing what I need to survive. This will make me happy. You too."

"No. You're... you're *reacting* to whatever's happening. It's affecting us. And I need to get the sail up, but I can't if I'm worried you're going to jump overboard." She looked back, terrified. "There's something out there."

"Um, yeah. Of course there is. They've been trying to talk to us for days."

"Stop!"

"They want us to join them, baby. We'll be happy. We'll be free."

"No. *No!* Whatever's out there doesn't want to help us. It probably wants to fucking eat us."

Sam rolled her eyes and began to struggle. "I'll show you," she said, arching her back and twisting. Sam finally wriggled free, rising, but Teresa grabbed her hair and yanked her onto her back again. Her head made a loud thwap against the deck.

"Fuck," Sam said. "Stop hurting me. I need to go. You don't understand."

Teresa was on top of her again, her knees pinning Sam's shoulders. But she knew it was only a matter of time before she struggled free again. It was then she realized that if she could knock Sam out, she would have time to raise the sail. Get them both away from there. She grabbed the sides of her head, lifting.

"That's enough, baby," Sam said, looking more serious now. "Let me go. I need to go. I promise it's okay."

"No," Teresa said, dropping her head down hard.

Sam grimaced, her eyelids fluttering. *Almost*, Teresa thought.

"Stop. Please. Just let me go." Sam began to squirm, kicking her legs. "You're hurting me," Sam said.

Teresa was hurting too—her head throbbing—but, so far, she had no desire to jump into the sea. She feared that could change at any moment. She had to hurry.

"I'm sorry, baby. I have to do this to save us." Teresa lifted Sam's head again, slamming it back down. Sam grunted in pain; her eyes went to the edge of the boat. She tried to arch her back and reached for the sea as if it would reach back.

"Just stop," Teresa said, crying. "I don't like hurting you."

"Let me go. I want to go. Please."

"No," Teresa said, smashing Sam's head onto the deck again. This time, Sam wilted. Her arm collapsed to the deck, eyes rolling back in her head. After a moment, Teresa rose, crying, stumbling toward the sail. "I'm sorry, I'm sorry, I'm sorry." She mumbled it over and over, slipping down next to the winch. She took in a gasping breath and turned it as fast as she could manage. The sail moved up by inches and she let out a satisfied breath. "We're going home, baby."

Then a voice said, "Jump for me." She froze, then whipped around to Sam, expecting to see her making her way to the railing. But she lay still on the deck. Then Teresa noticed the constant, squealing shriek was fading and being replaced by a soft, melodic vocalization. She felt a calm rise into her chest, her head. Her hands fell away from the crank. She sat there for a time listening, wondering if the voice would come again. Part of her wished it would. She began to wonder why she had been so frightened before.

She looked at Sam, smiled, and crawled to her side. Sam's mouth lay slightly open, her eyes the same. A pool of blood was spreading behind her head. Teresa smiled. "I'll go with you," she said. "I was just scared. But now I'm not. And I'll go with you." She positioned herself behind Sam and slipped her arms beneath her, lifting. Teresa stopped, looking out at the sea. "It'll be okay when I get you in there." And she dragged her, by inches, to the edge of the boat, next to the ladder. She stood as much as she could while lifting Sam. Then she grinned, falling backward into the sea, Sam with her.

They floated. Teresa stared up at the sliver of a moon, remembering her dream. She felt like it was important she took it all in. The stars, the moon, the light. Because it would be dark soon. And she would be different. As the first tentacle wrapped around her arm, stinging, then burning her skin, she gritted her teeth and smiled, squeezing Sam tight, hoping she had her eyes opened, too, so she could appreciate this last moment. Then there were more of them, wrapping around her, ripping at her flesh, pulling her under. The light above faded away as she tried to laugh.

Beneath The Waves

by Ollie Gill

C ODY, WYOMING
JANUARY 21ST, 1971

To whomever may find this,

My name is Daniel McLaughlin. I am an old man now. Eighty-four years old, to be exact, and I fear my time here is coming to an end.

As I lie in my bed writing this, a storm rages outside. I can hear the waves of the ocean crashing against the walls of my house, taunting me. It comes closer all the time. The damp, earthy smell of seaweed infiltrates my room, and I can taste the sharpness of salt upon my lips. I know this is not possible as I live hundreds of miles from any ocean. Alas, I also know anything is possible after what I witnessed on the night of April 12th, 1912.

It is common knowledge to most that an iceberg caused that ill fated vessel to sink, but if only that was the truth. There are some who survived who believe this also, or maybe it is easier for them to accept this version of events.

Did they see what I saw? I know some did. But the rest? I can't be certain.

My dreams are still filled with nightmares from what I witnessed that night. I wake screaming from time to time as the cold blackness of the sea surrounds me and pulls me down. And teeth... so many teeth.

What occurred on that oily black ocean was not a disaster caused by an act of God. I only wish this was the case. It would make sleeping at night a lot more peaceful.

I was raised a staunch Catholic, and my faith in God had always held strong. I truly believe in a higher power. But since that night, I have questioned where that higher power lies.

Somewhere in the distance I can hear the foreboding wail of a ship's fog horn beneath the turbulent wind that whips against the walls of my house.

I hope the pages I place in this steel box will survive. I only pray I can finish writing before it is too late.

I was born in Wicklow, Ireland on January 5th, 1887 to wealthy parents. My father was the owner of several textile mills around the country and had amassed a great wealth for himself in doing so. I lived a happy but uneventful life until both my parents died unexpectedly when I was 19 years old. Their deaths affected me great ly; I had a close relationship with them both, and their passing left a deep void within me. My father left behind a small fortune, so much so that I would never need to worry about money again in my lifetime.

It was a small consolation.

I trudged through the next few years of my life with little purpose or direction and would spend many afternoons dining in fine restaurants around the country, always with a beautiful lady by my side. Sadly, these flings bore no meaning, and most barely lasted more than a week; others little more than a night. I fell deeper into a hole of depression and used the power of money to buy myself friends.

After a time, I grew disillusioned. When news came to me of the floating behemoth they were building in Belfast, my ears pricked instantly with excitement. I longed for change, and the journey across the sea offered me just that.

From the day I first heard of the ship's construction to the day it was completed took almost two years. In that time, I set my affairs in order and tidied my act up. In New Orleans lived an uncle of mine, Fintan, whom I contacted and had arranged to meet with there. I was near bursting with excitement when the day of the voyage finally rolled around. It was a day I likely would never forget and the last day I would ever set foot in Ireland again.

It was early morning, close to 8:00 a.m., when I arrived in Queenstown, now more commonly known as Cobh. I enjoyed a leisurely breakfast in a local pub called The Siren. As was to be expected on such a momentous day of the year, a large crowd had gathered inside, and it was a small miracle I managed to get a table. The pub was cozy, and the fire was a warm blanket against the late spring chill which coursed through the country. When my food arrived, I sat back, and for the first time that day, I found myself content and relaxed.

Merry from the breakfast and two beers I had consumed, I ventured out from the pub to watch the ship entering the port. The morning was calm but chilly. I had not dressed appropriately, and the light brown jacket I wore did nothing to stop the constant sharp wind cutting through its fabric. The cold was quickly forgotten when I set eyes on the monstrosity making its way into the bay. I wondered in amazement how such a thing could even be built by human hands and in such a short space of time too.

When I entered the ship, my mind was baffled at the workmanship contained within. It was beyond anything I had ever seen before. I was mesmerized by the grand staircase with its polished oak banister and bronze cherub. Above me, the daylight shone through a dome of polished glass. Dull as the light was, it was still stunning to behold.

As I ascended the stairs, I stopped and looked at the clock on the wall that was embedded into a panel of wood. Two angels surrounded by leaves and flowers had been painstakingly carved into the wood, and I ran my hands over the elaborate scene, taking in every little detail.

My cabin was situated in first class, and I made my way there to relax for an hour or so before I explored the ship. I lay on the soft bed for over two hours, dozing lightly, and when I felt myself drifting into a deeper sleep, I pulled myself up and shook the tiredness from my body. I did not want to waste my time onboard sleeping the days away.

At a leisurely pace, I wandered the ship's interior then made my way outside to the top deck. In front of me, the ocean went on forever, and when I looked back, I could see Ireland fading away in the distance, little more than a speck now.

My father had been well known and liked around Ireland, and our name was held in high regard. Thomas Andrews, the man who designed the Titanic, had been an acquaintance of his, so I had been offered a place at his table that evening for dinner at 7 p.m.

I donned the finest evening attire I had and made my way to the first class dining lounge.

Joseph Bruce Ismay, the managing director of the ship, was also sat at the table, along with a host of other well-known and influential figures. Famous London socialite Ellie Leslie sat beside Isidore Straus and his wife, Ida.

Isidore was one of the co-owners of Macy's department stores. I caught a glimpse of Ellie's hand rubbing against Isidore's thigh as his wife chatted to me, oblivious to her husband's indiscretion. I said nothing; after all, it was none of my business.

There were other people sitting at the lengthy table. Most of them I did not recognize, but some of them I did. One of them was an extremely skinny silent film star called Gordon Gibson. He was puffing on a large cigar and tossing back double brandies, half the liquor spilling down his smooth-shaven chin.

The biggest star at the table that night was Harry

Houdini, who was set to entertain the passengers on the night of the 14th. He was a very serious man who did not partake in smoking nor alcohol and did not stay with us for long. He was deep in conversation with Joseph Ismay when I looked across at him. In my inebriated state, my gaze lingered longer than normal. There seemed to be some tension between the two as they spoke, and I noticed Harry becoming impatient with Joseph, who was clearly quite drunk now.

My gaze fell on a man with curly blond hair pulled back in a tight ponytail who smiled at me when he caught me looking. His eyes were drooping, and his pupils were constricted to a pinprick, accentuating their brilliant blue glare. I could tell he was high on opium. He waved at me, smiling like a simpleton, and I returned his friendly gesture.

After we ate, the captain, Edward Smith, joined us for a brief time, long enough to smoke a cigarette and drink a small cup of tea before returning to his duties. He said a quick hello and shook my hand when Thomas introduced us, before heading back to his post.

"I look forward to seeing you around the ship, young man," he said. His eyes fell upon Ida Straus, who was leaning in close to me, her hand now rubbing my back as she spoke. Beneath his well manicured white beard, he smiled and winked at me. "And enjoy your stay upon this mighty vessel." Then he turned and left.

Ida Straus bent close to my ear. "Isidore and I have been waiting for this trip with bated breath."

Her arm was touching my lower back. I could taste the sweet, floral perfume wafting from her skin. A rich person's perfume. One that lasted well into the night.

"It is an exciting time for sure," I replied cordially, my words slurred. I tried to pull away from her slightly.

I explained to her, as best I could, that I would be making my way to New Orleans to meet my uncle upon my arrival. When I mentioned his name, she perked up.

"Fintan McLaughlin? We know Fintan well, my young boy!" she almost shouted. Her burst of excitement led her to remove her arm from my back, much to my relief. She explained how they had business dealings together. But my mind was swimming from the alcohol, and I was only catching every third word she threw at me. I let her go on until she paused, and that was when I took my chance and excused myself. Just as I was about to rise from my seat, she pulled me back down.

She leaned close, her lips brushing against my ear, and whispered to me, "There's a place for you with us."

I did not know how to reply, for I knew not what she meant. She then nodded across at the blond haired man with the ponytail. He winked back at her and smiled.

"Edwin and I will be making a private film tonight in his room. You are more than welcome to join us."

Before I could even take her words in, the old woman's hand was making its way towards my crotch. Shocked at this, I almost jumped from my seat, my knees banging against the table as I got up, rattling the cutlery and crystal atop it. Everyone stared at me. After a brief silence, Joseph quipped, "One too many sherries, lad, eh?"

This was greeted by a round of laughter and giggles. I smiled back at them and cast my eyes over the group, doing my best to compose myself.

"It seems that may be the case," I chuckled. "It's been

quite some time since I have been drunk. If you will excuse my rudeness, I think I will retire to my room for the night."

Somehow, I managed to stand steadily on both feet. "God willing, I might see you all here again tomorrow."

They bid me goodnight in unison, and their voices merged together to create an unintelligible din. As I turned, I could feel Ida's eyes crawling over me. I made my way to my room quickly. I had sobered up considerably by this stage and lay on my bed, still disturbed by the old woman's sudden advances.

It made my skin crawl, to be quite frank. Some time not long after, I fell asleep. I woke late the next morning. My throat was drier than ash, and when I swallowed, it felt like razors cutting my throat. I drank deeply from the basin of water by my bed and splashed some on my face and prepared myself for the day. I decided to keep to myself for the rest of the journey. The previous night's encounter with Ida Straus had unnerved me, and I did not want to be in her company again if I could help it.

On the morning of the 14th, I bumped into Thomas Andrews while eating breakfast at approximately 8:00 a.m. He was in an upbeat mood.

He gave me a warm smile. "A great morning," he said. I agreed it was. "Are you looking forward to the show tonight?" he asked.

"Show?" I replied. It took less than a second for me to realize he was talking about Harry Houdini's performance that night. "Ah yes, of course," I said. "Very much so."

"It will be a night to remember," he said, and then he was waving at someone across the room. "I must go now, Daniel. I may see you later."

"I look forward to it," I replied, then went back to eating my breakfast.

Later that night after I donned my suit, I looked in the mirror and brushed my wavy brown hair into place. Once satisfied, I checked my pockets and made sure I had everything I needed. I locked my cabin door and made my way to the first class dining area.

The dining room was bustling with people. I still had over an hour to kill, so I ordered myself a drink and stood by the bar. I knocked back a shot of brandy and sipped on a glass of white wine. The first and second class passengers had been permitted to watch the show, but third class passengers were not allowed to join us.

Once the brandy worked its way into my system, I felt a weight lift from my shoulders and ordered myself another, a single this time. When the lights dimmed, I was already quite drunk.

Houdini took to the stage. When the crowd simmered down, he began with a series of card tricks, wowing the children who sat in front of him. I was beginning to see double at this stage.

After Houdini escaped from a steel drum filled with water, he levitated off the ground while strapped into a straight-jacket. It was at that time I began to feel ill and made my way outside. My mouth began to water. I knew I would be sick, so I quickened my pace and made it to the railing outside just in time and vomited into the black ocean. I slumped to the ground once the contents of my stomach had been emptied. Although my head still spun, I felt relieved. I sucked in deep; the freezing cold air filled my lungs and softened the fire in my chest.

Then I heard raised voices, and when I looked to my left, I saw Joseph Ismay being followed outside by the captain, Edward Smith, and my fathers old acquaintance, Thomas Andrews. They were engaged in a heated argument. I pushed myself as far into the shadows as I could so as not to be seen. They were no more than ten feet away, but they did not notice me.

The captain was waving his finger in Joseph's face. "You can't back out now," he growled. "This isn't a game!"

"Well I want out!" shouted Joseph.

The captain turned his head and looked at Thomas, then back at Joseph.

He let out a deep sigh. "You want out?" he asked. "Well, there's no backing out now, I'm afraid. What's done is done, so let's go upstairs and finish it."

I could not see his face, but I knew Joseph was weeping when he spoke again.

"But everyone..." He went to move past the two figures in front of him. "I can't let it happen."

That was when I got the first major shock of the night. Joseph tried to barge his way through the two men, but Captain Smith raised his fist and punched him straight into the mouth. The blow was savage, and Joseph cried out. Smith punched him again, and I could hear several of his teeth rattle across the steel floor. Thomas grabbed Joseph by the arms, and Edward sent several more blows into his face. The soft, crunching sound of his knuckles breaking Joseph's nose sickened me.

"You want out?" Edward barked at him. "Well, that's fine with me. All we need is the ship anyhow." He grabbed the stunned man by the legs, and before I could comprehend what I was seeing, both he and Thomas threw him overboard into the freezing Atlantic ocean. Joseph screamed as he fell, then he was sucked under the ship, all sounds of him disappearing.

Only for I was drunk I think I might have screamed and given away my hiding place.

The two men looked over the railings, then turned to each other.

Thomas muttered impatiently, "The time is nearly upon us. Harry's part is almost complete, so we must hurry."

"Indeed," Edward replied, and the two men took off quickly.

I watched as they climbed the stairs to the top deck. The shock of what I had just witnessed had not yet hit me. The alcohol gave me courage, so I followed them up. I had to know what was happening. Keeping my distance, I watched as they entered the wheelhouse. From within, I could hear the muffled voices of other people. It sounded like a chanting of some sort. Creeping low, I made my way over and carefully peered through the small window. Inside I could see ten people gathered in a circle. Among them was Ida and Isidore Straus and all the others who had sat at the dinner table with me that first night.

They were all stripped naked.

The dope fiend, Edwin, was chanting in a language I did not recognize. It was the same line over and over again. I never forgot those words, although their meaning is still lost on me.

Plathara Convis I, Plathara Anu, Thasa Ta Ocine, Vey Vallow Vu

I noticed something wriggling on the ground in the center of the circle. The room was dimly lit with candles, and visibility was low as Captain Smith bent and picked it up. He held his arms into the air. Squirming through his fingers was a shining, purple octopus.

A man with dark, slicked back hair came forward then. He held a large dagger. Tentacles slithered up the captain's arm, but he held the head tight in his fist. When the man stabbed the octopus between the eyes, its purple body instantly lost all color. He stabbed it again, and this time black ink leaked from the wound.

The candles shimmered in the room and almost blew out. The chanting continued. In the haunting glow of the candles, I watched Captain Smith walk around the circle and stop at each person. The first person he stopped at was Ida Straus, who was down on all fours. One of the young men was having sex with her, roughly pounding into her from behind.

The captain squeezed the octopus, and black ink sprayed across Ida's face and into her mouth. She groaned in pleasure as she swallowed. The captain hurried on and swiftly fed the rest of them.

Everyone in the circle now looked like they had been drinking tar, their mouths stained black.

Edward pulled out a pistol, walked slowly around the circle, and shot each of them in the head. When the fifth shot rang out, I heard a ripping sound from behind me. It came from the ocean. Fear had paralyzed me and I was rooted to the spot staring, voyeuristically, in through that window.

Inside the wheelhouse, each body dropped to the floor with a thud as their brains painted the wall behind them. After every gunshot, the ripping sound from the sea grew louder.

Captain Smith sucked the last drop of ink from the octopus and turned the gun on himself. Before he could pull the trigger, I slipped, and my head crashed against the window. My distraction caused the captain's hand to slip, and the bullet ripped through the side of his cheek, blowing most of the right side of his face off. He was still alive when I opened the door and went inside. He lay in a pool of blood, and one side of his face was completely missing.

"Kill me," he begged when he saw me with his one remaining eye. "It's not complete...."

Before I could open my mouth to reply, something massive smashed against the boat, rocking it furiously. I was thrown out of the wheelhouse and slid across the smooth deck, the wind sucked out of me as I smashed against the metal railing. I lay there choking and gasping for air. When I looked down into the ocean, I thought I had gone insane.

Something was trying to tear through the fabric of our reality.

Part of the ocean beside the ship had opened up, a circle of roughly twenty meters, and within it I gazed deep into another dimension. Giant nebulas and swirling galaxies shimmered brightly within this hole among giant stars. I was staring into deep space, only it was in the middle of the ocean.

My heart almost stopped when I saw what had rocked the boat, trying to force its way through the black hole. It was like a deformed version of a lobster claw covered in long, flailing tentacles.

Another one came into view and began pushing at the edge of the hole, trying to pull itself into our world. The hole seemed to be fighting against it.

The creature gave one great push, and for an instant, I saw its face. It resembled a giant fish with one single translucent eye embedded in the center of its head. When it opened its mouth, there were at least five other mouths within it, all lined with long razor-sharp teeth.

It was the most horrifying thing I had ever seen. Behind the creature, I could see the silhouettes of other giants swarming.

When the hole decreased in size, again a claw swung out in rage. It smashed against the side of the ship and tore a massive hole in the hull, the metal screeching in agony. I grasped the railing tightly.

Below, I saw the third class passengers spill out, screaming, into its gaping mouth. Some of the luckier ones were impaled on the teeth before they could reach the belly of the beast. The ones who missed its mouth fell into that endless space beyond, their bodies exploding as they hit the alien atmosphere.

One of the tentacles swooped over my head, and I saw that the suckers were filled with more tiny razor-sharp teeth.

The ship shuddered again, and I fell to the floor, smashing my head, the sudden pain bringing me to my senses. Again, from below I could hear the crunch of metal collapsing and the horrific screams as more of the passengers tumbled overboard. Then I felt the ship begin to tilt as it filled with seawater and was slowly sucked into the ocean.

Everything was happening so fast. Scrambling to my feet, I ran blindly to the other side of the ship. When I looked over the edge, I saw all was normal on this side. The ocean stared back at me. I uttered a prayer of thanks to God. There was still hope.

I descended the stairs, half falling down them, and banged into a man who was running past. He was well dressed and most certainly from first class.

"The ship is sinking," he cried, his face wild with fear. A thin layer of ice covered his pencil mustache. He pointed ahead of him in the ocean at a lone, floating iceberg. "It crashed into one of them!"

I did not know how to respond and decided to keep my mouth shut, not wanting to upset him any further.

"Quickly," I said, "We must make our way to the lifeboats." I knew where they were from my last few days wandering the ship. The man followed closely behind me. All around us was complete chaos. I am not too sure how many of these people knew exactly what was happening. When we got to the lifeboats, the crew were just about maintaining order, and several of them had guns drawn, waving them at the crowd.

"Come forward if you have a child," one of the crewmen was shouting.

A woman behind me tried to make her way through with her baby. "Please," she called, feebly.

The man with the pencil mustache who had followed me turned around, and when he saw the child, he ripped it from the woman's hands.

"Give me that," he hissed, "I have more to live for than you."

She screamed in protest. He butted his forehead savagely into her face, sending her falling to the floor. Blood squirted from her nose, staining her white gown.

I picked the woman up, and when I turned to confront the man, he was already being lowered down on one of the lifeboats, clutching the baby. He smirked at us both, the woman's child still screaming in his arms, reaching out for her mother as they disappeared from view.

Things had turned sour, and men were suddenly tearing women from the remaining lifeboats and throwing them overboard to save themselves. The sounds that came from those that hit the freezing water were haunting.

Suddenly, all the lights on the ship went out. That was when the terror really started to take hold of everyone still on board. There was a loud creaking sound as the ship started to split, and people scattered in fear, screaming and trampling over each other. The crew abandoned their posts, and the last lifeboats fell into the sea, smashing to pieces as they were taken down with the ship.

I looked down expecting to see the rip in the ocean with the creature crawling through, but it seemed to only be happening on the other side of the ship. Looking down at the surviving lifeboats floating in the water, I decided to make a jump for it. I stood on the railing and took aim for a boat just below me. The drop was not too far, maybe fifteen feet or so, and miraculously I landed on one and not in the freezing ocean. There were angry shouts of protest as I landed on top of two men. They tried to throw me over, but I fought back wildly and resisted them.

"Alright! Okay!" one of them panted. He had no strength left in him.

"Stay so," he said, and plopped himself down, exhausted.

Near to me I spotted the man with the pencil mustache holding the small child. It began crying loudly, and he looked at it angrily and tossed it into the sea. Horrified at what I had witnessed, I rose up in a rage and tried to crawl over the other men to get to him, but a roaring crash diverted my attention back to the Titanic. The last of the ship was dragged down into the ocean, and those who were looking would have seen the ghostly figure of Harry Houdini, still bound in a white straight-jacket, floating above it. Even though he was far away, I could hear him laughing maniacally. The rip in the ocean was closing rapidly, and hungry for more blood, the creature's claw rose one last time. It reached up and plucked Houdini from the air and pulled him into whatever hellish place it had come from.

As Houdini was dragged down, teeth from the tentacles tore him to shreds. Then the circle closed and the sea settled down as though nothing had happened. I passed out for a short time after this, and when I woke, the man beside me was staring at me.

"I did not se.......can't be real.....no, no, no....."

I looked across and saw the man with the mustache had fallen into a light sleep. Insane with anger, I barged my way over and grabbed him tightly by the throat, squeezing the life out of him. No one tried to stop me.

His eyes shot open in shock. He tried to catch his

breath, but I clamped down as hard as I could. I could feel his throat crushing under my grip. A pathetic yelp escaped his lips, and his bloodstained eyes were begging me to stop, but I felt no sympathy for him. Grabbing him by the collar, I tried to throw him overboard, but his clothes had frozen to the wooden boat. I turned to a large man with a black beard beside me. "Help me," I asked. He nodded and leaned forward. Together we tore the man from where he sat and threw him into the freezing water. Although his throat was destroyed, the man was still alive. He struggled briefly, but to no avail. When his body hit the water, his broken vocal chords let out a feeble cry. I grabbed one of the oars and gave him several sharp thrusts into the face, breaking nearly every bone. Then I lifted it high above my head and brought it crashing down on top of his skull. Blood spurted from the wound and he lost consciousness and sank. I sat down finally and burst into tears.

It took 8 hours for a rescue ship to find us, and when they did, there were only fifty-eight people left alive, myself included. The rest had frozen in the icy cold.

When we disembarked from the ship, I saw the man who had sat beside me on the lifeboat, recounting what had happened to a police officer. He sounded stark raving mad, and the officer hit him hard with his baton across the legs and told him to move on.

After witnessing this, I decided to keep what I had seen to myself for the time being. I saw my uncle Fintan in the crowd. He was squinting his eyes, scanning the crowd looking for me. I avoided him like the plague and slipped away quietly.

For six nights I recuperated in a hotel in New York. I chose a one star hotel for my stay and grew my beard out so as to disguise myself. I did not wash in all that time, either, as the thought of any water touching my skin terrified me. I barely drank and only did so when I was completely parched. Since that fateful night, I have developed a severe phobia of water. I read all about the disaster in one of the newspapers, and the official report was the Titanic had crashed into an iceberg, causing it to sink.

I left New York and wandered from state to state for a few years before finally settling in Wyoming. I knew I would never set foot on another ship, and it slowly dawned on me I would never see Ireland again. This saddened me greatly. Nor would I travel by air, for who knows what creatures lurk above as well as below.

For the rest of my life I lived an uneventful and boring existence and rarely left my house. My mind was constantly trying to make sense of what happened that night, but I never came any closer to the truth. One thing I am almost certain of is that if I had not distracted Captain Edward from killing himself with that gunshot, every one of us would have died.

The money that had been left to me had at least allowed me to live comfortably. I also used these funds to hire the best private detectives to seek out the remaining survivors of the Titanic. By the time I found them, most were already dead or institutionalized in mental hospitals.

They had all died in strange circumstances.

John Anderson was visiting an aquarium when he fell into one of the pools that held several sharks. He was torn to shreds in a matter of seconds.

Andrew Faye was found dead one morning by his wife. When they did the autopsy, hundreds of clams slid out from his belly.

In an institution for the mentally insane, a patient by the name of Fred Hansen was found drowned in his padded cell. It turned out Fred was the man who had sat beside me in the lifeboat.

Michael Maloney was found in an alleyway, strangled to death by a rope made of seaweed.

As the years went by, more reports came in of these mysterious deaths, until I was the only one left.

I am lying in my bed now, and just outside the closed door of my room, I can hear a man chanting. These are the same words I heard in the wheelhouse of the Titanic. The water is rapidly seeping into my room, and the foghorn from the ship outside comes closer. I know the man waiting outside is my uncle Fintan.

I am terrified of what awaits me on the other side.

I pray to God, but I do not know which one will answer me.

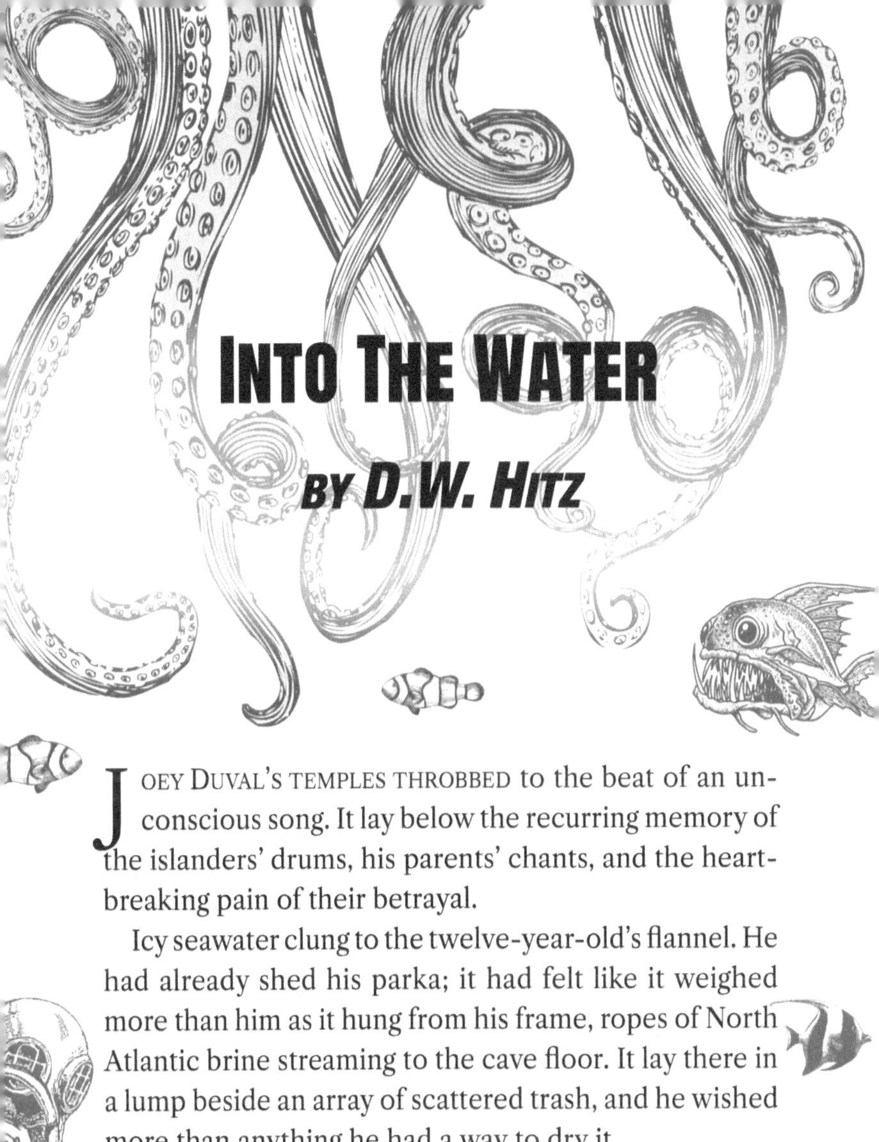

Into the Water

by D.W. Hitz

Joey Duval's temples throbbed to the beat of an unconscious song. It lay below the recurring memory of the islanders' drums, his parents' chants, and the heartbreaking pain of their betrayal.

Icy seawater clung to the twelve-year-old's flannel. He had already shed his parka; it had felt like it weighed more than him as it hung from his frame, ropes of North Atlantic brine streaming to the cave floor. It lay there in a lump beside an array of scattered trash, and he wished more than anything he had a way to dry it.

He was alone in an underwater cave, in the dark, and his head ached. But what agonized him more than anything was the tightness of his body as every muscle shivered, clenched, and trembled from the freezing air and his water-logged garments. He was afraid to shed any more clothes. Maybe his jeans and shirt could dry—maybe if he moved around enough?

Moved where? Was there a way out?

A musty, salty odor of dead fish and wet earth hung in the air. There was a dance of aquatic reflected light, the dark green sway and return of a lit water surface somewhere on the far side of the chamber. There was a passage on his left and another behind him. None of them told him how he got there. None of them explained why he had been tied and held under firelight below the waning moon, a hundred villagers calling the name of something he had never heard of. And his parents? Fire in their eyes with a stern glare that belonged to someone else—not Mom and not Dad.

How could they force him into that tiny boat? How could they send their only son out into those rough, icy waters?

But did that matter now? He needed to find warmth, or he feared he would freeze to death, a frozen corpse in a cave, not to be found until the next kid was sacrificed to whoever those damn villagers were trying to appease.

Between the darkened caves to his side and rear and the reflection ahead, Joey decided on the light. It didn't look like a fire, which was what he really wanted, but maybe there was something—a change of clothes would go miles toward making him warmer.

He walked, shivering, and studied what lined the cave's floor. It had looked like trash, but he saw now it wasn't only that. There were shards of wood, broken boats he assumed. There were dirty, shredded toys, stuffed animals, and... were those clothes?

His heart jumped. He gathered pieces of fabric from the ground and held them up. They were caked in dirt and mud, illustrations of puppy dogs, kittens, and unicorns. And they were shredded. And—was that blood?

He tossed aside the rags and continued scanning over the mess. More rags seemed to stand up and announce themselves. More blood. He found a small, pink parka made for a girl half his size. His shuddering flesh insisted he try it on.

His shirt and flannel hit the ground with a wet splat, and he forced his arms into the holes.

Dry, gritty nylon caught on his wet, sticky skin, but he forced his limbs through. The cuffs rested halfway up his forearms once he secured the pink zipper. It was tight around his chest, exposing the lower quarter of his stomach, but the warmth in his chest instantly rose.

Joey imagined how silly he looked in a girl's coat almost half his size, and his eyes ran over it. Tears exposed stuffing in a dozen places. Dried mud clung in blotches, looking like perverse polka dots. Dark brown stains ran from the collar to the elastic base. He forced himself to believe it wasn't blood.

If he could find a pair of pants to replace his frigid jeans, maybe he wouldn't die from hypothermia while trying to get out of there. He saw nothing. Maybe in the next room, where that light was coming from?

Something brushed against rock and echoed from the cave behind him.

Joey swung around, the voices of villagers in his mind, the drone of the strange words and the almost painful way they screamed. It hurt his throat to imagine making that sound himself.

"Hello?" he spoke softly. Maybe it was help? Maybe it was a villager coming down to see if the ritual was complete? There was no way to tell. There was only him, standing in the dim cave in cold, wet pants and a coat way too small, and the sound of—*what?*—in that cave.

He thought of calling out again. Something in the pit of his stomach told him *no*. There was a chill about that direction. A feeling in the recesses of his gut warned him: *you don't want anything from over there.*

A pair of noises echoed. They were indistinct. Maybe rocks clattering against the floor, maybe footsteps from hard-soled boots? Maybe it was the thing with the name they were chanting.

An image came to Joey's mind: bows of a half-dozen boats he had seen along the small dock as they carried him and bound him in that wooden dinghy. There were carved faces of things that shouldn't have been above the water. He remembered the head of an eel, only it had the eyes of a man. There was something like an octopus carved into another, but fangs extended from the center of its mouth. Black eyes watched from that one as they carried him past, as he screamed and called for help and Mom and Dad just followed alone, a look of sleep on their faces.

But those were just stupid carvings of superstitious people. Whatever those islanders believed, it couldn't have been real. But what they did to him was, and it was just as likely one of them was coming down to finish their job.

He didn't wait for the next sound. It came as he took a running step the other way. This time, it was a thump and a scraping sound. His mind formed the image of claws running over rocks as some shadowy thing moved toward him, but that was just silly—it was his mind being as dumb as those damned islanders. But still, he ran.

The next chamber was massive. Joey stared up as he entered, unable to break his gaze from hundreds of carvings in the rock walls—full-bodied depictions of beasts exactly like those villagers' boats. They were twice the height of a man and nestled inside stone, staring over a pool of water the size of an Olympic swimming pool. Wavering light passed over their faces, monstrous and sickening yet too real to disregard. Bulging eyes, glistening fangs, muscular bodies topped with aquatic heads.

If Joey wasn't sure nothing like that could exist, he would have been worried. They were so lifelike. They were watching him.

Joey walked to the water's edge and scanned the rest of the chamber. He knew there had to be an exit, but he saw none. Only his way in.

Rocks fell behind him, echoing from the previous cave. Prickles of worry ran over his back. His jacket, while now starting to actually rebuild his warmth, was way too snug. He felt like he was being strangled by a pink mass of stuffing; it was too tight on his chest. Too tight on his arms. It seemed harder to breathe with each second.

Water lapped at the edge of the pool, pulling his gaze downward, and he gasped. What he saw in the shimmering depths below was... It made no sense.

Tens, if not hundreds, of beings swam, but they weren't fish—they weren't people, either. They were human-shaped things with webbed hands and webbed feet and bulbous, black eyes. They worked inside a cavernous gap, moving rocks and boulders, chiseling the walls—it was some sort of underwater construction site. If Joey wasn't filled with unease at the creatures' very existence, he would have been in awe of the process.

But what were they doing?

His eyes were transfixed by their movement. As he watched, he sensed someone watching him. It wasn't a physical being he felt, but a sensation almost like being held, like something was moving into his thoughts and—was it calling to him?—calling him to climb into the water?

There was a scraping sound, then two, from behind him. It was closer than the last, and the image returned to Joey's mind, a picture he was sure couldn't be; he was just being silly, a crazy kid in a scary situation. He saw a thing coming, its claws on the hard cave wall, its claws on the floor below, its eel-shaped mouth with jaws wide and seawater shining on rows of spiked teeth.

He scanned the room again. There had to be a way out of here. Darkness hung from the farthest corners, but even in that gloom, he saw nowhere else to go other than the pool ahead.

But those things, man-shaped beasts, what would they do if he got in that water? And where would he go? It wasn't like there was another cave with air he could swim to...

Footfalls from the cave. It was just beyond the opening. He turned to see what was coming, his heels against the water's edge.

"Hello?" a small voice echoed, a child's voice.

Was it a trick? Was the vicious thing he knew was

coming trying to fool him?

Eyes shone in the darkened tunnel ahead. Something splashed in the water behind him.

Joey spun, sure that one of those creatures from the black lagoon had come to the surface to drag him down. He saw a rock crash into the water.

It had come from above, from—

"Hello?" It was the voice again. "Is someone else here?"

Joey spun back to the cave entrance. He looked around the room again. He was sweating in the cold chamber. His heart thudded in his chest. That thing, whatever it was, would grab him and tear him to shreds, turn him into chum for the army of workers in the waters below.

He held his breath, wincing as *she* walked in.

It wasn't a monster at all. There were no claws or fangs or gills. It was a blond-headed girl, maybe eight or nine, dripping wet and clenching her arms to her chest in fear and frigidity.

"Can you help me?" She stared at Joey. Sure, he wasn't much older, only a few years, but as far as kid-world went, that meant he should have more answers than her—and she looked like she had just showed up in a boat, same as him.

"Uh—" was all Joey could say before a flood of rocks showered the far side of the pool, and movement and groans called him to turn around.

He didn't feel the wetness; his pants were already wet, but he felt the heat as his bladder released and his legs warmed.

Some of those carvings, the beasts twice as tall as men

and a hundred times as ugly, were crawling down the face of the wall.

Their black eyes were fixed on Joey. They slithered as they descended, hugging the wall with inhuman appendages, arms thick like the tail of an eel, their legs—Joey could see they had more than two—flopped and sucked and gripped the rock.

The girl must have seen them. She belted out a howl of terror that rang in Joey's ears, yanking his gaze from those things and bringing it to her. And thank God she did. It sunk in at that moment he needed to run.

There was no place in that cave, no chance he would dive. He had to go back the way he (they) came. That was the only choice.

Joey ran, his pants starting to cool, and grabbed the screaming girl's arm. She nearly toppled over as he pulled her backward, but she spun and ran with him.

She whimpered as they passed into the next cave.

Joey scanned over the piles of trash, wondering if there were any weapons mixed into all that mess. It dawned on him just how much was there and how many other kids must have been sent here.

All he could think to do was grab a hunk of boat debris as they ran past it. A splinter hooked into his skin as he snagged a board. It was like a bite, and for an instant, he wanted to drop the thing, toss it away, but he held on. Blood seeped from his grip into the wood.

Joey remembered the room had two exits, and he tried to figure out which to use.

"What was down there?" He pointed to the far side of the cave, where the girl must have come from. She had been what made those noises,right?

"I don't know." She stared at him, bewildered. How was she supposed to know that? She pointed to the side. "I came from there."

Something moved in the shadowy crevices beyond the trash. It was like the wall had come to life, and part of it was lurching toward Joey and the girl.

"Shit!" He wasn't one to cuss very often, but his mom's mouth had taught him how. This moment felt like the perfect time to use it.

Joey didn't wait for his eyes to decipher what was in those shadows. He took the girl by the arm and moved across the cave into the passage she had come from. He saw shadows move as he darted into the cave, long-armed shapes—they were catching up.

He screamed as they went through the opening.

Joey had never felt his heart throb so hard against his chest. It was like the thing was going to burst through if he didn't slow down. Add that to the list of horrible things in here!

The girl was running pretty well now. He still had no idea who she was, but obviously, she understood how horrible those things back there were. He saw the tears on her face glisten in the low light and was both sorry and angry. He wished he could help her not cry, but he also knew crying wouldn't fix any of this. So why was she doing it?

Heavy breathing and stomping followed them through the tunnel. The sounds were low, echoing against the walls, loud and forceful—as unnerving as any growl, only these creatures didn't need to do that; they were horrifying enough.

The cave took a hard turn to the right, and Joey had to brace himself as he shifted directions so he didn't crash into the rock wall. He had just regained his balance and started moving again when something grabbed his coat and yanked him backward. The board fell from his grasp. He opened his mouth to scream, and a grimy hand covered his lips.

A voice in his ear, "Shh."

Joey's breath hitched, and he quelled his urge to shake off the hand and run. The girl didn't.

She took a step and dangled mid-air, one foot out to run, the other pushing, as the shadowy person held her back.

"You can hide here." The hushed voice was lower now, speaking to the girl.

She turned, her face wrinkled in fear.

"Quickly. This way." Their hands released, and Joey could faintly see a chest-high hole in the rock. The shadowy form retreated inside.

Around the corner, the heaving breaths, the heavy footfalls—they were closing in.

"Come on," Joey hissed at the girl and gave her a tug toward the hole.

She looked around. More tears. She followed him inside.

After a few feet, Joey had to drop to his knees to pass under the sloping cave roof. He wondered how that adult (he assumed) had fit in here. He could hear the girl crawling behind.

The sounds of beasts behind them stopped moving. They were paused, likely at the entrance to this smaller path.

A rush of fear and imagery flooded Joey's mind. If they followed them in here, there was no way he could escape. It was too confined for him to move any faster. He just—

Joey's heart skipped a beat as he heard the creatures' footsteps again, thumping, booming, crushing the dirt and mud beneath them. They began to fade.

They were going the other way! Maybe they wanted to follow him, but—they couldn't fit!

Joey had to stop and regain himself. It took that moment for him to realize how abnormally his body was reacting. His fingers were twitching. His breathing was fast and shallow. His mouth was dry. God, he just wanted to be back at home in his room, playing Zelda. Why did they have to take a stupid vacation?

Pressure on his back leg. It was the girl urging him forward.

"Okay," he whispered. He breathed deeply and crawled.

They went through at least a hundred feet of twisting, turning tunnel. It widened and narrowed, and Joey got the distinct feeling he was crawling through the bowels of the Earth or some arterial system that pumped molten rock eons ago. But as the path continued with no outlet, he felt more and more this could have been a mistake.

Yes, they had eluded those *things*, but maybe they should have just waited for the monsters to pass and gone back out. He didn't know where this was leading or who that person was ahead. What if they were crazy and drawing him into a maze? What if this was all a trap, and he was being lured to his death?

He didn't want to think those things, but the longer they crawled without end, the more his thoughts darkened. Until there was light ahead.

The next cave was the size of Joey's living room, but instead of a couch and television, it was littered with the same type of trash Joey had seen when he arrived. Clothing was scattered between three exit tunnels and bunched into a bed-like mound against one wall. Trinkets lay scattered over the floor: broken cell phones, wallets, a fidget spinner, a few dingy toys, the head of a stuffed bear. The walls glowed with damp fungus, and their savior sat against the far wall, toying with something in her pocket.

She wore a thick, puffy coat, ripped in a hundred places, and her face was smudged in every direction with dark mud. She wore a blank expression—only her eyes moved as Joey and the girl circled the room, examining the new space.

Joey stopped in front of the woman and sat cross-legged on the floor. "Thank you," he spoke softly, then immediately glanced at the other two cave openings. A spike of fear hit his gut—what if those things could come through the other entrances?

She nodded and raised a hand. "It's okay. They can't get in here."

The girl sat several feet from Joey, forming a triangle of strangers, all gauging, all wary of the others. "Where are we?"

"Why are we here?" Joey said.

The woman took a breath, and for the first time, emotion showed on her face. She raised both hands in explanation while her face said *I'm sorry*. "You were sacrificed."

"What does that mean?" Joey said.

"Where's my mom and dad?" the girl said.

The woman shook her head. "I don't have all the answers. All I know is we're stuck here. And when those things grab you, one of two things happens: they eat you, or they throw you in the pool with the others."

"With those other things? Those... sea monsters?"

"Yeah."

"But what do we do?" The girl was crying again. "How do we get home?"

The woman took a deep breath and yawned. "All I can tell you is you're safe here, for now. You should try to get some rest. Whenever sacrifices come, it's always the middle of the night, so I'm sure you're tired. I can show you how this place works after that." She motioned to her bed and the rest of the clothes. "Make something like mine. It's not a hotel, but it'll work."

Joey didn't like the idea, but she was right. As the fear waned in his system and the adrenaline wore off, he realized how tired he was. It was one a.m. when they dragged him from his bed and threw him in that boat.

But before he moved, he had to know at least one thing.

"What's your name?"

The woman smiled. "Tina."

"I'm Joey." He smiled back and glanced at the girl, gesturing.

Her eyes darted between them. "Jessica."

"Okay." Joey stood and made a bed against the wall, a few feet from Tina's. He ensured he could see each tunnel from where he was laying. Then, he helped Jessica with hers.

She had pulled a small, plastic pig from her pocket and clutched it tightly as she worked with one hand. It slowed her, and Joey was about to say something when he realized what she was doing. It was Mommy Pig from that TV show he hated, but as her hand flexed white, desperately holding onto it, he knew to her it was just Mommy.

They finished her bed, and she smiled, thanking him. He wondered if this was what it would be like to have a sister. As terrifying as this whole experience was, this part wasn't bad. He could do that. He flashed with an image of them ten years later, surviving in the cave, their faces as dirty as Tina's, helping each other to last another day. That wiped away the good feeling as he settled in bed.

"Good," Tina said. "It'll all be easier after some rest." Her hands were in her pockets again, fiddling with something. Joey wanted to ask what it was, but he didn't want to be rude—the woman had saved them after all.

He stared at the tunnels and the ceiling, wondering how he would get any rest in a place like this. He didn't have to wonder long.

There was a low tone in the back of Joey's mind. It warbled as he flew through caves. He saw rock walls and shimmering light, the reflected water patterns across stone. And as he moved closer, as it grew brighter, that sound became rhythmic, a pattern of... Was it speech?

He didn't know what it was saying. The words were distorted, and he was sure it wasn't English. But he knew it was directed at him.

He found himself in the room with the pool. He floated above an army of monsters. Their faces were slime-coated, their hands webbed. They bulged with massive muscles on inhuman limbs. And they said the same words as the thing inside his mind.

He hovered over the water, watching the creatures below, and suddenly, he knew what they were doing.

He dove into the water, and time ran at a frantic pace. The beings moved rock, uncovering something beyond—a door.

It wasn't an everyday door. It was massive. Bigger than the humanoid fish, bigger than the monsters above the surface, ten—twenty times that. It was a door meant to hold back Godzilla or some planet-killing kaiju.

Joey knew the voice in his head was coming from in there, and soon, it would be out.

There was a slurping noise. It echoed in the small cave above the crackling of underfoot rocks.

Joey's eyes fluttered, catching glimpses of the glowing fungus on the ceiling.

The slurping reminded him of his friend Bruce eating an ice pop at the park back home. That kid always slurped, and it drove Joey nuts to hear it. But right now, dry throat and empty belly, he wondered if Tina might have something good to share, something to drink, even just water to soothe his parched tongue.

He followed the sound with his eyes.

It wasn't coming from Tina's bed, and Tina wasn't there.

As he turned, he found her leaning over Jessica's bed. Tina's hands were in front of her face. Dark liquid dripped from her elbows, soaking her forearms. If Joey could see her mouth, he was sure it would be covered in whatever that darkness was.

"Tina?"

She spun, her eyes wide. She clutched a raw piece of meat as she rose toward him. Shock rippled through Joey as he realized where she had gotten it from, what was dripping down her forearms and elbows, what was on her face that he had misinterpreted as mud.

It was blood. It was Jessica she was eating. And he would be next if he didn't move.

Something in her other hand glinted in the faint fungal light, and Joey didn't need to think about what that was coming from—his mind replaying the question: *what was she toying with in her pocket?*—she had a knife.

Joey raced to his feet and ran into the nearest tunnel.

"Hey!" Tina called from behind.

Joey heard the dripping wetness of the sea reaching through the cave walls. He heard his shoes pounding into the floor as his feet thrust him forward. He heard his breath rushing through his gaping mouth.

"Joey, wait!" She was following him. "Stop! It's not safe!"

He turned a corner. In his mind, he saw crimson liquid dripping from her jaw, the piece of Jessica's flesh in her hand.

"I'm trying to help you, Joey!" She wasn't far behind.

Help me? She was insane, right? She was *eating* Jessica!

The tunnel opened up into a larger chamber. Joey scanned for exits. He needed to get away from her, but that was hard to do running in a straight line. If there were at least two ways out, he'd have a 50/50 chance of losing her.

He spotted them, two large openings on the far side of the space. Now, which one, right or—

His foot sank into a puddle, and as the wetness splashed onto his leg, a sharp pain ran through his calf.

It was like the limb had disappeared. It was instantly numbed, gone, and without it, his body dropped, skidding on the gritty cave floor.

Joey's face slid over rock, and hot, burning pain lined his nose and cheek. He heard Tina's footsteps—she was closing in—and he groaned, trying to climb back to his feet. He would figure out what happened to his leg later. He had to move.

But as he tried to get back up, his numb leg refused to hold weight. He crashed back down to his knees. Hot wetness streamed to his chin and patted against the ground.

The footsteps stopped at the chamber entrance. Tina gazed at Joey with wide, gleaming eyes, and he gazed back. All he could do was crawl on his belly, so he did.

She strolled toward him. Her knife swung in her hand gleefully. "I was trying to help you."

He groaned and pulled, then yipped as a nail popped off his finger.

"There wasn't going to be enough food for three. Who knows how long it'll be before another sacrifice shows up."

Tears ran from his eyes. He saw Jessica's young face. He imagined it drenched in her own blood. That would be him, too, if he didn't get away from this crazy girl.

"I was going to share her with you. Believe it or not, I actually thought you were kind of cute in that ridiculous coat."

"You're crazy!" He huffed and dragged himself on.

"I told you! I wasn't going to kill you. Well, not as long as another sacrifice showed up reasonably soon..."

Her pace rose, and she closed the gap between them in seconds. She raised the blade. "But I guess I don't have a choice anymore."

There was a sound Joey couldn't identify at first, but seconds later, he would recognize it as his brain played it back. It was rock against rock, then a whipping, a sound like a stick through air, reminding him of when he used to play swords in the woods. Then, it was gurgling and a thump.

Joey didn't want to look, but he did.

It was so tall. Its chest could have been made of stone, and its limbs, like eel tails, swayed at its sides. Below it, Tina's throat pulsed with surging blood as she twitched at its feet. White glistened from the exposed bone in her neck, and though her eyes blinked, her body was still.

Joey opened his mouth to scream and heard a faint whistle before he went numb all over.

Joey sank into the depths of the pool. At first, he was unmoving other than his eyes, which sought out each sea monster. They would come after him; he knew it. He was being tossed in as chum, a snack. They were going to swarm him and devour him, and it didn't matter because he couldn't fight them off. He couldn't even breathe.

But they paid him no mind.

He sank to the bottom, screaming in his mind, *I need to breathe!* waiting for his body to convulse and drown. But as he touched the floor, his lungs sucked in the salty brine, pushed it back out, and he stood.

Stood!

He was breathing the water. His limbs could feel and move again.

He watched the line of creatures lugging boulders in one direction and swimming back to get more. Suddenly, he knew what they were doing. They were clearing the way, opening the door. They were doing their righteous duty, making clear the path for God to return. He saw the release. He felt the awe swell inside him, and though he knew he was a nothing, an insignificant dot of grease within the universe's cogs, he could do something great. He could move a rock. He could help usher in the return.

He swam, scooping water with his webbed fingers, and darted forward. His webbed feet and fin-lined limbs cut through the sea as he joined the line with his brothers.

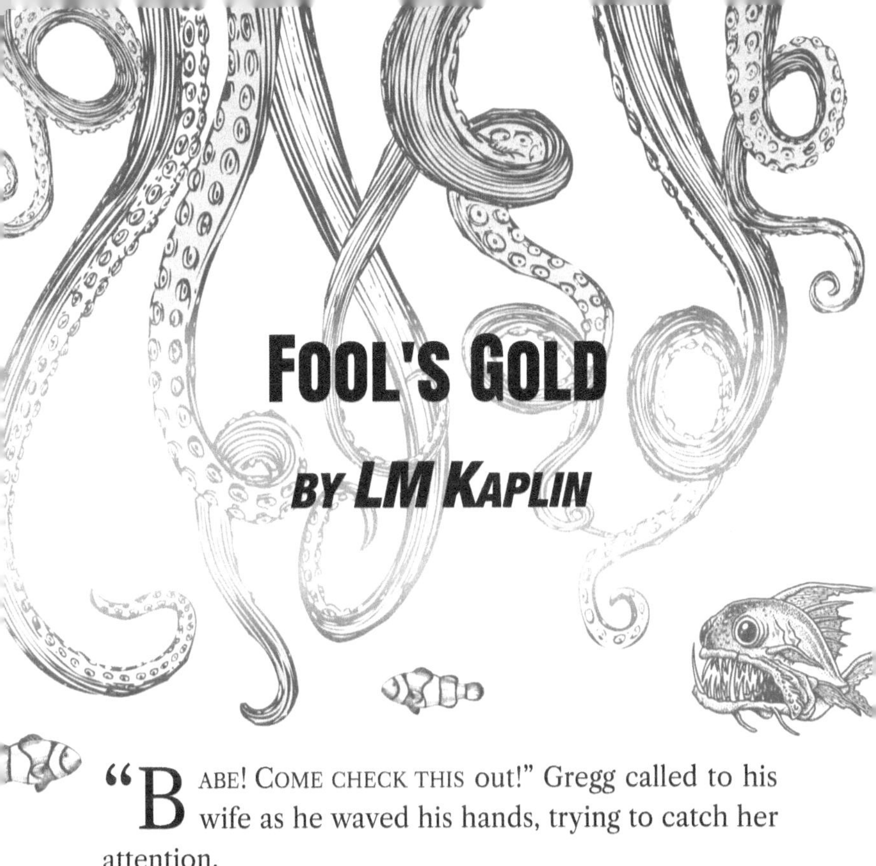

Fool's Gold

by LM Kaplin

"**B**ABE! COME CHECK THIS out!" Gregg called to his wife as he waved his hands, trying to catch her attention.

Between the sounds of the wind blowing through her mask and the water lapping against her ear, Cheryl barely heard his call. She looked up and rolled her eyes. She hadn't been a 'babe' in years. Gregg was on his best behavior and had been flattering her all week. He knew this romantic getaway was a last-ditch chance to save their struggling marriage after almost thirty years. He framed it as a week together on the open seas to rekindle their romance. She had a feeling that by the end of the trip, she would be more sick of him than ever.

Gregg waved wildly to her across the open gap between them. He had floated away from their group while she was looking at the rainbow of brightly colored fish swimming below her. She glanced at the other snorkelers in their party. Each of them was interested in their own sights, none seeming to hear or care about Gregg's find.

"Come back!" yelled Cheryl. "Don't drift too far away!"

"Just check this out real quick. It will only take a second," he called back to her.

Reluctantly, Cheryl kicked her legs and swam towards her husband. She preferred to be lounging on the top deck of the cruise ship, working on her tan, but Gregg had been looking forward to exploring the coral reefs in Grand Cayman the entire trip. He hadn't shut up about them being the largest living reefs on this side of the world. The least she could do was patronize him during his favored activity. There would be plenty of time for tanning on their way to the next island.

The swim to Gregg took longer than she expected. She was either swimming against the current or the distance across the open water was farther than it looked. Finally, after what seemed like an eternity, she made it to her husband.

"What's so important?" she asked. "They're getting ready to board the boat and head back to the ship soon."

"Look down there and tell me what you see," Gregg said, pointing into the water.

Cheryl adjusted her goggles and bobbed her head underwater to see what the fuss was about. The crystal clear water gave a stunning view of the coral reef. Intricate patterns of living rocks containing an entire ecosystem sprawled in every direction below her. A small school of orange fish swam along the edge of the coral, weaving in and out of the openings as they went.

When her vision adjusted, she followed Gregg's finger to something shiny and gold lying in the coral, about ten feet underwater. She paddled closer for a better view of the circular object.

"Is that a coin?" she asked.

"Sure looks like it to me," Gregg replied. "It could be worth a lot of money."

"It's probably just some local currency that a tourist dropped. Do you know how many snorkelers come out this way? Plus, remember the captain's speech on the ride out? He warned us not to touch or take anything while we're out here. There's already been a lot of damage to the habitat in this area. There's a huge fine for disturbing the reef."

"Yeah, but that isn't part of the reef. Technically, it's garbage, so I'd be helping clean up the ocean by taking it."

Cheryl rolled her eyes again, the gesture going unnoticed behind her goggles. She saw no point in arguing. Once Gregg made up his mind, there was no talking him out of it. With only a few days left on the trip, at least she wouldn't have to put up with his stubbornness much longer. "Whatever, just hurry before anyone sees."

Gregg took off his snorkel, handed it to Cheryl, and gave her a big grin before disappearing into the water below. Four years on the high school swim team gave Gregg plenty of confidence in his swimming skills. He often had to be reminded he was a long way off from high school.

Opening his eyes underwater, Gregg gave himself a moment to adjust to the sting of the salt water. The shining object caught his eye almost immediately, and he swam deeper towards the coral below. As he closed in on the mysterious item, the object came into focus and he knew his first instinct was correct. It looked like an old coin with an image stamped into the metal.

Placing one hand on the reef, he reached through an opening in the coral towards the coin. Squeezing his hand through the tight hole, he wiggled his fingers along the rough coral, moving the coin closer until he could grasp it. With the coin clutched between his fingers and the air in his lungs almost depleted, Gregg was ready to return to the surface with his prize. Eager to inspect the coin, he withdrew his arm from the coral but quickly realized his hand had become stuck. He twisted his wrist in an attempt to free himself from the reef, but no matter which way he turned, he couldn't pull free.

With the coin between his fingers, his hand was too big to fit back through the opening. Alarm bells rang inside his head as he knew he needed air soon. He considered the obvious option, to drop the coin—except during his struggle, he pulled his hand into a position where he couldn't open his fingers to drop it.

He looked up at the surface and saw his wife's shadow floating on the water above. He waved his other hand up towards her. She made no movement in reply. He doubted she would see a signal from down here, but with his lungs desperately low on air, he was running out of options.

His body needed oxygen, but he fought the urge to inhale, instead pushing out what little air was left inside his lungs. In full panic mode, Gregg punched at the coral holding him, causing sharp pain to shoot up his arm. Ignoring the pain, he repeated the action, smashing his fist into the rock-like coral. After multiple blows, blood from his ruined knuckles clouded the water surrounding him. The reef did not give.

With only moments before his lungs filled with seawater, Gregg arched his lower body up and brought his leg down, kicking the reef with all of his might. Finally, the coral broke, freeing his hand and allowing him to shoot quickly towards the surface. Gregg emerged gasping for air, his wife giving him a look of half-concern, half-I told you that was a bad idea.

After Gregg caught his breath, he looked down into the water, realizing he still clutched the object that almost cost him his life. He opened his hand, revealing the golden coin in his palm. The glowing piece of metal lit up the water around them and pulled Cheryl away from the disapproving glare she had aimed at her husband.

The visibly worn coin was misshapen but gave off an astonishing shine considering its age. Gregg recognized the image etched on one side. A Crusader's Cross–a commonly used symbol on a wide variety of medieval coins throughout Europe. But two large gouges formed an X through the front of the coin, obscuring the face.

Gregg raised his hand slowly, bringing it out of the water for a closer inspection of his treasure. Surrounding the cross was an intricate design of interlocking lines that seemed of Celtic origin. Oddly, the words around the edge looked to be some sort of Middle Eastern language.

A horn from the small dive boat broke Cheryl's attention from the coin. She looked over to see the other snorkelers in their group had already boarded. Everyone was waiting for them.

Gregg, still examining the coin, didn't look up until Cheryl called his name and said, "It's time to go. They're waiting for us. You'll have plenty of time to look at your precious back in the cabin."

With his wife's back turned, Gregg brought his other arm out of the water to inspect the damage to his hand. He winced when he saw the torn skin hanging from his knuckles. Blood seeped from the wound, but the injury was superficial and would heal quickly. His biggest concern was getting another earful from his wife. The trip hadn't been going according to plan, but he could tell his luck was turning. The coin was proof of that. His mind was dancing with the riches it would bring him. Gregg finally looked up and, with a huff, followed his wife to the waiting vessel.

By the time they reached the boat, the other passengers had grown impatient. Embarrassed by their disapproving looks, Cheryl took a seat in the corner, hoping to stay unnoticed for the return trip. She would be perfectly happy letting her husband be the source of their ire. After all, he's the one who called her away from the group. He had better hope the coin was worth a small fortune if he wanted to avoid her wrath later for the embarrassment. She made a mental note to ensure her lawyer included half its worth in the settlement offer he was preparing.

Dinner on the cruise ship was awkward, but not in the way Cheryl had expected. After multiple attempts at being snarky with him, she expected Gregg to ask why she was being so standoffish. Instead, he gazed into the distance as if she wasn't even there.

His thoughts remained focused solely on the coin

and its origins, while his fingers fidgeted with the gold piece in his pocket. Gregg just wanted to get back to their cabin and fire up his laptop. He planned to look for similar coins online to see their value, but he had a feeling the one in his pocket was unique. He knew he would have to contact a specialist to find out the true value. In his mind, the single coin had already made him rich beyond his wildest dreams. He would never have to work another day in his life. A smile crossed his lips as he pictured his next cruise on a private yacht instead of this overcrowded petri dish.

As the night progressed, Gregg became even less responsive, ignoring not only his wife but his meal as well. She wanted to be angry with him, but by then the color had drained from his face and thick beads of sweat appeared along his forehead. When he spilled his drink on the table, Cheryl knew something was wrong.

She suggested they retire to their room for the night, to which Gregg gave no reply. She stood and moved to his side, placing her arm around him and lifting him gently. Gregg rose from his chair, giving no opposition to her guidance, and followed her as she helped him back to their cabin.

"Should I call for a doctor?" she asked, worried about his sudden illness.

With less background noise in their room, he finally acknowledged her. "No, I'm just tired. Probably sunstroke from being out on the water all day. I should be fine by the morning."

Although still concerned for her husband, hearing him speak eased her mind. Maybe it was just sunstroke. She conceded to letting him sleep. If he didn't improve by morning, she would call for a doctor. Cheryl wondered if she should stay with him but he looked peaceful, and given the early hour, she didn't feel like sitting in a dark room all night. She could at least head downstairs, get a cocktail, and check out the scene in one of the ship's many ballrooms. She would be back to check on him in an hour.

Down at the bar, Cheryl sipped on a mai tai and nodded her head along with the music. A scruffy DJ played classic 90's hits to a rowdy crowd of middle-aged soccer moms and over-the-hill frat boys partying like they were still in their twenties. Even with the cheerful mood in the room, her thoughts kept returning to Gregg.

What if his condition worsened with no one there to help him? Even though it had barely been a half hour, Cheryl couldn't enjoy herself out alone while she worried about her husband. She didn't know why she cared so much when she planned to be rid of him anyway. She guessed she would always have some feelings for him, even if she usually hated his guts. Not one to waste a perfectly good drink, she took a moment to finish her beverage before heading back to the room.

Afraid of what she might find behind the door, she swiped the key card and entered. With the room in near total darkness, Cheryl moved to the bed and switched on the small light to get a better view of her sleeping husband.

Cheryl breathed a sigh of relief when she saw Gregg was sleeping peacefully. She placed a hand on his forehead, expecting a slight fever, but upon contact, the hairs on her arm stood on end as a chill ran up her arm. His skin felt surprisingly cold. His breathing seemed normal and he looked fine, so she prepared herself for bed and lay next to him. With the mai tai running through her veins, her worries faded and she fell asleep quickly.

Sleep didn't stay with her for long, because a short time later, a commotion outside the door woke Cheryl from her slumber. She glanced at her husband, who slept through the noise even as the ruckus grew louder.

Cheryl rose from bed and opened the cabin door to see what was happening. Looking out, she saw guests running and yelling in the hall. These patrons didn't seem to be in the same good spirits as those at the bar earlier. Instinct told her to go back inside and secure the lock, but curiosity got the better of her. She poked her head out farther, looking for the source of the disturbance.

A man glanced at her, giving a fearful look as he hurried by. Following him was something crawling along the floor. Not just one something, many somethings. An army of them. Marching in a single file line like soldiers. A clicking sound accompanied the creatures' advance.

As they drew closer, Cheryl saw that each had two large appendages raised in the air. The pincers opened and closed in tune with the noise echoing through the hall. Mesmerized by the approaching creatures, she snapped out of the trance when one fell from above and landed on her head. Taken by surprise, she shrieked as the creature buried itself in her hair. Screaming and shaking her head, she ducked back into the cabin and attempted to remove the crab, but the crustacean had become entangled in her long hair. No matter how hard she pulled, it held onto her roots with a vise-like grip.

She looked like she was headbanging at a heavy metal concert as she whipped her head around trying to get rid of the water-spider. Finally, she tore the creature away from her scalp, ripping a large chunk of hair along with it.

She locked eyes with the crab in her hands. For a moment she knew the shellfish wasn't just some unintelligent sea creature. She could've sworn she saw hate and purpose in those tiny beady eyes. Shaking the thought away, she raised her arm and threw it with all her strength. The creature hit the cabin wall with a cracking noise and fell to the floor, injured but still alive.

The clamor next to him finally woke Gregg, who shot up in bed. Yanked from a deep slumber, the sudden arousal broke him free from the terrible visions in his sleep. The pictures in his mind faded quickly, leaving only remnant images of a pirate ship sinking to the bottom of the sea along with its crew. Except the crew of this ship were no originary men. The stolen treasure had been cursed, and all aboard were doomed to wander the bottom of the ocean for eternity. Gregg shook away the thoughts as he chalked his nightmare up to an overactive imagination, but the feeling of unease persisted.

Cheryl watched her husband for a moment, expecting him to help or at least ask what was going on. Anything except lay there motionless without saying a word. Not willing to wait for Gregg to come to her rescue, she marched to the corner and stomped on the crab, sending its organs oozing out through the cracks in its shell.

With the crab neutralized, she looked back to Gregg. His complexion looked paler than ever, and his whole body was visibly shaking. "We have to get rid of it," he said.

"Don't worry, it's dead. But there's more in the hall. What do you think is going on?" she asked.

Gregg opened his mouth to reply, but instead of words, a gurgling sound emerged as he dry heaved. Loud noises erupted from Gregg's belly, followed by an eruption from his stomach. Streams of vomit came out of his mouth in between gasps for air. Cheryl watched in horror as her husband expelled what looked like gallons of seawater.

Gasping for air in between heaves, Gregg raised his hand to his mouth and put his fingers inside, pushing them to the back of his throat. He withdrew something gripped between his fingers, but a stringy, mucus-like substance coated it, obscuring the object from view. Gagging as he yanked harder, long strands of a green, slimy material emerged. Another heave and larger clumps of what looked like seaweed came spilling out of his mouth, along with an impossible amount of water.

Cheryl remained motionless, transfixed by the nauseating sight in front of her, until she felt a cold splash on her ankle and looked down. Gregg had puked up enough water to coat the cabin's entire floor, high enough for the small waves to splash up against her socks.

She didn't know if her husband was going to drown or suffocate, but it didn't matter. She would prefer either to this revulsion. At this point, she just wanted him to stop this disgusting scene one way or another before he filled the entire cabin with regurgitated salt water.

Just as these hateful thoughts crossed her mind, his anguish slowed and came to a stop. Breathing heavily, his body worked to restore the oxygen levels in his bloodstream as he wiped the remaining bits of seaweed from his chin.

Feeling weak and drained from the ordeal, he struggled to reach into his pocket and remove the gold coin within. With what felt like the last of his energy, he held the coin out to his wife and said, "Here. Get rid of it. Throw it overboard."

His wife just stared at him, still trying to come to terms with what she just saw. She held out her hand and let him drop the gold coin into her palm. As soon as it touched her skin, a feeling of peace came over her and her fears floated away like the tide. Cheryl laughed at how just a few minutes ago, her husband said the coin would make them rich beyond their wildest dreams. Now he wanted to throw it overboard all because of... some food poisoning? She didn't understand him sometimes.

Gregg noticed the confused look on his wife's face and added, "I saw it in my dream. It's cursed. We have to throw it back into the ocean."

Cheryl could barely hold back a laugh. She couldn't explain her feeling, but the events of only minutes ago had already faded from her mind. And she certainly didn't believe in curses.

Seeing her lack of urgency, Gregg raised his voice as best he could considering his aching lungs and said, "Go! Now! Get it out of here."

Surprised at her husband's stark command, she patronized him and followed his orders, leaving the cabin to dispose of the coin. The deck was littered with broken crabs shells, but the majority of the creatures had vanished, returning to the sea from which they came. A few bewildered passengers huddled in corners as they recovered from the attack.

Not wanting to stay on the exposed deck any longer than necessary, Cheryl stole one last glance in each direction before returning to the safety of her cabin.

Back inside, she found her husband had already fallen back to sleep. As she neared him, she saw his complexion had turned from the pale color to a light shade of blue. Panic swept over her as she feared the worst. She moved in closer to feel for a pulse but found none.

When the realization that he was dead finally hit her, the panic lifted and a sense of relief washed over her. Cheryl watched her husband lie motionless in bed and, for the first time in years, had hopes for the future. She never put much faith in this trip rekindling their romance, already having made up her mind to end the marriage months ago. She planned on serving him the divorce papers soon after they returned. Things were a lot easier this way. Now she wouldn't have to worry about court hearings or custody battles. And if this gold coin in her pocket was worth half as much as Gregg had claimed, she could live the rest of her life in luxury.

Sapped of energy from their ordeal, she didn't feel like dealing with the ship's security until morning, so she slipped into bed next to her husband for one last night's rest with him. She laughed to herself as she realized that without his snoring, it might be the best sleep she would get with him in years.

As she settled in, a soft clicking noise lulled her off to sleep. She recognized the sound but couldn't place the source. She knew she had heard it recently, but being so exhausted and apathetic, she couldn't remember where.

As she lay in the darkness thinking about the noise, it grew louder and louder until it echoed inside her head. The more she searched her mind, the less certain she knew what she was searching for.

Laying there in the dark cabin, she wasn't even sure if she was awake or dreaming. With the room in complete darkness and her eyes trained on the spot she knew the ceiling was, she never saw the hundreds of tiny crabs flowing from Gregg's mouth. The newly hatched creatures tickled as they crawled across Cheryl, covering every inch of her body. She couldn't explain why her internal alarm never went off, even as the crabs began prodding and nipping at her body. The small creatures were hungry. Using their tiny pincers they ripped at her flesh, tearing hundreds of small incisions in her skin.

Somewhere in the recess of her mind she wanted to scream, but she felt them on her face and lips. She knew the moment she opened her mouth to scream, the creatures would pour into the open cavity, stifling any noise she tried to make. Instead, she lay silent with her lips sealed tight as the crabs enjoyed their feast. Some explored her ears, while others worked their way up her nose. Many just engorged themselves on the closest exposed flesh they could find. One curious creature tore at her eyelid until it reached the soft cornea beneath. The sweet juices ran down her cheek like tears as the creature drove its claw into her pupil.

Within minutes, the army of crustaceans had picked her bones clean and began their march single file back towards the ocean. Working together like ants, they carried the gold coin back to their home at the bottom of the sea.

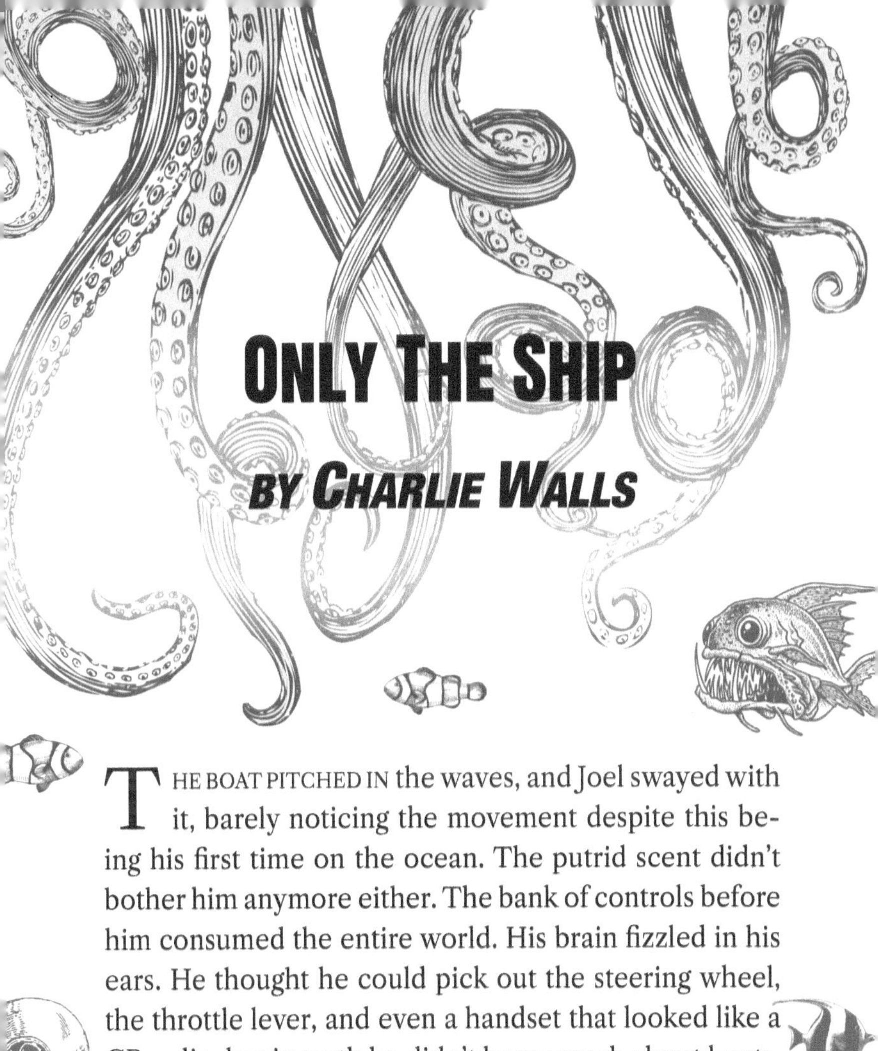

Only The Ship

by Charlie Walls

THE BOAT PITCHED IN the waves, and Joel swayed with it, barely noticing the movement despite this being his first time on the ocean. The putrid scent didn't bother him anymore either. The bank of controls before him consumed the entire world. His brain fizzled in his ears. He thought he could pick out the steering wheel, the throttle lever, and even a handset that looked like a CB radio, but in truth he didn't know much about boats. He wasn't even sure what kind he was on, except it was the type used to take tourists deep sea fishing.

He checked his phone again, but it was useless out here. He put it back in his back pocket, disgusted as he considered the amount he paid each month only for the damn thing to not work when he really needed it.

Numb fingers took up what he hoped was the radio. He depressed the switch on the side and started to speak. Nothing came out. He cleared his throat, blinked several times, and shook his head. *Come on. Get it together.* He said, "May day, may day," into the radio, released the switch, and waited. After several minutes without a reply he said, "Breaker, breaker one-nine. I'm on this boat (he failed to recall its name and refused to go check) and need help."

Waited.

Nothing.

Is this thing even on? There were so many switches and buttons covering the dashboard; he couldn't begin to decipher which one, or ones, to press. "Help me," he said over the radio. Over the next hour, he fiddled with the machine and attempted to call for help several more times, but not only was there no reply, there wasn't even static, and none of the switches he tried made a difference.

He twisted the wheel, but it wouldn't budge. The lever he suspected as being the throttle went untouched for fear of going further out to sea. The fishing boat floated in the open water. He couldn't see any buildings or landmarks on the horizon in any direction, nor had he seen another boat or a plane since before the incident occurred. Hell, there weren't even birds flying around anymore.

His thoughts turned to Amara and Nia, back at their condominium. He pictured Amara lounging on the balcony, reading while the baby took a nap. If he wasn't back by dinner, she would call the police, a search party would be sent out. Someone would find him. The thought of upsetting her, of giving their vacation a black eye, pissed him off, but in this situation, her worry might be the only thing that saved his life.

He considered the marina. The boat was a tourist rig with schedules and insurance, and the captain and crew probably had families as well. When they didn't return on time, a report would be made, the calvary called in. Each of the chartered boats probably worked their own territory, so he reasoned the authorities would be well on their way to him before Amara even became concerned. Though once help did arrive, he didn't have a clue how to explain the situation. No one would believe the truth. He wouldn't have believed it if he wasn't here. He decided against thinking about it, decided to wing it once (if) the time arrived.

But what if they never found him? He imagined some yacht or cargo ship coming across the fishing boat years from now, deserted. Another ghost ship. Happened all the time. A Filipino fisherman sets sail one morning, twenty years later his skiff washes ashore in South America. Or never reaches shore. How many empty vessels were floating out there now, completely unknown, forgotten? The *Mary Celeste* was one he had read about. It was found abandoned by the crew but in otherwise perfect condition. He remembered there still being plates set out on tables, personal effects left in bunks like everyone just vanished. None of the crew was ever located. No one ever learned why the ship was abandoned. The *Ourang Medan* was another one. There was always another one. Human seafaring history was chock full of stories, myths, and legends. Not to mention the movies. There was a shitty one called *Ghost Ship* that came out several years back, but his favorite was probably John Carpenter's *The Fog*, with the ghost pirates.

Joel shivered. What if that was his future? He looked around the little vessel, imagined it so empty it barely existed. Barnacle encrusted. Rust leaking from seams and rivets. Sea bird shit blanketing the skyward surfaces. Paint peeling, melting in the sun. He stared at the lifeless controls. Where would it go unsteered? Where would it take him? Swallowed into nothingness by the sea? Unbidden, unavoidable, the day's events replayed in his mind.

He had been in the bathroom—the head—when whatever happened, happened. He flushed, washed his hands, and was busy drying them on his cargo shorts as he stepped into the cabin. From outside came a grunt, a splash, and then another splash. He glanced up in time to see a pair of legs and flip-flopped feet disappear over the side. Rushing out to help, a strong carrion odor swallowed him. He bent over, gagging. The stench seemed to hover around the vessel. Finally, he called out for someone to come help, and it wasn't until he reached the back rail that he realized he was alone on deck. A minute prior, twelve others shared the boat, including the two crewmen helping the tourists bait their hooks and the captain up at the wheel, which was now also vacant.

The water lapping at the boat and sometimes splashing inside was black as pitch. It was a deep green before his visit to the head. Despite the cloudless sky and calm, green ocean farther out, black water twisted all around the vessel.

His first thought was an oil spill. A large one occurred nearby in the Gulf several years earlier. But there were no structures in sight, and the sludge surrounded only the boat. Maybe there was a malfunction of some kind and they were leaking something. But if so, where was everyone else? His stomach turned at the thought. He knew where they were—he had seen the last one go there—but he couldn't fathom what happened.

Creatures swam around the hull. Surely they were some species of fish, but the murky water made it impossible to see them clearly. A fin here. A swath of scales shimmering in the sun. But none of them breached long enough for him to get a clear view.

He was sick all over the deck, heaving until nothing came out. Then he frantically rushed up the ladder to the control panel where the captain belonged.

A particularly nasty wave struck, skipping the craft across the surface. He was nearly knocked off his feet but managed to snatch one of the canopy support rails to keep from going overboard into the blackness. When this fresh bout of turbulence abated and his heart and breathing calmed, he climbed down the aluminum ladder to the deck. He was careful to keep his eyes on the boat housing. It was white and metal or plexiglass or some type of plastic. All that mattered was that he not look at the water or back toward the deck where everyone... where it happened. Once his feet struck the deck, he kept his eyes down and waddled into the small cabin.

There was a wrap-around sofa built into two walls and a narrow set of steps leading to the bathroom. *Head*, he reminded himself. There was also a kitchenette with a sink, mini-fridge, and hot plate. This was an all-day excursion, so everyone packed their own lunches, either in bags or coolers. He opened his lunchbox, the one he carried daily to work, and a folded sheet of paper fell out. With trembling fingers, he opened it.

'Honey,

'Have fun and catch all the fish you can. Me and Little Bird will be waiting for Daddy to get back. Hopefully we can eat your catch tonight for dinner.

'Love Always,

'A.'

His appetite fled. He looked longingly at the now ownerless coolers set on the floor. He remembered at least two of the other tourists had beer, and he suddenly felt the impulse to rummage through them until he found a brew that didn't taste like cat piss. Instead, he pounded a bottle of water. Getting drunk in this situation was probably not the best idea. Exhaustion, both mental and physical, crashed over him like a tsunami. Taking another bottle of water from his lunchbox, he plopped onto the sofa and avoided looking through the windows that stretched along the opposite wall.

His stomach grumbled, and without much thought, without really tasting it, he chewed down the pair of ham sandwiches he had packed. While eating, he reread the letter. He survived a tough time after returning from deployment, and Amara helped turn him around, brought him back from the desert. He met her at the funeral of an Army buddy who had killed himself. It was the lowest point of his life, and then she was there. Amara knew he had always wanted to go deep sea fishing and volunteered to stay behind with the baby while he went. Part of him wished she was there with him, but if she was, maybe she would have met the same end as the crew and the other tourists. Maybe the baby... He forced himself not to think about it. The sole positive aspect of the day was that his wife and child were safe.

He ate and dozed.

Everything was dark, yet he could see. He floated in an amniotic pocket of warmth but could feel the freezing water creeping in from the edges. Startled, he thrashed about. He hadn't been holding his breath, didn't have one of those diver's breathing things. But he also wasn't suffocating. In fact, he felt fine aside from the sudden shock at finding himself there. Below stretched a coral and boulder-strewn expanse of sand from which rocky, salt-caked spires rose, appearing both intentionally placed and naturally formed.

Shapes swam outside his pocket, serpentining this way and that. Due to the darkness and the speed of the creatures, he still couldn't tell what they looked like. They could have been a species of fish or simply amorphous shapes.

A film of gloom pervaded everything, and he suddenly felt much colder. Goosebumps rippled his flesh, his teeth chattered, and he wrapped his arms around himself to preserve body heat. His fingers and toes were already draining of color, appearing ashen, rapidly growing numb. He panicked, but it was a distant emotion, like he was watching someone else go through a traumatic or dangerous event while he was safe on the other side of an impenetrable wall of ice. Everything seemed far away, miniscule. What was happening was not important—it just was—and that spark of panic shrank further into the dark, deep water of his mind.

From behind, a wave of warmth enveloped him and realization struck—he was about to freeze to death and hadn't even cared. This thought disturbed him nearly as much as the situation. He cared for his family more than anything... Amara and Nia. He had to return to them. The sudden thawing of his extremities brought with it a feeling of well-being, of action. Goodness. The warmth was good. *Find the warmth*, he thought. *Go into it.* It had to be the way out, or up, or wherever.

Turning over, he found a great chasm yawning from the seabed. The place he floated was dark as night, but inside was abyssal. He couldn't stand to look directly at it for more than a couple of seconds without his vision glazing over and his head pounding. Instead, he concentrated on a particular gnarl of coral that grew along one edge.

Heat radiated from the abyss. He basked in it, thankful for the respite from the cold despite the ominous circumstances. He felt rather than saw the presence within. It was large and old, old as the sea itself. Teeth of shattered masts snapped in centuries-old gales. Barnacled, salt-crusted scales. Eyes larger than the moon and just as pale swallowed him in the warmth of their gaze. It spoke with a million luminescent, writhing tongues.

It was neither angry nor bestial. It was hungry though. It *wanted* him, longed for him, loved him. It was the sea, and It loved all creatures within It. It knew he was in trouble, that he was caught in a situation of which there was no hope of freeing himself. Being lost at sea was dangerous enough for an experienced seaman, but he had never stepped foot on a boat before today. It could help him. Would help him. All he had to do was reach out for It, reach for salvation.

Mesmerized, Joel stretched an arm toward the chasm, into that warmth.

He reached out as another wave struck, and for a moment he teetered on the rail at the stern of the fishing boat, arms thrown wide for balance. Night had fallen. Clouds blanketed the sky. The entire ocean was as dark as the chasm.

The carrion odor draped over him like a sheet. His stomach churned, and he puked a stream of turgid fluid into the water. Below, the seething creatures splashed as they slurped up his refuse. Fin and scale were all he had seen of them earlier, and even though he could see even less now, he added the smacking of fat lips and snap of razor jaws to his mental image of the damned things.

Jesus! He had nearly leapt overboard, and those things down there; those snapping, circling things were waiting for him.

Arms still out, he shifted, looking for a place to step back onto the deck.

The hull bucked in the frenzied sea. Joel nearly slipped from the rail, rocking back and forth, over the deck and then back over the water. His arms pinwheeled about as wave upon wave battered the craft.

And he fell.

Captain Emily Brown steered her vessel toward the fishing boat. A crew member spotted the craft while it was still on the horizon, and after several failed attempts to radio the crew, she decided to investigate. It wasn't in good shape, but as far as she could tell, it rode the water just fine. Nearing the boat, it became clear it was abandoned. Captain Brown warned her crew to look alive. Barnacles climbed the hull, and the gulls had taken full advantage of the fortuitous perch out here in the ocean. Bird shit covered everything.

Pulling alongside, they lashed the ships together. She sent one crew member aboard to search and another to scrape away the barnacles obscuring its name. As she expected, it was completely empty, but surprisingly, everything appeared in working order. The search turned up no conclusive reason the ship, *Point of View* (*shitty name*, she thought), would have been abandoned. She ordered the radio operator to call it in to the marina and the Coast Guard. And then they waited.

Finally, the call came in. "Captain," the radioman said. "That boat's been missing for two months. There's a big ass finder's fee for it, they said."

She grinned. "Let's pull her in then."

The sun burned into him. Joel's eyelids felt cemented together and hurt when he opened them. He grimaced when he sat up; his back popped and pinched. He could have been made of wood. His throat felt like a dried creek bed, and it cracked and bled. His tongue was stuck to the roof of his mouth. Head spinning. Body weak, limbs shaking. It took a long time for him to stand using the rail on the back of the boat to hold himself up.

Head throbbing, he ran his fingers over the back of his head where a knot as large as a softball protruded. He felt like shit, plain and simple. But at least it was daytime now. He survived the night and whatever those things circling the boat were, whatever that Thing was down there. He was alive and it was a bright, cloudless day.

Then came the blast of a ship's horn, and he nearly leaped overboard. The sight of the ship, an actual ship, one of those big cargo rigs nearly the size of a skyscraper on its side and loaded with shipping containers, filled him with a mixture of excitement and disbelief, of hope. He waved his arms and jumped as high as his weakened legs would lift him. He screamed his throat ragged.

He feared the gigantic vessel wouldn't see him and would pass on by, possibly overturning his tiny boat in its wake. But they did see him, someone did at least, and finally he was ferried up onto the deck. Crew members bombarded him with questions, but it all sounded like gibberish. Faces crowded in, blocking out the sun, smothering him. When they backed up and let him catch his breath, he could see individual faces; looking at each of his rescuers, he found them all to be Asian. Then the gibberish clicked into place; they were speaking their native language. Joel didn't care who they were; he was glad to be off that fishing boat. All of it was over. They could radio someone and get him back to his family.

One of the crew, someone important he guessed but could not be sure, led him below deck and down a narrow corridor to a medical officer. His chaperone spoke to him during the physical evaluation, but he only shook his head, shrugged his shoulders, or repeated, "English." The medic gave him a pair of white pills and gestured to his head. Joel accepted the pills and a small paper cup of water that left a chemical aftertaste at the back of his throat.

Next, the crew member led him to another cramped room with a small metal desk bolted to the floor, a handful of chairs stacked in the corner, and a computer monitor affixed to the desktop. He handed Joel a chair and gestured for him to sit before the monitor. He turned it on and loaded a display. It was a weather report, with most of the screen covered in symbols he couldn't read. But there was a map and the date. Joel stared, disbelieving. His body was numb and distant, his mind filled with static. *This couldn't be right*, he thought. They had left the marina yesterday and only went a few miles out into the Gulf of Mexico. But the display said...

He looked away, looked up at the crewman with wide, frightened eyes, and shook his head, begging the screen to be wrong.

According to the map and the date, they were currently in the middle of the Pacific Ocean, six months after he left on the loathsome fishing trip that should have only lasted a few hours.

There was neither light nor dark. Joel didn't breathe nor drown. He had no bodily control but was not pulled by the current that ripped along the ocean floor. The cold from before was absent, and so was the warmth it had promised him. He was nothing. Stagnant. Repose. Static.

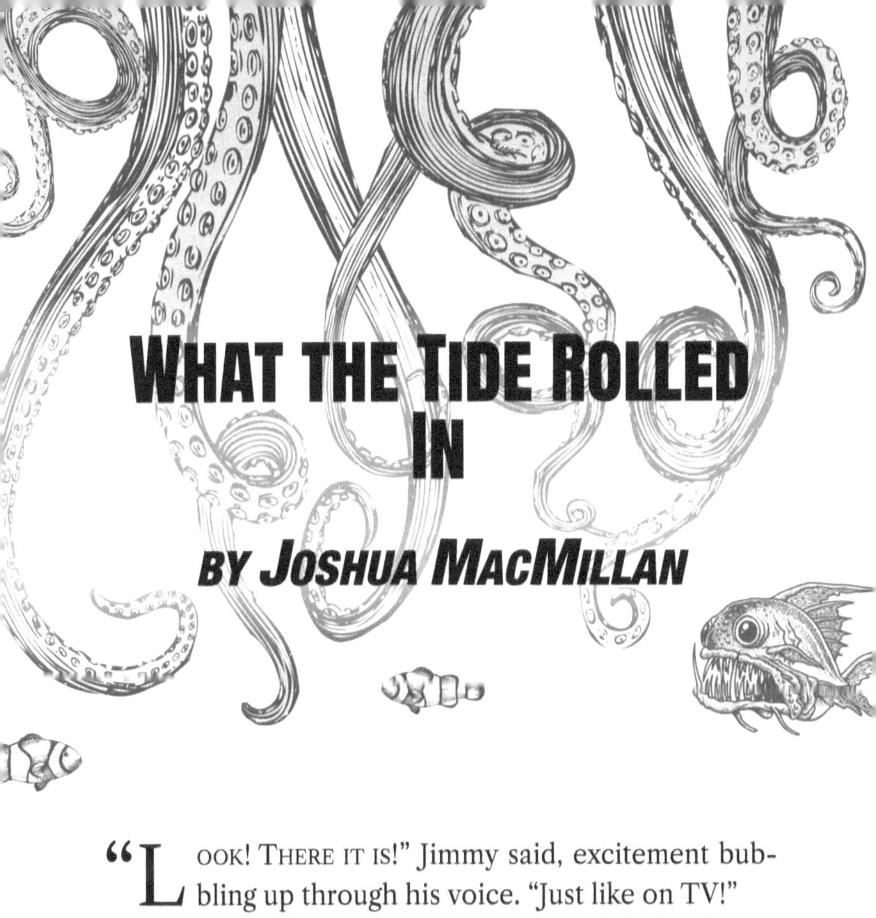

What the Tide Rolled In

by Joshua MacMillan

"Look! There it is!" Jimmy said, excitement bubbling up through his voice. "Just like on TV!"

Ted smiled. He had caught glimpses of the land mass through the breaks in the trees as the two of them peddled their bikes up the road that snaked its way along the highway. Their mother would have killed him if she had known Ted had allowed Jimmy to cross the main highway to come with him, but he figured what she didn't know wouldn't hurt her. Now that they had gotten through the section of the bike path that took them through the woods, the area opened up and they could see the vast Galveston coastline.

Jimmy had been bugging him all day about going out and seeing the island that had washed up. The young boy's badgering had only increased when he had heard

Ted and some of his friends had planned on going out to the island for the day to investigate and explore it. That alone hadn't been the downfall of Ted's real plans though. His mistake had been mentioning how they were going to have a cookout with a bonfire on the island.

"Oh man, can I come? Please?" Jimmy had whined.

"No."

"PLEASE!" Jimmy continued.

Ted turned his back on his younger brother and began scrolling through his text messages. He found the message thread he shared with his two best friends and typed out a quick message about how frustrating Jimmy was being before he turned to look at the boy and tell him to shut up about it. However, when he turned back towards the hallway he had been in with Jimmy, the hallway was empty.

"Jimmy?" Ted called out, looking further down the hall through squinted eyes before looking back in the direction he had turned when he sent the text message. There was no one in the hallway. Moments later, his mother's falsetto voice rang down the hallway.

"Teddy, would you please take your brother with you? I could use the help; I have a lot of work I need to catch up on."

Ted groaned, leaning against the hall and gently rocking the back of his head into the drywall in frustration. He didn't want to be saddled with his younger brother all day, especially not if he hoped to have any shot at spending some time with Brittany. He lifted his phone back up and stared at the screen. There were four new messages from Brent and Sam telling him to ditch the little brat.

No such luck on his end though.

Ted led the trek as he and Jimmy coasted down the winding road toward the boardwalk. A few minutes later, they were chaining their bicycles to the bike rack on the north side of the parking lot and were walking briskly down the boardwalk, taking in the sights and the smells of the final days of one of Galveston's many festivals. Their mouths watered at the smell of frying dough and grilled meat. Carnival barkers hailed them, trying to draw them near, but the boys were on a mission.

It took them a few minutes, but they managed to weave their way through the sparse crowd and cross the boardwalk. Ted was the first to reach the guard rail they would have to slip under to get down to the section of beach that would take them away from the prying eyes of the numerous adults. In the distance, he could see Brent and Sam standing on the beach.

Ted waved casually before ducking below the lowest bar of the guardrail. He slid over the edge, dangling his right foot and wriggling it around as he slowly lowered himself to the sand, feeling blindly for the soft firmness the beach had to offer. He turned and aided his brother down the short drop.

Ted turned and briskly crossed the sandy beach at a jog to catch up to his friends. As he neared, he could see the two had managed to drag out a large Igloo cooler on an old, rusted-out wagon.

"Everyone else make it out there yet?" Ted asked.

Brent shrugged his shoulders and glanced over Ted's shoulder, nodding his head in the direction he had come from. "I thought you were going to ditch him."

Ted looked at the ground for a moment, embarrassed at his inability to leave his younger brother behind. "My mom made me bring him," Ted started, looking back toward Jimmy, who was just now catching up to him. He lowered his voice to a whisper. "I'll keep him in line, don't worry."

"Hey guys!" Jimmy's voice rang out, excitement permeating his words between deep, gasping breaths. "I had to actually run to catch up to you."

"You'll survive," Ted said glumly.

Brent gestured toward the expanse behind them. The beach ran in an arc that curved to their right and then slithered back to the left. "The island is just around the other side of that bend there."

Without saying anything else, the four of them began their trek again with Brent and Sam leading the pack. Ted had taken hold of the wagon. He felt as if taking the load off the other two would ease the annoyance of having to drag along his twelve-year-old brother to some degree, he hoped.

After a few moments, Jimmy found himself ahead of the older boys. He had tried to talk with the three older boys, but none of them would give him more than a grunted one- or two-word reply. This bothered Jimmy some. He loved his older brother, secretly admiring the older boy. He wanted to be just like his brother, but he knew he could never be as popular as Ted. Ted could make friends with anyone anywhere he went. Jimmy couldn't even get the most playful of puppies to lick his hand. Still, he tried to be friendly with everyone, especially Ted's friends. He could tell he wasn't going to get anywhere with the older boys though; it was clear, even to Jimmy's younger mind, that he wasn't wanted here.

He decided to leave them be. He would stay within sight of his brother, but he was going to do his own thing. He broke away from the boys and put some space between himself and them. His mind pushed the sting of the older boys' rejections away with surprising ease and quickness. He whistled as he searched the shoreline for shells or maybe a crab.

He looked behind him, seeing Ted and the other two were still somewhat visible. His mother had constantly droned on and on about how he needed to remain in Ted's line of sight whenever he would go out with him. *If you can see him, he can see you*, she would tell him. This little saying always struck him as being a bit off. He was familiar with the concept of spies, and those guys always got away with watching people without being seen. They hid in plain sight, and you would never be able to tell they were watching you. Still, his mother's words kept him rooted where he was for a bit to allow his brother time to catch up.

He bent and removed his flip-flops, burrowing his toes in the golden sand and wriggling them. He relished the feeling of the sunbaked earth. He slowly began prodding along, whistling once more as he swung his arms and clapped the flip-flops together in time with the tune. He watched the tide as he waited for the others to come closer, feeling his impatience growing. His mind raced with excitement as thoughts of what he might discover on the strange island flashed before his mind's eye.

Jimmy could see it all now, clear as day. There he was, standing on the shore of the island, shaking hands with some important-looking people in shirts and ties while a massive crowd of people formed in front of them. TV news anchors swarmed the area and reported the huge discovery live as Jimmy broke away from the handshake and turned toward a large object concealed with a heavy velvet cloth. He gripped the sides of the drapery with his fists and gave the growing crowd a knowing smile. He waited a moment longer before he pulled the cloth away to the sounds of excitement, and fear.

Jimmy shook the daydream off, glancing in the direction of the older boys. He cocked his head to see if he could hear them talking amongst themselves yet. He thought he could hear the quick, barking laugh of one of them and decided that would be good enough. He felt like he had waited long enough. He was beyond ready to get to the island and explore. He picked up the pace, coming around the bend and finally, for the first time in person, saw the island that had drifted from unknown origin. His excitement was too much; he broke into a sprint, clearing the remaining three hundred yards or so in no time at all.

He slowed to a jog as the island drew closer. It was much larger than it had looked on tv. Looking around, he was surprised to see there wasn't anyone else here. How was it that something as strange as this floating island could just appear overnight, yet no one in the overpopulated city of Galveston thought to come and check it out for themselves? Jimmy pushed the thought away, contented with the fact this meant he would be able to explore the island for as long as he wanted while his brother and his friends did whatever it was they wanted to do.

He took a quick glance over his shoulder and found the three older boys were little more than bouncing dots on the horizon. He hadn't realized he had put that much space between them. *Oh well, it's not like they care anyway*, he thought as he turned back toward the island.

On his left, a downed tree trunk lay on its side, half on the island and half on the shore of the mainland. He tested the strength of one of the limbs that jutted upward. He found it spongy but solid enough to hold onto.

As he stepped onto the island, he eased his right foot onto the mossy ground. The land felt firm but had a springy give to it that excited and scared Jimmy at the same time. It felt as if the ground could give at any moment. He allowed his full weight to press onto the island, gently bouncing a few times on his right foot before bringing his full body onto the island. He could immediately tell the island would hold his weight without issue.

He moved forward a few steps, walking cautiously until his bare feet began to feel the warm sand making up the majority of the island's surface. His heart trip-hammered in his chest, and the moment he had fully arrived on the sandy surface, his chest eased as he sucked in a deep breath after releasing the one he had been holding.

Jimmy turned, looking back in the direction from which he came. The overgrown vegetation prevented him from seeing the path he had taken and so prevented him from being able to see his brother. His immediate thought was to remain in place; the last thing he wanted was to keep moving farther onto the island only to get his ass chewed by his brother for not waiting up for him. He knew deep down his brother wouldn't care though. He would only care if Jimmy managed to get lost or hurt. Ted would catch the blame. With this thought fresh upon his mind, he turned back towards the island's center and began to walk.

Jimmy had been correct about Ted not caring whether Jimmy had run off ahead of them or not. He had watched his younger brother disappear around the bend and had felt the tension ease inside his chest. This also brought a sense of guilt through his heart, but he quickly buried that feeling. He turned toward Brent, who had been telling him about the hook up he had gotten from their dealer of a new strain of some truly stellar buds. "Did he say where he got it from?"

"Nah, man," Brent said, passing the rolled-up sandwich baggie to Ted. "You gotta smell this though. It smells a-maze-ing!"

Ted hated it when Brent would space his words out like that, announcing each syllable as if it was made from capital letters. But, after one sniff of the pungent weed, he forgave his friend's aggravating phonics. He rolled the bag back up and passed it back to his friend, who quickly stuffed it in the front pocket of the oversized hoodie he wore.

Up ahead, Ted watched his brother stop just before the bend leading to the island. The smell of the aromatic dope touched his nostrils and he quickly glanced around, stretching out his left arm. "Hey, let's slow down some. The last thing I need is for the little narc to smell or see us smoking."

"Well, you should have left him," Brent said, clearly uncaring whether Jimmy caught them or not. "I bet he'd love to try some of this. Might be good for him."

"Seriously, dude."

"What?" Brent said, chuckling to himself.

Without further conversation, the group slowed their pace, passing the pre-rolled blunt between them. All three of them took turns hacking their lungs out as they puffed it quickly.

Jimmy found himself a little let down after climbing on the island's surface. He knew it had been wishful thinking to believe he would find some sort of long-lost monster like those in the old Japanese *Godzilla* films he and Ted would sometimes watch together, but the wonder of the idea had been an incredibly strong drug for the young boy.

For safety reasons, he opted to stick near the outer edge of the island, walking and enjoying the refreshing waves of salt water as the tide rolled across his feet. He resumed humming the tune he had been whistling earlier as he took in his surroundings. Large palm trees grew tall; he had never seen palm trees in person before, and he was in awe. He turned toward them, approaching them, thinking that he might find a wild coconut growing. His mother loved coconuts, and he liked the idea of bringing one home to surprise her.

A sudden jostling amongst the bushes at the base of the tree caused a jolt to course through him, stopping him mid-stride. He squinted, the way one does while studying something and trying to figure it out. There was something in the bushes, but he couldn't make out exactly what it was. What he could see was that it was something alive, and it was watching him. An icy chill wormed its way down his spine as the pungent odor of rotten fish and decaying flesh touched his nostrils.

He inched forward, sliding his toes through the sand rather than picking his feet up and taking actual steps, his eyes locked on the shape concealing itself around the base of the palm tree. Every fiber in his being was telling him he shouldn't be moving toward whatever it was that lay in wait, but his natural curiosity pulled him closer and closer. After a couple of steps, the shape darted off, scampering through the thick underbrush that made up most of the island's topography, a low mewling trailing behind it as it vanished.

Jimmy quickened his steps, grabbing hold of the tree's trunk and peering over the bush. He could make out the wake of the thing's path by the broken branches and the bent limbs weaving through the underbrush. His body continued forward, moving along as if on autopilot. The trail became more sparse the farther he trekked into the dense woods.

Up ahead, the woods thickened, but a shimmering

glint broke through the trees and brush, reminding him of the way the sun would glint off the ocean. *Is that the other side of the island?* His mind wandered, trying to imagine the overall layout of the chunk of land that had washed up along the beach of their ocean-front town. The trail he had been following had just about vanished, like the shape behind the trees. Still, the horrible smell stung his nostrils. It seemed to be everywhere around him.

He smelled his hands, grimaced, and rubbed them on the front of his board shorts. The odor was all over his hands. An oily, sticky substance that had stuck to his palms while he pushed his way through the woods. At first, he had thought the substance was sap, but the faster he rubbed his hands across his legs, the more he could feel the goop balling itself up and clumping together like congealing fat. With the pads of his index finger and thumb, he pinched a chunk of the substance and peeled it away from his shorts, bringing it up and examining it. It looked similar to potter's clay.

He tossed it aside and looked back toward the shimmering he had seen through the trees. What was it he had seen? More than likely it was just some stray animal, a dog perhaps, that had been stranded on the island before it washed up. He didn't think so. No, his gut was telling him the thing had been something else entirely.

Jimmy crossed the remaining stretch of the woods in a trance-like state. His mind was telling him to turn back, that it was stupid to continue moving forward when his animal instincts were screaming at him there was danger ahead. *This must be how those dumb characters in all those stupid horror movies Ted watches feel*, he thought.

The thought of his brother nearly pulled his mind away from the task of breaking through the other side of the trees, but before the thought had fully formed within his young mind, he found himself standing in the open, direct sunlight.

He brought his hands up to shield his eyes. As he did so, he felt something warm and slick drip onto the backside of his cupped hands, a warm fluid that pooled itself between his fingers and forehead. He pulled his hand away, his pelvic floor falling as he spread his fingers and examined the thick, translucent substance that coated his hand and formed sticky webs between his fingers. His eyes slowly worked their way from his hands to the treetops overhead, taking in the nightmare looming directly above him, perching like a gargoyle ready to pounce at any moment.

Even in the sunlight he couldn't make out its precise shape, but the smell had become overpowering. His stomach flopped, quivering, feeling as if it was rolling over within itself. He could taste stomach bile as his legs gave out beneath him. Within moments, he crumpled to the sandy ground, icy tendrils of fear lacing his bloodstream as white-hot bile spilled over his lips.

The thing in the treetops had coiled back onto its haunches, like a snake on the verge of striking its prey, and he had just enough time to pick his hand back up, briefly examining the substance he now knew was the creature's slobber. He had enough time to take notice of the yellow-white rings around the thing's eyes. He could hear the sucking, gasping sound that emanated from slits on either side of its blue-green neck.

The horror that leaped down upon him was humanoid

to some degree but had a ridge-like crest that ran from its snake-like snout towards the back of its head, jutting outward. He saw the webbing between the creature's claws turn translucent as swiped at him. White-hot pain seared its way down the left side of Jimmy's face and neck. He could feel hot blood pouring out in runnels and sticking his tank top to his bird-like chest. The wet, gurgling, mewling sound turned into a bubbling snarl as the full weight of the creature came down upon the small boy. Jimmy reached up, grasping at anything he could get his hands on. His hands raked across hard, knobby scales that felt glossy and sticky. Tendrils of seaweed pulled away from the thing's torso.

He tried to open his mouth to scream for his brother, or anyone at this point, but the only thing that came out was a silent hiss of pure terror and pain. A new sensation washed over him and, with it, the unfiltered loss of sensation. Pain at first, as if the thing had punched him between the shoulder blades, but this gave way to a feeling of losing oneself as the only thing that came to Jimmy's mind before permanent darkness was the feeling of his spine coming unzipped from his being.

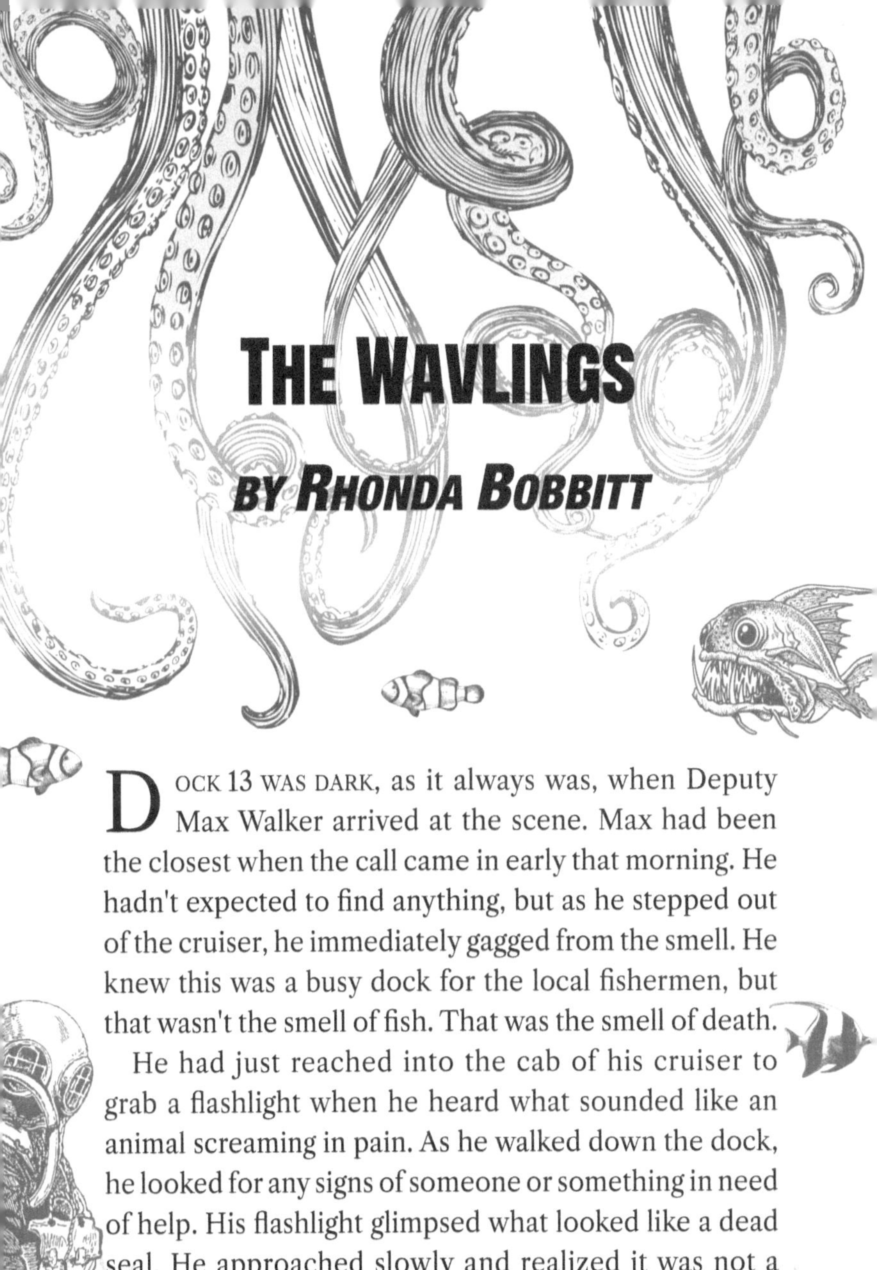

THE WAVLINGS

BY RHONDA BOBBITT

DOCK 13 WAS DARK, as it always was, when Deputy Max Walker arrived at the scene. Max had been the closest when the call came in early that morning. He hadn't expected to find anything, but as he stepped out of the cruiser, he immediately gagged from the smell. He knew this was a busy dock for the local fishermen, but that wasn't the smell of fish. That was the smell of death.

He had just reached into the cab of his cruiser to grab a flashlight when he heard what sounded like an animal screaming in pain. As he walked down the dock, he looked for any signs of someone or something in need of help. His flashlight glimpsed what looked like a dead seal. He approached slowly and realized it was not a seal but half of a human body. Before he called it into dispatch, he glanced around and saw body parts all over the dock. The torso of what he thought was a man was ripped in-half, containing no organs or blood. The head was laying just feet away, also drained. Even the legs had been eaten clean to the bone, and there were no arms in sight.

"Dispatch, this is Deputy Max Walker. I'm down on Dock 13. We need to get everyone down here immediately."

"Copy that, Max. Do you need the sheriff?" the dispatcher asked.

"I need the whole damn force, and call the coroner too. This is a nightmare."

When Max released the mic, he felt as if something was watching him. Just my nerves, he thought. But then he heard that screaming again, and before he could turn towards the direction of the sound, the creature shot straight up out of water and tore his body in half.

Sheriff Sean Booth arrived at the scene twenty minutes after he had received the call from dispatch. It seemed as if the entire department had been called out as well he thought as he stepped out of his cruiser.

"Hey Tony, where's Max? I need a full detail of what's going on here," asked the sheriff.

"Not sure that's going to happen chief," said Tony Pride, one of his deputies.

"And why the hell not? This is his crime scene."

"Yeah, unfortunately Max is now part of the crime scene, boss."

As Sean looked around in confusion for Max, he heard James Daley, the local coroner, yell for more body bags.

Sean turned back to Tony in shock.

"Are you telling me Max is dead?"

"Yeah, as far as we can tell it's Max. What's left of him anyway," Tony replied.

For the next hour, Sean and Tony worked the scene, trying to match the different body parts to the correct bodies and looking for any evidence that could answer the question of what the hell had happened here.

"Hey Tony, did you notice anything strange about the body parts?"

"Yeah, there was no blood anywhere," he responded.

"How can someone kill two people and not leave a single drop of blood?" asked Sean.

"No idea. And that smell, it's not coming from the bodies. It's coming from the water."

Sean noticed the smell was a lot stronger near the water, but he thought it was just the fishermens' discarded, rotten fish.

The early morning sun had just started to rise when Sean suddenly heard the most horrifying scream he had ever heard, coming from the ocean.

The entire police department and town locals used all their efforts in the next few weeks to find the source of the screams and the murders.

It had been almost four weeks since the murders on Dock 13 when Sheriff Booth got another call that two more bodies had been found on the pier. This time, the bodies belonged to a fisherman named Frank and his first mate, John. They had just returned after a five-day fishing trip. Frank's son had been the one to find the nearly unrecognizable bodies when he had gone to pick up his father.

Sheriff Booth called a town meeting the next day and informed the town there was to be no fishing and no one out after dark until they caught the culprits. The town's fishermen had flown into a rage, screaming the sheriff couldn't stop them from fishing. Over half the town were fishermen, including Sean's father and brothers. Gloucester, MA was a fishing port and nothing more.

After the town hall cleared out, Vincent Brody, the town's most successful fisherman, along with his crew, Sam, Tim and Jack, held their own meeting.

"There's no way in hell that pompous-ass sheriff is telling me I can't fish in these waters. He needs to get his town in order and leave the waters to us," yelled Vincent.

"What are you suggesting we do, go against the sheriff's orders?" asked Jack, Vincent's first mate.

"You're damn right we are. We leave in three hours, just like planned, to get our quota in for the month," said Vincent.

The three hours went by fast as the crew set the boat up for a three-day fishing trip. Vincent and his crew stocked the boat with plenty of liquor, food, and bait. Jack grabbed his rifle and ammo just in case the sheriff was right and there was some crazed killer out there. There was no way in hell they were letting any young sheriff tell them to stop fishing.

"Everyone set to go? We're leaving in five minutes," said Vincent.

"We're all set, Captain. Everyone's onboard," Jack

said.

"Alright then, let's set sail. We should be at the first spot in about two hours."

"Aye, Captain," yelled the crew.

A little over two hours later, the captain killed the engine and yelled, "Drop the anchor boys, it's time to make that money."

Just as the anchor hit the bottom, there was a loud screeching noise.

"What the hell was that?" Jack asked.

"Sounded like someone screaming, but there ain't no one around here but us," replied Sam.

Sam, Jack, Tim, and Vincent stood deathly still waiting for another sound, but nothing came.

"Do you hear anything, boys?" asked Vincent.

"No, nothing, nothing at all," replied Jack quietly.

"That's what I thought. I don't even hear the water. It's dead silent," said Vincent.

"How's that even possible?" Tim asked.

"It's not. Must be some strange weather phenomenon. Let's get these lines into the water. Damn fish won't catch themselves."

After they put all the lines into the water and finished setting up all the gear, they grabbed some grub. It was going to be a long night. The first twenty-four hours of the trip were always the most exciting. Not many of the crew would get sleep.

"Who is our chef tonight?" roared Vincent.

"Sam's up first, Captain, frying up some chicken," replied Jack.

"Thank God. The rest of y'all can't cook for shit," laughed Vincent.

With their bellies full, they took turns watching the lines. Tim was up first. This was his first fishing trip with this crew, and he was eager to please everyone so he took the first watch. As he settled into his seat, he heard a loud splashing off in the distance. Thank god, there are some fish out here, he thought. Within minutes, several lines came alive.

"Hey boys, we got some live ones out here tonight!" he yelled back to the crew, causing the crew to jump in excitement and head up to the deck.

"Captain, get the hell out of here fast. You're not going to believe this!" yelled Tim. His voice then froze in fear as he watched fish of all sizes fleeing from around the boat.

"Where the hell are all the fish going?" he asked as the others joined him on the deck.

The boat rocked violently from the waves the hundreds of fish were causing.

Before Vincent could ask what was going on, a god awful smell arose from the water.

"Where is that damn smell coming from?" he asked.

Nobody said a word, shocked by the movement in the water.

"Was that a damn whale?" asked Sam.

"Captain, something is chasing the fish," yelled Jack.

"What in the hell would a whale be running from?" asked Vincent.

"Hold on to something, I think we're about to find out. Look at that wave coming!" screamed Tim.

The wave was not like anything they had ever seen before. It was black as night and reached to the sky.

"Raise the anchor and bring in the lines fast men, this wave is a fisherman's nightmare," screamed Vincent as he reached to reel in a line.

Before they could bring up the anchor, the wave took hold of the boat with such force they heard the anchor line snap in half.

"Everyone get below NOW!" yelled Vincent.

There was that screaming again. Tim held on as tight as he could to the boat. He was frozen in absolute fear. He couldn't believe his eyes. There, in the darkest wave he had ever seen, was a creature swimming swiftly against the water. He screamed as he kept his eyes shut and, waiting for the wave to pass, he held on as tight as he could to the boat.

"Tim, where are you?" Vincent yelled.

Not hearing him, Tim stood still as he watched the wave vanish into the ocean.

Sam slowly approached Tim as to not scare the terrified man. "Hey buddy, it's me, it's ok to let go. The wave is gone," said Sam in a soft voice.

Tim's face was ghost white. He started screaming as

soon as he saw the other men coming toward him.

"We need to leeeeave NOW... right now! There is a monster in the water," screamed Tim.

"Calm the hell down. It was just a rogue wave. Nothing to freak out about," said Vincent.

"Did you see that wave?" screamed Tim. "No, you didn't because you hid below and left me here. I'm telling you there was something in the water."

"Yeah fish... and some big ones from what we saw fleeing," said Jack.

"I've never seen fish flee from waves before. It makes no sense," replied Sam.

"Well, whatever it was, it's gone. Let's get the anchor replaced and drop new lines," ordered Vincent.

"Jack, take Tim down below and fix him a drink. He needs to calm down," yelled Sam.

With Jack and Tim below, Sam and Vincent set out to fix the broken anchor.

"Hey Cap, do you smell that?" Sam asked, trying not to gag.

"Yeah, probably a dead seal or whale. Let's get back to fixing this thing," ordered Vincent.

They dropped the new anchor in the dark water, only briefly pausing to catch their breath.

"Let's check on Tim and get those lines into the water," said Vincent.

"Hey Jack, how's Tim?" asked Vincent as they went below.

"Captain, he's totally freaked out. Says he saw a monster swimming against the wave. He said it was bigger than any fish he's ever seen," replied Jack.

"Aye, it's probably just his imagination. Let him sit a few more minutes while we get these lines dropped," said Vincent.

Before the three men could get back to the deck of the boat, something slammed into the side of it.

"It's back...it's coming for us. I told you there was something out there," cried Tim.

"Calm down, probably just a whale," replied Vincent.

They all heard the screaming coming from the depths of the ocean.

"That's no damn whale. Do you hear that screaming? Whales don't scream, fish don't scream... That's a MONSTER," screamed Tim.

"Jack, grab the rifle and ammo. Sam, grab the spotlight," yelled Vincent.

Tim remained below as the three men took to the deck, not knowing what they would see once they reached the side of the boat.

"Sam, shine that light over here where we heard that scream," commanded Vincent.

"What the hell is that?" asked Jack.

Blood covered the entire deck and side of the boat. The smell was horrendous, and the screaming was getting closer.

"Watch your step boys, there is blood everywhere," Vincent yelled.

"Blood? How the hell is the boat covered in blood?" asked Sam.

"There in the water? What is that? Bring the light over

here," said Vincent.

"Holy hell, that's a half eaten whale. What in the hell can bite something that big in half?" cried Sam.

There were sounds coming from above the boat that caused the men to look up. Before anyone could yell, the creature dove down onto the boat and grabbed Jack by the head. With one swift move, the creature and Jack's body were pulled deep into the ocean.

"Run! Now, before it comes back, get below now, Sam," screamed Vincent.

"Captain! Come on, you can't stay up here."

"Throw me that rifle. That son of bitch just killed Jack. I'm not letting it get away that easy," cried Vincent.

The monster circled the boat, causing it to spin violently. Both Sam and Vincent were losing their balance. Vincent started shooting blindly into the water, not knowing what he was shooting at.

"Where is that damn thing?" yelled Vincent.

The spinning slowed down, and the men were trying to catch their breath as another wave reached the boat.

"It's coming back, it's in the wave," yelled Sam.

"Shine the light into the water. Let's see what that damn monster is," commanded Vincent.

"There it is! Jesus, it's swimming against the wave just like Tim said," yelled Sam.

"Get back. I'm going to shoot it as soon as the wave is closer," said Vincent.

As Sam stood back and watched the creature rise from the water, he could hear Captain Vincent shooting at the monster. But none of the shots made contact with the target.

The monster looked like a dragon but had fins where

the arms and legs should be, with scales of pure black and no visible eyes.

The creature screamed as it grabbed Vincent, blood spraying the entire boat and covering Sam. Tim raced to the deck of the boat when he heard Sam's screaming. Shocked from all the blood and seeing only Sam remaining, he yelled at him to get back. The monster was coming.

"Sam, we have to go now!! It's coming back," yelled Tim.

"That thing killed Jack and Vincent. I think it's what killed all those people on the dock too," said Sam.

"Well, I'm not waiting on it to kill us too. Let's get out of here NOW!" cried Tim.

"We have to kill it. We can't let it kill anyone else."

Before either of them could speak again, they saw a flash of black scales just below the water's surface.

"How the hell are we going to kill a monster in the damn water?" replied Tim.

"We have a gun. We have to shoot it in the head," said Sam.

"No freaking way are we going to be able to shoot that thing while it swims in the water. Did you see how big and fast it is?" said Tim.

"We have to try... we have to for Jack and Vincent," Sam said.

"Well, here's your chance. There's another wave coming, and it's a big one."

"Grab the ammo fast, we need to reload the gun," Sam said, running toward Tim.

Sam loaded the gun and prayed it would work. As the monster crested the wave, Sam stood frozen in fear. He had never seen anything so terrifying. It was an ancient creature straight from Hell itself. He was so afraid he wasn't able to shoot the gun.

The monster didn't approach the boat this time; instead, it swam around the boat several times before it left.

"Sam, we need to get below. You're in shock."

Tim grabbed Sam by the arm and dragged him down below. They sat in silence for what seemed like hours before Sam finally said, "What was that, a dragon with no eyes and fins? How can it be possible? How has no one ever seen that thing before?" asked Sam.

"I don't know, but I don't ever want to see it again," replied Tim.

"I agree. Let's get the boat started and get the hell out of here."

"I think the anchor broke again. You go check, but be careful. I'll get the engine started," said Sam.

Sam had been right. The anchor was broken again, and they had no way to fix it. They definitely needed to leave. Sam was trying to start the engine when Tim walked in.

"Anchor is completely broken, no way to fix it," said Tim.

"Well, I can't get the engine to start either. It may be water logged from the waves. We gotta go to the engine room," said Sam.

"Damn man, that could take hours. We need to go now," said Tim

"There's nothing we can do if the engine won't start. Grab the tools and keep lookout in case that thing comes back," replied Sam.

After a few hours, Sam and Tim got the engine running. They feared the sound of the engine would draw the creature back, so they made sure everything was tied down on the deck before they headed back. They didn't know how they would explain to the sheriff how half the crew was dead and that there was a monster in the waves. Although those were the least of their worries, getting back alive was their biggest fear.

"Ok Tim, are you ready to get this engine started?" asked Sam.

"As ready as I'll ever be. Let's pray it doesn't hear us," replied Tim.

"Are there any bullets left in the gun or any other weapons on board?" Sam asked.

"Gun is loaded, and I found a few flares too."

"Let's hope we don't need either, but I have a bad feeling about this."

Both men stood in silence as they waited to hear if the screams would come back from the monster. But nothing came. It was eerily quiet. No birds were flying above and the ocean stood still.

"Let's get the hell out of here. This place is freaking me out," Tim yelled.

A few minutes into their trip back, they heard the scream from below the boat. The boat began to rock as the waves picked up. Before Sam could say anything, Tim started screaming.

"It's following us. It's right under the boat!"

"Get me the gun and grab the flares. We have to try to kill it before we get back to the dock," Sam ordered.

Tim threw the gun to Sam and lit the flare, staring into the water, waiting for the monster.

"Wait for it to come around again and shoot it!" Tim yelled.

"It's going to be impossible to get a shot. Hold the flare down so I can see it," said Sam.

The monster circled the boat several times, making the waves stronger, causing both men to lose their balance on the deck.

"I don't see it anywhere. Where the hell is it?" Sam said. They knew it was close by; they could smell it.

"Over there, watch that wave... Here it comes, be ready!" yelled Tim.

The monster swam silently with the wave. It circled the boat several more times before it lunged out of the water to attack. Tim waved the flare into the air, trying to see where the monster was, but all he was really doing was letting the monster sense the heat. The monster rose high above the boat and dove straight down to the men.

"It's coming, get ready to shoot it, Sam!!"

Sam emptied the gun into the monster, but it kept coming straight for them. Not knowing what to do, Tim threw the flare right into the monster's mouth just as it reached the boat. The monster screamed and threw itself around, trying to retreat to the water. Sam remembered there was a fishing hook hanging on the deck. He grabbed the hook and hit the monster several times in the head, causing it to fall onto the deck.

"Kill it, NOW! We can't let it back into the water!"

yelled Tim.

With one last swing, he heard the skull crack. Both men stood in shock as the black goo seeped from the monster's head.

"What the hell are we going to do with it now?" Tim asked with fear in his voice.

"We have to take it back. No one will believe our story unless we have proof," stated Sam.

The creature smelled horrible when it was alive, but now the stench was so bad the men both vomited over the side of the boat.

"If we're taking this thing back, we need to go now. I can't stand that awful smell," cried Tim.

Half an hour later they arrived back at Dock 13. The sun had just come up, and the local fishermen were gathering at the pier. Sam had called the sheriff's office to tell them what had happened and have the sheriff meet them there. The boat was a horrific sight to see, covered in blood and black goo. No one would go near the boat due to the smell.

Tim, still in shock from the ordeal, was sitting in the back of the ambulance when the sheriff walked over to him.

"Tim, how ya doing? I need to take your statement if you're up to it."

"Sure Sheriff, but I'm not sure how much more I can tell ya than what Sam said," Tim replied.

"Well, I'll be the judge of that," said the sheriff.

After taking both mens' statements, the sheriff was still not sure what to do with the monster's corpse; it still hung off the boat. He yelled over to the fishermen standing near the dock to get them to unload the monster from the boat.

"Hey, can you men get that thing..." he paused, not knowing what to call it.

Sam replied to the sheriff, "The Wavling; it swims with waves, waiting to attack."

"Okay then. Can you men get this Wavling off the boat?" asked the sheriff.

The fishermen all stared at each other, unsure how to complete the task.

"Well, at least we know what's been killing things around here, but why did it come so close to land?" asked the sheriff.

Sam had gazed off into the water, dazed and still in shock, when the sheriff tapped him on the shoulder.

"You alright, Sam?" he asked.

Sam jumped and nearly fell over. "Yeah, I will be, Sheriff. It's just been a shitty night. Losing Vincent and Jack like that was horrifying."

"Well, it's all over, Sam. Why don't you head home. I'll call you tomorrow; I'm sure we'll have more questions."

"Sounds good ..." Before he finished his sentence, a scream pierced the early morning air. Everyone at the scene froze with fear. When the screaming died out, they all heard what sounded like giant fish or monster jumping in the water.

"Hey Sheriff, I don't think it's over yet! Sounds like there are more of those things. The Wavlings are back!"

The End..... or Is It?

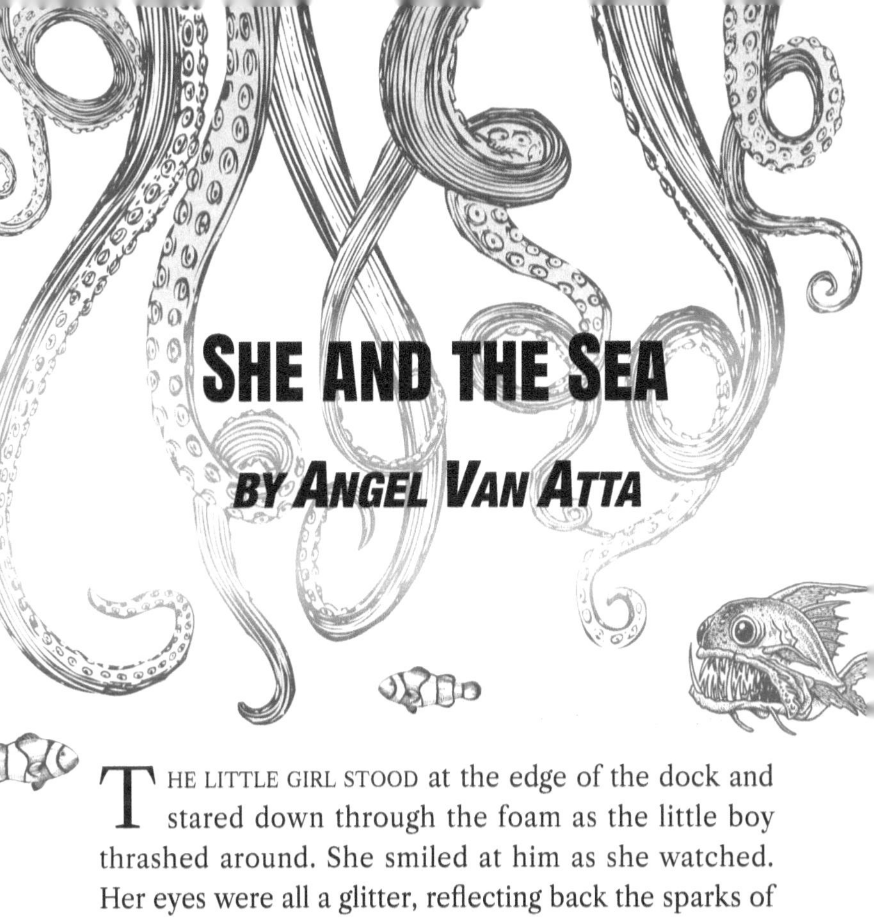

SHE AND THE SEA

BY ANGEL VAN ATTA

T HE LITTLE GIRL STOOD at the edge of the dock and stared down through the foam as the little boy thrashed around. She smiled at him as she watched. Her eyes were all a glitter, reflecting back the sparks of sunlight dancing off the water below as the waves came and went toward the beach, which was rather far away, especially for two children so young to be out without adult supervision.

The little boy had come along happily enough. She had only had to say there was a baby seal, and if they were quiet enough and quick enough, it would still be there, splashing about. The boy could not resist. The thought of snapping some pictures with the shiny, little Polaroid camera his grandma had given him for his birthday just the day before and showing it to his ma was just too much. How delighted she would be. How proud.

The little girl picked up the camera, which was now

lying on the rough and swollen wood beneath her soft-soled feet, and she pointed it at the little boy. She watched his swaying hair, which was beautiful to her in some removed way she didn't understand, as the current tugged at it softly, and her smile widened.

The way he looked through the viewfinder as he struggled to unwrap the netting she had wound around him before pushing him in was mesmerizing to her. The snippets of panic on his face she could see as he moved his head about in his ever-escalating despair seemed magical through that lens. It was a magic intensified with the ebb and flow of the water around him as the waves moved in toward the sandy beach at her back.

She pressed the camera's button over and over, again and again. With each click, her smile widened until it was stretched as far across her face as possible. A horrid, thin line that seemed to transform her adorable little face into something evil and dark and terrifying.

As the boy struggled to keep his breath held within his tightening chest, he looked up one last time before that breath was lost to him. And what he saw caused him to lose all hope. What he saw was pure evil.

Their eyes locked. The camera fell to her feet, forgotten atop the small pile of miniature Polaroid pictures. Her bright blue irises saw only his dark brown ones, and for an endless second, they were the only two who existed in the whole entire world. And then he could hold his breath no longer, and the air rushed out of him in one burning gush as the water raced into his mouth and down his throat. His body's desperate struggle for air doomed him to death.

The little boy's open mouth was a dark and endless

hole to her. A cave she imagined would soon be home to tiny fish and crabs looking for food and sanctuary from the larger creatures who swam around in this ocean's deep blue depths. His face jerked forward as the water filled his lungs, and the saltiness burned him in places he had never known could burn.

She watched all of this, and a part of her was alight with the most pure form of excitement. He watched her watch as he died. Through a veil of moving glass, he watched her. Through the swaying of his bangs before his eyes, he watched her. As the world around him darkened ever slowly, his lungs screaming out in pain and his heart racing with fear, he watched, and still their eyes stayed connected. Until his life drained away from him as the darkness overtook, their eyes were locked.

She stood there for a few moments more, after she knew he had gone away from this place. Finally, after what must have been mere minutes but was some kind of wonderful eternity for her, she kicked the camera over the rough wood's edge and knelt and gathered up the pictures of the boy's final struggle. She looked through them slowly, as if they were nothing more than images of rocks or shells, images of meaningless things and not of this poor child's last moments of life.

She chose the one she liked the most and slid it nonchalantly into her pocket. She tossed the rest atop the water above the poor lad's lifeless body, and she turned and walked back down the pier. Back toward where her parents waited on a blanket the color of bright red blood freshly spilled upon the sand when a predator rips apart its prey. The symbolism of it calmed her wicked little heart.

She thought about this moment years later as she stood staring into the sea, her belly pressed against the railing of the boat. She let her body sway with it as the ocean rocked the vessel in which she stood. She could almost see the little boy down there, even though his body had been found and buried and there was no way it could be. She could almost see him drifting up from the deep, dark depths as she stared down into them.

She saw him often, the boy whom she had ended all those years ago. Every time she bathed or swam or ventured over or into any body of water, she saw his struggle and his eyes and reveled in his despair.

So this time seemed no different. She yearned for it, to see his face again, to watch the life drain away from him. She wanted to eat it up and soak it in, and she yearned for that feeling once again.

She had taken many others in the years and years that stood between that first poor boy and now. Many others, but none of them had been the same. None of them had held that same feeling of magic that first time had. None of them had been so pure.

The second had been the school bully, in the public pool when all the other kids had been running and splashing about. Too many people to notice her in the crowd as she wrapped one hand around the bottom ladder rung and held his ankle in a firm, tight grasp after jumping in and landing on him, kicking him in the gut as she did before swimming down and grabbing hold. It had been a move she had practiced in her mind for three whole days before finally deciding it was time.

He lost his breath when her foot had slammed so forcefully into his soft belly, as she hoped he would.

As he tried swimming up, she quickly swam down and pulled, and he had had no hope of escape. It all happened so fast he hadn't had a chance to even understand what was happening. He had tried to kick and yank away, but the water was rushing into him as it had that other boy, and he had lost his fight to keep it out just as that other had. That first.

The next had been her little baby brother. She was supposed to watch him as her mother ran to get the phone. She was older now, and he had been a surprise to all of them, an adorable little distraction her mother loved in a way the little girl had never felt from her. And her father had been so proud. She felt invisible when he had come.

She waited for the chance, and it had come as if a gift. Her mother told her to sit there and ensure he didn't fall, and she nodded that she would. But as soon as her mother left the room, she slid the baby under and held him tight. It had taken little effort, and as the baby thrashed about, helpless against her, she watched the light fade from his little baby eyes as her mother prattled on and on in the other room. Again it had not been the same as with her first. It had not been as exciting or as memorable.

As soon as she had known the deed was done and that her baby brother's life had faded from this place, she pulled him up and started screaming out for help, fake tears coursing down her cheeks and the excuses pouring from her mouth as the water ran from his.

She had thought for countless hours late at night, tucked safely away in bed, about how to get away with this most heinous act as her mother cooed away at him in the very next room. With every soft giggle her baby brother made and every delighted sigh her mother made in return, she had thought. Over and over she had pulled at the threads of her deadly desire, and every scenario she painted for herself ended the same way. It had to look like an accident. And so it would, and so it did.

The next had been her rival at swim camp, a beautiful little girl with the blondest hair and brightest blue eyes and whom all the other little girls wanted as their best friend forever. She had hated that girl from the second her mother had dropped her off and fled.

For her mother had known something was wrong with her only surviving child, something off, but her grief blinded her to it all. It numbed her. So she pushed her away instead of pulling her close. She blinded herself and avoided her daughter when she could so she wouldn't have to examine the clues and see.

The blonde little girl was faster than she was. The blonde little girl was funnier and kinder. The blonde little girl was to be the next to die.

She waited until the other children had all run off to lunch, just as the bell had rung. The blonde little girl had been easy to fool, a simple secret for her ears only had been the only bait she needed. So as the other children climbed up the ladder on the dock and ran toward the shore, leaving tiny wet footprints in their wake, the blonde little girl had ducked under the boards after her, excited to know who had said what about whom.

She had lured her into the secret place all the kids had loved to go. The water was high enough so nobody could see in from the sides, but low enough to leave a pocket of air the children could whisper their secrets in as they peeked up through the cracks at the staff as they blew their whistles and called out games or positions or yelled to stop Sally from splashing Sue.

This secret place beneath the boards was a forbidden place, as well, which made the going that much sweeter. That much more desired. That much more acceptable when the offer had been made. Like a fly to a spider's web, the blonde little girl had gone in agreeably enough.

This had been an easy kill for her to set up. She had thought this one out as well. At night, as the counselors laughed and shared drinks from flasks outside the cabin windows, she had planned. As the coaches shared their own bits of juicy gossip on the pier when they were supposed to be watching the kids practice their backstrokes and breaststrokes, she had slipped away under their feet to plan, unnoticed.

Everything she needed was there; she had made sure of that already. It had been no hard task to slip from her bed the night before. The thin rope used for hanging wet towels on the line was already tied in a slip knot on one end. She had wrapped it around her arm as she went, her flip-flops softly flapping against the smooth dirt path. She had felt alone in the world as the mist rose up from the water's glassy top, stars and a sliver of moon reflecting from it between the thin rivulets of foggy air. She felt alive.

She slipped her foamy sandals off once she reached the end of the dock and smiled at the way the cooling wood felt all rough against her soft little girl's feet. It had reminded her of that other time, that first time, at the ocean, with the boy. She dropped her towel onto her shoes and slid slowly off the side and into the water. The cold chill climbed up her toes and feet and legs as she went in as quietly as she could, not wanting to make a splash.

Once she was under and in the place where she planned to lure her prey, she took three deep breaths before dunking and swimming down where she had already found the large metal spike which had, for some reason unknown to her, been pounded into the round soggy wood some time ago. Perhaps it had been to hold a buoy. Perhaps not. Either way, it was a perfect and welcome sight.

It took her three whole tries of diving under and back up before the rope was securely tied. She was shivering and cold by the time she pulled herself back up onto the rough planks, where her towel waited patiently for her to wrap around herself, and she did. She thought it would be hard to fall asleep that night, with so much excitement to come, but she had slipped under sleep's gently flowing surface as easily as she had slipped into the water to tie the rope that would the next day ensnare her unlucky catch.

The blonde little girl was eager to hear the juicy secret. As she ducked under the edge of the wood which held the planks of the dock above in place, she didn't notice her wicked little friend had gone under as well. When the blonde little girl popped up on the other side, she was puzzled by the fact that she found herself alone. Alone in this wet and dripping place beneath where the bored twenty-somethings put in charge of watching over them all usually stood. Alone beneath where the green algae clung to the slowly rotting wood and where a tiny brown spider struggled to keep a web.

"Liza?" the blonde little girl called. Her excitement in finding out who had been caught kissing whom behind the boy's cabin last night was instantly gone and replaced with confusion and an ever-growing dread.

The blonde little girl couldn't hear a thing aside from the slapping sound the water made against the underside of the wood. No children laughing or calling out to each other or splashing. No whistles being blown, instructions being called out, and no Liza whispering secrets in her ear. Suddenly, the blonde little girl didn't want to be here anymore. As she turned to duck back under and swim toward the ladder down a bit, something slipped around her foot and tightened with a bite around her ankle.

"Oh, what the fuck?" the blonde little girl spat as she tried to kick her foot. But whatever held it held it firm, and as she kicked, it tightened into her tender flesh, scraping against her ankle. The pain was even worse.

Liza popped up then, closer to where the ladder was than where the blonde little girl bobbed, and the blonde little girl's heart was filled with not just fear but also relief as she was grateful not to be alone. "I'm so glad you're here! I need help. Something's got my foot! It's wrapped around my ankle. Can you help me? I wanna go in now." She was on the edge of tears as the terror slowly built, and something about the smile on Liza's face made that terror bloom and anxiety grabbed her heart in its wet and icy grip.

Liza didn't answer, not with words. Instead, she wrapped a leg around and through the lowest ladder rung, as she had done at the community pool not that long ago. She lifted the rope tip out of the water, wanting the blonde little girl to see it. Needing her to know.

"What is that?" the blond little girl asked, but suddenly she knew and didn't need the answer Liza wouldn't give. She knew, and that's when she started to scream and splash about.

Liza let her do it for a second or two, wanting to see the panic in that blond little girl's beautiful eyes. She wanted to see the beauty lose its shine and watch as the ugliness of fear devoured it. But the blonde little girl was a good swimmer, and Liza almost lost the rope. She tightened her leg's hold on the cold metal of the ladder, and she tugged.

The blonde little girl was instantly pulled under, then Liza loosened her hold. She bobbed back up again, water pouring out the blond little girl's open mouth as it had her little baby brother's. The blond little girl coughed and gagged, and just as her breath was almost back to normal, Liza pulled again. Again and again, she played with the girl this way.

Again and again, Liza let her think she would be okay before getting tugged back under once more. Sometimes, as the girl struggled to catch her breath and cough out all the water, she would beg and plead for Liza to stop. To let her go. She would promise not to tell a single soul what Liza had done, but Liza didn't care. The blond little girl was shiny, and Liza loved what water did to shiny things. It ate away at them and turned them an ugly color. Liza knew that soon, this little girl would be ugly too.

When finally Liza grew bored with this and knew there wasn't much life left in the blond little girl, she dunked the blond little girl under once again. Liza tied the rope tightly to the bottom rung. She pulled it enough so that the line from the ladder to the metal spike then up to the nearly lifeless girl's purpling foot was tight. She wanted there to be no way for the blond little girl to reach the surface and struggle to breathe again.

Liza didn't care to see it this time. Liza had seen it enough to know it wouldn't be as exciting as that first had been. She knew the girl would make that gasping "o" with her mouth after her body's desperate fight to keep from sucking in all that water instead of air into her lungs was over. She knew the girl would jerk and that her face would be filled with pain, and she didn't care. She was bored of it. All she really cared about was that the blonde little girl wasn't going to be pretty anymore. That the pretty blonde little girl wasn't going to be anymore. And that was enough for Liza. It had to be.

She had always been careful when she took them. Calculated. She knew she must never ever be caught. And so she hadn't, though that time at swimming camp had been the closest call.

She may have even been caught had there not been a man who had murdered a goat and sacrificed it to a god no one had ever heard of but he. He had covered himself in the blood of that unlucky beast and ran naked down the streets that very night in a town not too far away from where the camp sat nestled by the lake. But the two things were too close together for the sheriff to consider them coincidence, and murdering little girls was a job for sadists, as far as that wily old policeman cared to think.

So she had done it over and over again throughout the years, and always in bodies of water. There was something about the way the water made them move that called to her. That beckoned to her. That fed her evil hunger. And seeing the water often brought him back. Though she knew it was just a cherished memory that she was replaying in her mind, she longed for it.

So she had borrowed her father's boat and taken it out far, far, far into the sea. Farther than her father would have liked to see her go, and farther than she had ever gone. She had taken it and stopped the engines and pressed herself against the side, and she had looked over the edge and waited. She hoped to see her oldest friend, who was really not a friend at all. She hoped to see his ghost.

So when he finally came, she was not surprised, and she smiled at his rising form. Up, up, and up he came, emerging from the shadows of the depth as if being born from it. It was as if his molecules assembled one by one as he emerged, and pieces of him came into existence a little at a time the closer he came to her.

But she knew it was him, as it always was, and this time was no different. Not at first, at least. For as he rose, she watched his hair swaying lazily about. And as he rose, his eyes turned and fixed on hers, as they always did, as they had that day when the life left his body and she watched it go. But this time, they were not full of that fear that always filled the eyes of those she took. This time they were filled with glee, and he was laughing.

She could hear the sound it made through the water. With that sound she heard another, but this one from behind, a wet and flapping sound rushing toward her from the other side of the boat. A squelching flap, flap, flap as something ran across the deck. Before she could even begin to turn and see, she felt the hands plant firmly into her back. The force of it pushed her forward and over and in.

The water was colder than any water she had ever felt before. She was shocked it could ever be this cold without freezing hard and turning into ice. As her head swung around in the water and her body twisted and tried to right itself so she could begin to swim back up where her salvation lay above the surface, she saw them. Not just him; she saw them all.

Her baby brother reached out to her. His tiny bluish fingers opened and closed as he did. His fine, little baby hair swayed in the ebb and flow of water that pressed against her chest and lungs, which were screaming at her for air.

The class bully was reaching for her, too, a look of angry gratitude upon his water-swollen face as his out-stretched fingers inched closer and closer to her foot. The blonde little girl was also there, and Liza's heart sank as she took in the beauty she still held as a beam of sun lit up her flowing mermaid hair.

Dozens of others were here, as well, and Liza re-membered each and every one. Every kill played itself out before her as they came. Each of them edged ever closer as her mind screamed at her to swim and her lungs begged for her to open her mouth and breathe. Just breathe.

Finally, her spell was broken as the first soggy fin-ger wrapped around her ankle. She instantly began to thrash, pull, and kick. But there was no use, and she knew it. There was no escape. That didn't stop Liza from trying, though.

She lunged out her hand and tried to hit the memory of the man she had murdered in his own jacuzzi. Before her fist could even start to swing forward from its backward path, another firm but waterlogged hand grabbed that wrist. At the same time, three more hands wrapped around her ankles, then five more around her thighs. Suddenly, instead of them all floating up, they were sinking, dragging her down.

The pressure in her chest burned, and when she could no longer keep from breathing in whatever would come when her body took control, she marveled at the beauty of them all. She had taken them because of jealousy and simple hate. But as soon as they were gone, she no longer cared about what they had had that she had so badly wanted.

The little boy's camera had become instantly unimportant. The mother's attention had been overbearing at times and intrusive. The friends of the blonde little girl had been boring, bratty, and the list went on and on and on.

She had thought that by taking these lives she would leave them swollen and ugly and somehow rusted and covered up with slime. But these creatures, who pulled her farther and farther down into the darkest depths as the water rushed into her, taking the place where the air belonged, she saw they were even more beautiful now. More tranquil. More seraphic.

Their hair flowed and swayed, and their limbs, though swollen and purpled, were graceful. It was as if they danced with every movement. And as the fire the water brought inside her filled her and her vision darkened, death approached and, with it, her final thought. She hoped but one last thing as the life drained away with the light as they sank. She hoped that in her death, she would find the beauty in her too.

ABOUT THE AUTHORS

Broken Brain Books is an indie publisher dedicated to helping authors share their stories with readers around the world. Please visit our website for more information about our releases, signed copies of our books and information about submissions.

www.brokenbrainbooks.com

Angel Van Atta
Angel Van Atta was born into a sea of rough waters. Her father was an evil man and her mother was taken from this world, too soon. She turned to horror as a way to hold on to hope. To remind her good can triumph over evil. She now lives a quiet life in a little town, writing stories and spreading as much joy as she can while drinking copious amounts of chocolate flavored coffee.

Chad West
Chad West is a writer and graphic designer in Arkansas. You can find him at cwest.substack.com

Charlie Walls
Charlie Walls lives with his family in Mississippi. He writes in the horror, science fiction, and fantasy genres. His short stories have featured in anthologies such as Below the Stairs-Tales from the Cellar, Beneath the Waves-Tales from the Deep, and Hammer of the Gods: Ragnarok.

D.W. Hitz
D.W. Hitz lives in Montana, where the inspiring scenery functions as a background character in his work. He is a lover of stories in all mediums. He enjoys writing in the genres of Horror, Extreme Horror, and Science Fiction/Fantasy.

Derek Heath
Derek Heath is the author of a dozen published short stories (so far!) and a growing number of self-published novellas and collections. He lives with his beautiful partner and together they hoard board games and houseplants. You can find him at derekheathhorror.com.

Gage Greenwood
Gage Greenwood is the best-selling author of the Winter's Myths Saga, and Bunker Dogs. He's a proud member of the Horror Writers Association and Science Fiction and Fantasy Writers association.

He's been an actor, comedian, podcaster, and even the Vice President of an escape room company. Since childhood, he's been a big fan of comic books, horror movies, and depressing music that fills him with existential dread.

Heather Ann Larson
Heather Ann Larson is an up and coming editor and avid horror reader. Although Christopher Pike was a favorite, Stephen King's The Dark Tower is what pulled her in and kept her on the journey. She has several edits under her belt, including The Children and The Gods series by Angel Vn Atta, They are all Monsters by Justin Boote, and their collaboration They End of Things as He/She Knew Them. She continues to grow her journey by taking Aces editing courses and delving deep into the Chicago Manual of Style. In her spare time, she... Who are we kidding? There is no spare time!!!

Joshua MacMillan
Joshua MacMillan is a lifelong horror fan. He grew up in Texas but currently resides with his wife Audree in Eau Claire, Wisconsin. Joshua has short stories published in multiple anthologies, but his main focus is novella and novel writing. Joshua has written for the award-winning horror website Dread Central and is currently a staff writer for House of Stitched Magazine. He is a fanatic of all things dark and disturbing, and his passion is for the horror genre as a whole.

Leigh Kenny
Leigh was born and raised in the garden county of Wicklow, Ireland. She lives by the Irish Sea with the love of her life, two wonderful son's, a black Labrador, and a three-legged cat that hates people. You can find out

more about Leigh's work and any upcoming releases on her social media: LeighKennyWrites
Her debut novella, Cursed, is available on Amazon.

LM Kaplin
LM Kaplin is an author from upstate New York who has been a horror enthusiast in all forms his entire life. His morbid obsession with the macabre began one night while watching Poltergeist as a young child. The next morning, he began searching for ancient burial grounds in the backyard. Dismayed at not uncovering any evil spirits, he buried his own demons for future generations to find. It's time to start digging them up.

Megan Stockton
Megan Stockton is an indie author who lives in rural Middle Tennessee with her husband and two children. She primarily writes dystopian, horror, thriller, and science fiction/fantasy novels that are character-driven and immersive. She is known for delivering works that are raw, thought-provoking, brutal, and cinematic.

Ollie Gill
Ollie Gill is a writer of short horror and fantasy stories. His love for horror began at a young age after receiving a Christopher Pike novel as a gift. He grew up in Co Galway, Ireland where he still lives to this day. As well as writing, he enjoys creating heavy metal music and also works as a tattoo artist.

Patrick McNulty
Patrick McNulty is an author, screenwriter, husband and

father to three amazing children. He has served in the Canadian Armed Forces as a Medical Technician and now works as a police officer. He lives with his family in southern Ontario, Canada.

Rhonda Bobbitt

Rhonda grew up in a small town in East Texas and currently resides in Central Illinois. Mother of four wonderful children and grandmother of five amazing grandchildren. Rhonda is a published photographer and loves to travel. In her spare time, she loves to read and spend time with her family. Horror, thrillers and dystopian are her favorite genres.

RJ Roles

Hailing from West Virginia, RJ Roles is the founder of Books of Horror, and From the Ashes. He is an author and publisher of horror fiction. You can find his work on rjroles.com.

Wil Forbis

Wil Forbis is an author of horror and suspense fiction that simmers with tension before exploding into action. His novel "What Waits in the Shadows", a tale of the monsters that dwell in the mind (and elsewhere), was released in January 2024. "Anonymous", a twist on the classic 'masked slasher' premise will follow. His story "Too Many Cats" can be obtained by signing up for his newsletter at https://www.thehorrorofwilforbis.com/